Dearest St...

Thank you so very
much for attending
the launch event.
We appreciate all you
support!
All the best,
J. Cole &

PERCIVIOUS

PERCIVIOUS

ORIGINS

J J Cook & A J Cook, MD

A J
J J
PUBLISHING

Published by AJ JJ Publishing, Calgary, AB Canada
Percivious.com

Edited and designed by Girl Friday Productions
www.girlfridayproductions.com

Cover design: Emily Weigel
Project management: Dave Valencia
Editorial production: Abi Pollokoff
Image credits: cover © Shutterstock/DDus, Shutterstock/Maryna Stamatova, Shutterstock/Marta Ruiz Vera, Shutterstock/solarseven

ISBN (hardcover): 978-1-7773774-6-5
ISBN (paperback): 978-1-7773774-3-4
ISBN (e-book): 978-1-7773774-4-1

Percivious (per-siv-e-us)
Noun
The ultimate in altruism. Self-sacrifice in order to benefit others with no regard to reward or reciprocity.

PROLOGUE

XYZ EVACUATION DAY

GRYNN

3.02 (Late Afternoon) / Orbyss / 280 Million
Years Before Humans Appear on Earth

A torrential rain, the kind that deafens you, one that drowns your thoughts and amplifies your fears. That was the sound of ten thousand passengers proceeding in unison towards fifty space elevators, just as they had practiced each day for twenty weeks prior. This time it was quicker, no words spoken, just footfalls pounding against the pebbled, well-worn path up to the launch promontory.

The percussion they produced offered no comfort. Marching was foreign to a species without war or the need of it. Their configuration did not reflect their collective strength over the approaching enemy. The departure scared them with its regulation and restriction, because, in actuality, it was not an evacuation at all but rather a funeral procession. As they knew, all too well, they had already lost . . . already lost their home. They continued on together within the mass assembly, with no one to comfort them, as they all would suffer the loss.

Nine days earlier, the high-pitched frequency of the alarm, together with flashing red lights, made it impossible to concentrate. Grynn had become desensitized despite the asteroid's impending arrival. Similar to how we accept the eventual end of our own existence, he had adjusted to its countdown of sorts. The capacity to function under one's impending doom was critical to survival, just as important today as it had been millions of years before.

Leaving Orbyss was like getting a tooth pulled before a cavity formed or cutting an invisible bruise from a perfect apple. The seemingly superficial summer day made what they were doing almost ridiculous, like buying into a sordid fairy tale because your older sibling told you it was real, and the XYZs doubted their plan one last time. It would truly be the last time, as this was the final group to board the *HELIX*.

No choice but to fall in line, lemmings approaching the edge of a cliff. Hating the fear but desperate to rid oneself of the pending sensation of plummeting downwards. It was almost preferable to jump instead of suffering the previewing. Panic was the enemy. Panicking would undo everything. It could be catastrophic, potentially reducing their numbers beyond restoration. The months of practice focused largely on overcoming fear regardless of the cost. They were trained to think of small things, stationary things. To watch and listen for those in front, to each side, and behind. Extending oneself had become a reflex, and it was exemplified in real time as a motherly XYZ reached out to comfort and encourage a youngster who had become separated from his assigned group. As always, being aware of others first—even before oneself. To anticipate and prevent the panic was everything. It was a word, a look, a touch, whatever would keep the masses on track towards their assigned elevators as they made their last trip up.

Despite his loss and trauma, Grynn was far from panicking. He could already picture himself on the *HELIX*. Could see it happen. Upon boarding his elevator with forty-nine fellow passengers, he knew the ride up would only take minutes. But in the moment—as part of a slow-moving congregation composed of individuals that he felt, at times, he knew better than himself—it was like being in a dream. A dream where he could run, but only in slow motion. Or one where he was swimming through thick, invisible mud. His instincts cried out to speed up his walking, but he knew that this, as with everything they did now, had been optimized for the whole. There could be no deviation; trepidation could cost them their lives. They would follow the rhythm, a pulse of safety, the optimal beats per minute. It was a tempo of survival derived by the very best of them—commanders of their involuntary trip to the stars.

An impact crater would have been a welcome sight, a testament to a small meteorite or insignificant asteroid grazing Orbyss's surface with little repercussion or casualty. Instead, this five-hundred-kilometer-wide iron relic of the big bang would immediately liquefy central Pangea into a brilliant orange-red molten carbonaceous slurry. The second act of this complete annihilation involved the simultaneous tectonic cracking of Pangea and the expulsion of tetra tons of debris into the surrounding atmosphere, rendering Orbyss a dark speck in the cosmos for millions of years to come. They were all well versed in the impending disaster, and they were keenly aware that the ramifications would be immediate and profound. Instantaneously, all life on Orbyss would perish; every valley, every mountain, every nuance would be homogenized into a flat, barren landscape. The fertile oceans where life had begun, and one day would begin again, would be vaporized into atmospheric water, their remnants quickly obliterated and filled in with molten metal.

Grynn played out the epic disaster in his head, and it was as if his thoughts conjured the attack into existence. He entered the elevator through transparent doors framed with a biological concrete-like shaft made from biomineralized nutrients and CO_2, a process similar to the production of seashells in the ocean.

The ride up was spectacular; his favorite part was the moment when the see-through elevator left Orbyss's atmosphere and day became night. Orbyss became space. The cylindrical tube that was his elevator, a perfectly aerodynamic bullet, rose ever upwards to the largest structure ever conceived or built by unwilling creators—the *HELIX*.

"What time do you have?" Grynn's best friend, Shal, coyly asked.

"Why?" responded Grynn, obviously preparing himself for yet another of Shal's epic punch lines. Grynn played along with more enthusiasm than he felt, endeavoring to lessen the guilt Shal obviously felt. Pushing aside his own grief, Grynn attempted to make his friend realize he would never blame him, that nothing that had happened was his fault.

"I want to document the only time you will ever match my speed."

Grynn laughed half-heartedly, for Shal's sake. For Grynn, leaving everything he had ever known behind felt surreal. He tried to focus on the fact that he would be heading into the future with his love, and soon his newborn son or daughter by his side. Inherent in their genetic code, and a consequence of millions of years of evolution, relationships meant everything to the XYZ species. The friends and family Grynn surrounded himself with were the answer to how he continued on, how they all continued on. For them, love and connection superseded all else.

Grynn and his father, Aricis, had taken to playing a game. His father's way of coping with the loss was to go out of his way to lift Grynn's spirits. As an extra precaution, family members were not permitted to travel within the same elevator. However, they weren't very far from each other, their respective elevators side by side. Father and son assumed a position as close as they could to one another where glass-like carbon-fiber openings in between the thick partitions put them in clear view of one another for most of the ride up. Once they began their ascent, they would start a competition of sorts. One they had crafted mostly out of boredom in an attempt to overcome the monotony of innumerable drills. They had become quite good at it, enjoying the reaction of the respective winner or loser even with an interrupted view during the breaks where the support beams blocked their sight, a few milliseconds at a time.

Grynn leaned on the glass in anticipation; he was sure that his father would have something profound if not at least entertaining for him today, on their last ascension from Orbyss.

He began the transmission, a mind-to-mind, emotion-to-emotion communication that appeared to occur in silence but, in actuality, offered deeper elucidation than words could ever hope to achieve. Their transmissions were so much more than words, perfected between him and his father only after many years of practice. Grynn's father took the lead with their customary riddle, a comforting ritual to mark their final ride up, the end of a chapter, so to speak.

The riddle he transmitted to Grynn was: "The more you take, the more you leave behind. What am I?"

That one was easy. "Footsteps," Grynn replied.

His father nodded and threw his head back in obvious laughter. This steadied Grynn. To watch his father standing across from him as they both left Orbyss in synchronicity was so very familiar. At a time like this, familiarity was akin to comfort. He felt a combination of relief and fortitude that he could so easily say something that would lift his father's spirits, despite his grief.

It seemed enough to just laugh with each other, separated but closer than ever. They would be OK, even after the loss they had both suffered prior to the asteroid making its debut. It was going to be a challenge, but together with his family and loved ones, Grynn, for the first time, considered the transition more of an adventure than a mass evacuation required to escape extinction.

It was at that moment that the speed of the elevators increased. A message transmitted from the HELIX to each passenger simultaneously explained the terrifying news that the asteroid was travelling at an increased speed and they could not predict its impact now or guarantee their safe transport. The calculations had been flawless, computed more times than could be counted in order to ensure they were all well away from Orbyss when the asteroid hit. The asteroid was never meant to cross paths with the HELIX or the space elevators. However, now its orbit was altered as the procession of Saturn's orbit was in resonance with its own. The asteroid's plotted course had changed, as had its speed. Something none of them had anticipated.

Seconds later, Grynn shuddered with fear and disbelief as a blazing ball of fire ripped through the barrier between the atmosphere and the dark emptiness of space and hurtled through the air towards them. Terror cascaded through the group. It started out as ripples, then grew to a crescendo of waves crashing against a rocky shoreline during a storm. The shadow the asteroid cast on Orbyss below them grew in size until it covered the ground as far as Grynn could see. The asteroid was so enormous, Grynn could not believe it was real until they felt the tremor of the asteroid's impact as it hit Orbyss's surface at forty-two thousand kilometers per hour. Only milliseconds lapsed as the asteroid buried itself far into the crust of Orbyss with absolute force, intent on ripping it apart.

The debris from the impact travelled across the surface of Orbyss, rising up to destroy anything in its path. From the elevator shaft, Grynn witnessed the firestorms decimating everything. He clamped his eyelids shut for just a moment, hoping to wake up from this nightmare. Upon opening his eyes, they locked with those of his father less than thirty meters away.

"I love you, son," his father transmitted. "May you be everything you have always dreamt of becoming. Remember when I taught you to stand, to run, to be so very proud of who you are and from where you have come. We loved you so much when we first learned you were conceived, when your mother and I first knew we would one day meet you. That you would be with us. I wish you could remember your first breaths in our arms as I do. You are and will always be everything to me, to us both."

Escaping screams of terror transmitted at large from the passengers in the preceding elevators as they were swallowed in debris and fire, interrupting the transmission from father to son.

Grynn was close now, close to reaching the *HELIX*. The increase in speed shook the shafts, and he held tightly to the safety bars to stabilize himself. He didn't want to die. Not this way, arms around his elevator mates, who had become like family; he had been staring desperately just moments before into the terror-filled eyes of his father helplessly ascending towards freedom—only seconds away. But would seconds be enough to save them?

Then the words of his father broke his train of thought as Aricis sang the lullaby he had when Grynn was a toddler, every night until his son had asked to him to stop, every night he could remember until he decided it was no longer necessary, and even then, Aricis would hum it to him next to Grynn's ear when he thought he was already sleeping.

This song rang in his ears as he watched a tongue of fire encompass his father's elevator. He shook with fear, and they all screamed in terror, just seconds away from the *HELIX*.

Grynn could no longer grant himself the fantasy that this would be an adventure, that they would all be OK, that his wife and child would be OK. All he felt was agony, clinging to Shal, with his father's lullaby still ringing in his ears.

CHAPTER 1

LENAC

3.42 (Sunrise) / Orbyss / 50,000 Years
Before XYZ Evacuation Day

Alone in the forest, the soft foliage felt cool and wet against her legs as she maneuvered through the dense trees and vegetation. She was almost two kilometers from home and more than two hundred meters away from the marked path that made travel between the villages both swift and safe. This was the first time she had ventured off alone in search of argus root, their staple food source. Nutritionally sound, it had become scarce due to intrinsic competition from other foraging mammals in the gathering spots they typically harvested. Today she was determined not to come back empty-handed.

Lenac had not only been the bravest but also the strongest youth in her village for as long as she could remember, dwarfing both female and male counterparts her age. She took pride in the respect it garnered and was in awe of her own abilities as much as others were. Her training had become more advanced than that of others in her cohort, even those one or two years older. Fifteen was an important milestone;

it marked the end of adolescence and the beginning of life as an adult in her village. She would soon pair with a mate and start her own family. It was the topic of choice amongst the young females, discussed at every opportunity. How would they survive without the constant female companionship, both day and night? Some hated the prospect and vowed to run away—others could not wait. For Lenac, it meant taking on a great responsibility. She wanted to be a valuable partner, and today these thoughts translated into bringing back as much argus root as possible, despite the potential danger.

The foliage was so lush that leaves were layered like armor in the trees. Life was green at that time. The forest floor bloomed with ancient ferns and grasses in every shade of emerald and jade with only the grey bark of the tree trunks sporadically interrupting the display. The wind blowing the crisscrossed ferns back and forth was hypnotic. Combined with the high temperature and humidity, Lenac felt light-headed as she continued her search another hundred meters off the path from the village.

If not for her curiosity, she never would have come across the most important discovery anyone in her culture had ever made. In that simple serendipitous finding, she would unknowingly change the history of not only her species but every species that was to follow on Orbyss for millennia.

The subtle whistling of the thermal vent was what initially drew her attention. Almost inaudible, easily overlooked amidst the constant cacophony of the forest. At that one brief moment, however, the trees, the wind, life itself seemed to temporarily pause and reveal its most significant treasure. Spiral columns a meter high of brilliant-green cylindrical leaves, illuminating the dark forest floor. Crowding together yet thriving despite their proximity to each other. No need for competition amongst individual plants, as these unique organisms were not only utilizing an accelerated form of photosynthesis but also geothermal energy to coexist, flourish, and grow at an unprecedented rate.

Lenac had never seen vegetation of this nature, and she considered collecting a sample to bring back with her. However, the quiet of the forest continued, and its silence was always a warning. A lullaby that generations of parents sang to their infants filled her head. She needed a distraction, and subconsciously chose a lullaby that would provide comfort as she ventured farther into the forest, spear in hand. The voice of her mother repeated in her head, whispering to her that sleep would bring peace to the darkness. But the words were interrupted as she stumbled upon the bloody body of a recently hunted ranceva still warm from the kill. The bleeding mammal, its viscera not yet consumed, meant that the terrodon would still be nearby. Deep gashes from the beast's reptilian front claws ran the length of the primitive sheeplike creature's spine, confirming her assumption.

Three meters behind her, the terrodon's sail, like that of a reptilian shark, cut effortlessly through the lush foliage of the primordial forest. Terror struck her chest as she realized she had interrupted its midday feeding. She started to sprint, heart pounding in her ears as she raced through the forest. It was futile, as she would not be able to avoid the attack. As the nearly six-meter-long creature closed in on her, she could see the tree branches ahead shake while the mottled greenish-grey apex predator disturbed the canopy less than a meter behind.

She could not discern between the deafening sound of her pulse pounding in her ears and the thunder of the terrodon's gallop and labored breathing, like a misplaced echo. Lenac darted left and right, trying in vain to evade the predator's incessant reach. In ultimate desperation, she buried her spear deep into the trunk ahead. The beast's claws grazed her right forearm, etching a jagged tattoo that would serve as a reminder of the attack for the rest of her life. As she leveraged her spear to vault to the safety of the branches above, the terrodon pummeled the tree with its front legs and shoulders. It reared up, attempting to slice it in two with its powerful jaws, but missed, and the spear remained lodged in the tree just inches above its teeth.

Tears streamed down Lenac's cheeks as she fought hard to climb higher into the branches. She needed to slow her heart rate and consciously attempted to stop her own shaking as the beast charged the tree just half a meter below.

She closed her eyes and attempted to block out the reality of the situation in order to call out to the others for help. Her transmission was frantic and desperate but not futile. If she could get through to even one individual in the village, they would make every effort to save her. She just had to hold on.

CHAPTER 2

POLST

10.67 (After Midnight) / Orbyss / 50,000
Years Before XYZ Evacuation Day

Lenac was back in the forest running towards the tree responsible for her survival, with the charge of the beast still ringing in her ears. Sweat saturated her clothing, constructed from natural fibers woven tightly together and pieced strategically across her body in order to provide ultimate mobility and comfort. They glistened on her moonlit skin as her ragged breathing and muffled scream woke her from her fitful reprieve.

Lenac sat up in the bed, her heart drumming out the same rhythm it had just hours before. It had truly been a nightmare, a living nightmare, a surreal event that would shape who she became despite her best efforts to escape it. She had never been as terrified in her young life, and she had known that the chances of escape were slim. Not until she had seen the warriors she had summoned, the ones who had answered her transmission, had she been able to give hope access to the recesses of her mind. The terrodon had continued to ram the tree until it shook with such force that Lenac could hear the trunk crack from within. She had climbed as high as she dared in the ever-thinning tree branches. The smaller branches touching the neighboring trees were too thin to facilitate her migration. She feared that if she crawled too far out onto the longest branches, her weight would not be supported as the creature pelted the tree's base from below.

She had continued to transmit, as best she could manage. Venturing off the path made transmitting her location more difficult, but she knew that as long as she kept it up, they would eventually find her. Her transmission was a homing signal that would resonate more intensely the closer they came. She kept her gaze set on the terrodon so that, through her eyes, they could see what they would be up against.

Her spear had remained lodged in the tree trunk below despite the terrodon's attempt to reach it. She considered retrieving the weapon so that she could aim for its abdomen or eye, injuring the terrodon sufficiently enough to cause it to recoil and possibly retreat. But it would have likely been a fruitless attempt at warding off the enormous predator, a creature evolutionarily equipped with incredibly thick plated armor covering the vast majority of its body, a combination of keratin protein and rudimentary bony outgrowths that would render the spear no more than a passing nuisance. As its jaws snapped with singular purpose just inches from where the spear protruded, she could not risk its retrieval as the terrodon's six-inch teeth relentlessly destroyed the trunk below.

Lenac had continued to transmit her signal with intensity, hoping to relay the desperate nature of the situation. She needed them to hurry. The beast had become frustrated, but instead of giving up and consuming the rest of his meal, he grew ever more determined to have Lenac as a second course. If he were successful in bringing down the tree, she wouldn't have enough time to climb to another for safety, nor would she be able to dislodge her spear in order to fight him off, which would be an unlikely win even if, by some chance, the odds were in her favor during this mismatched battle. The XYZs did not hunt the terrodon, even as a group. The closest they came to hunting was catching fish, which was their main source of protein. They lived at one with all life-forms around them, taking only what was required. Hunting terrodon was counterintuitive and counterproductive. Even if they were successful in killing one, gaining access to any sustenance past the scales of these dragons was not worth their while. Instead, they avoided them successfully for the most part. The terrodons' preferred habitat was the saltwater marshes far away from the dense high ground of the village. The ecological buffet at the marshes provided more than ample nutrition, enabling the beasts to grow to a formidable size. It was alarming to encounter one so far from its home yet so close to theirs.

The transmission had come from her rescue party just as the terrodon struck the trunk with such a force that the leaves pitched and twisted around her, making it difficult to hold on. "We see you!" She had felt ill with relief when they found her. She went cold as she absorbed the reality of the situation. The danger she had found herself in, the danger she had put them all in.

The half dozen warriors had approached, each taller than two meters in height, and closed in on the terrodon from behind in order to save her. They synchronized their formation, three on each side of the beast. With surgical precision, a razor-sharp quarterstaff pithed the terrodon in the back of the head through its cervical spine, instantaneously rendering it motionless.

Lenac physically shook in her sweat-drenched bed, trying to stop reliving the attack and rescue yet again.

"You are safe now, Lenac," came the transmission from behind her. Polst chose to transmit instead of speaking to her, not wanting to scare her or wake the others in the lodge.

Upon returning to the village, the rescue party had delivered Lenac immediately to the healer, and he had insisted Lenac remain in his care until he was satisfied with her recovery.

Lenac had been shaking as much from terror as cold. "You are soaking in sweat; we need to get you out of these clothes," Polst had said as he helped her stand and led her to the dressing area. He washed and re-bandaged her fresh lacerations that had bled through the dressings. He left her only to retrieve some broth to nourish and warm her at the same time.

"You are a brave girl, Lenac, perhaps too brave," Polst had said. Lenac understood that Polst wanted to get her talking in hopes of helping her past what had happened.

She managed a smile from behind her soup. The last thing she wanted to do was talk about what had happened. She just wanted to forget it all. She wanted to run from the lodge back to the comfort of her family, back to the comfort of her sisters. The constant shaking of her right leg, up and down, up and down, gave away the anxiety she felt within.

"Do you know where the term 'brave' came from?" Polst had deliberately taken a seat on the lodge floor beside her wooden stool so that she would feel more in control. Lenac watched as he sipped at his own cup of the broth.

She shook her head no, taking another sip of the soup and observing him from her perch intently, ready to listen to what he had to say.

"Well, as you know, our language has changed many times over millions of years as part of our own evolution. Brave originated as *barbarus*, and it meant uncivilized, ignorant, wild, rough, cruel, fierce." Her face fell slightly as he went on with his list.

"Yes, Lenac, it was only as our territory came under attack and we were forced to defend ourselves that being brave has become a necessity, the word itself morphing into something good instead of bad." Her eyes widened slightly.

"Millions of years before us, our ancestors did not live as we do today. We evolved from the whale/dolphin lineage—our ancestors came from the sea. Our lineage gifted us with mammalian brains. Our ancestors developed low-frequency communication that could span entire ocean basins, language, abstract thinking, social conscience, and altruistic behaviors that enhanced our migration to land. We were the planet's first tetrapods. While it is true that most of our ancestral cousins returned to the sea, it is our ancestors—yours and mine—that were able to use advanced intelligence and social conscience to adapt to land out of the water." Polst could see that he was starting to lose her with his history lesson. Perhaps he needed to have it hit a bit closer to home for her.

"So, you see how different our evolution was from the terrodon you so closely escaped from. How diversely we have evolved over millions of years."

She surprised him by asking, "Why would we stay on land? For that matter, why would the terrodon?"

"Yes, you are quite right, the oceans are abundant with life, but they are also fraught with danger, Lenac. The instincts and social structure required to ensure the safety of our numbers that we experience today could never have been achieved if we had stayed in the water. As often is the case, great hardship is required to achieve great change. An awakening and much suffering were required in order for us to prosper as we do now. Evolution is not kind; it has its favorites, and the traits that made existence on land possible for our ancestors are the ones that protect us all today."

Polst continued, "Unlike the terrodon, once we had adjusted physically to life on land, we had the ability to manipulate our environment to our advantage as a result of our cognitive abilities. The laws of nature, of science, apply to all life regardless of if you reside on land or in the sea. It was our intelligence that made life here not just possible but also allowed us to uncover endless possibilities for our Orbyss and the heavens and beyond.

"You see how special you are, Lenac, and what a waste it would have been if we had lost you to the terrodon today. The fact that you carry inside you the DNA of millions of years of evolution of the most advanced species on the planet would have been a grave loss indeed. Especially to a greedy reptile who wouldn't have had any idea of the magnificence of the creature he was feasting upon."

Lenac wanted more. She no longer saw this as a history lesson; it was more of a biology lesson now. She wanted to learn all there was to know about the breadth and depth of her abilities and how she could refine them.

The fact that she had moved towards him as he looked up at her, balancing on the edge of the stool, was not lost on Polst, and he decided to go on with his bedtime story of sorts.

"You were very lucky today with the terrodon, especially a male, who, as you know, outweighs the female by up to five hundred kilos. A female would probably have left you alone, but a male during mating season directly following a kill is a different beast entirely. Reptiles such as the terrodon, and even other mammals on land, evolved in a similar pattern, the males markedly larger in size than the females. Males evolved to a larger size in order to maximize reproductive success and to aid in competition for resources; females became smaller for feeding, camouflage, and caring for offspring.

"Our species evolved first with a reversal of sexual dimorphism. The larger female whale is coveted by the smaller males because she will produce a larger calf. As we evolved as tetrapods on land, size became less important a trait than speed, memory, and agility. And we continued to evolve in the absence of sexual dimorphism, resulting in males and females of equal proportion, intelligence, and ability."

"If we are the most advanced species on the planet, as you say, then why do we fear the terrodon? Why are we hunted and killed by predators? Why do we avoid them at all costs, living high above our main food source?" Lenac was getting tired, but she still did not have the answers she was looking for. She was still afraid.

"Lenac, you already know the answer to this. We must exist in harmony. If we resort to killing in excess or expanding our borders beyond what is required, if we kill for fear or sport instead of nourishment, then we are no different than the terrodon. Orbyss provides us with an abundance we could have never dreamt possible in the sea. The beauty and richness of the planet are ours, and we must cultivate its longevity not only for ourselves but for all of the creatures it hosts. We are all connected, and as the most advanced species, the responsibility to facilitate life in its every form is ours."

"How was I connected to the terrodon today, Polst? Only as a meal, that is all." Lenac had grown weary and fatigue was setting in.

Polst quietly considered her outburst and then gently replied, "We have already strayed from our nature; we have already accommodated the harshness of the land. You are considered brave, are you not? You don't know what the terrodon is evolving towards, Lenac. One day we may rely on them not to eat us but to save us instead."

CHAPTER 3

RANA

5.09 (Early Morning) / Orbyss / 50,000
Years Before XYZ Evacuation Day

There was an unmistakable shift in energy just before Rana made her arrival. It was like something in the air changed, as it does just prior to a storm. A warning of sorts. A welcome warning, as it was never in one's favor to be surprised by Rana. She was spectacular, just like the storms on Pangea. A symphony of electricity and precipitation creating celestial fireworks with the acoustics to match. An event that illuminated the sky while it swirled apart the sea below.

"Ah, I am relieved to see you in one piece, Lenac. You were almost a terrodon breakfast from what I have heard. Few live to tell the tale." Rana was the head of their group, the chief matriarch, and she'd had her sights on Lenac for some time. She was always keeping an eye out for potential successors. While Lenac's strength and bravery made her stand out from the others, Rana now had to question her judgment. She had no desire to have the young girl relive the trauma, but she did want to know why she made the seemingly foolish decision to stray so far from safety.

Rana's lucid eyes were the deepest color of brown, almost black. Once you locked your gaze with Rana, everything else fell away. She had the ability to mesmerize her people, whether it was an interaction with an individual or with the group as a whole. Her eyes held secrets and truths, a lifetime of wisdom, and the collective inheritance of their past.

Rana could see Lenac's unease. She needed to give the girl time to collect her thoughts, so she instead turned her attention to Polst, who had been quietly observing from the corner.

"How long do you advise Lenac remain in your care?" Her pointed question brought Polst to attention. He and Rana were oftentimes at odds. She had accepted the testaments of health from the often wounded warriors of the village above his own recommendation for further rest much too often, in Polst's opinion. This time was different. Lenac was far too young to make the call herself.

"Her injuries are nearly healed; another two days within the lodge should suffice. However, it would benefit her to spend some time in your care, Rana. If we are encountering terrodon within our territory, then perhaps further consideration should be given to her training."

He expected her refusal to be swift. However, she remained still and did not answer him immediately; instead, she considered his advice. She had been contemplating the same thing and now believed that Lenac might be key to their change of strategy. She may be key to delivering the message to the rest of the tribe. Especially the young, sometimes reckless warriors amongst them.

"Polst is right, Lenac. A couple days' rest will do nicely. Tomorrow morning, you and I will talk. We have much to discuss."

Rana nodded goodbye to Polst and left without waiting for a reply. Once she was out of earshot, he let an exhale escape, which earned him a smirk from Lenac.

CHAPTER 4

LENAC

6.82 (Morning) / Orbyss / 50,000 Years
Before XYZ Evacuation Day

As Lenac wove her way through the warriors, they stalled at their respective tasks long enough to briefly acknowledge her presence. Their silent stares were a mix of pity and disbelief, and some even held an energy of anticipation; they all wanted to make sure she was OK. The best she could manage was a small smile as she devoted her attention to the ground just in front of her own steps. As she made her way to Rana's quarters, she regretted her decision to gather argus root at all that day.

Being who they were, altruism at their core, meant that apologies were unnecessary and unrequired. In spite of that, Lenac remained embarrassed.

She was ushered in by Rana's mate. Yarsig was the village favorite. His was the widest smile amongst them. He always put Lenac at ease despite his towering height and mass, surpassed only by Rana herself.

"You will join me in the inner courtyard, Lenac. There is some-thing I want to show you." Rana was already headed there, leaving her words hanging in the air behind her, like the scent of an impending rainstorm, with the expectation that Lenac would surely follow.

There was a beautiful fountain in the center of the courtyard. It was carved from a solid piece of stone. A spiral slide led the water from the top in two opposing directions around the perimeter, its mirrored flow followed by the fish that swam in opposite directions in the basin below. The skirt of the stone pool was decorated with ancient carvings Lenac had never seen before. She stood mesmerized by their intricacy and the steady rush of the water. It was impossible not to be soothed by the motion as much as the sound.

"It is beautiful, is it not? It rests at the heart of our village and sig-nifies the heart of our people. As it tells our story, it describes our past. One we can never forget, Lenac." Rana moved to the far side of the fountain and signaled for Lenac to follow.

"Can you imagine what we were before now? Can you identify with the images?" Rana gestured for Lenac to look specifically at the carving she pointed towards. "Here, see the whales layered by the thousands amongst the waves. Our ancestors, from whence we came. If you close your eyes and listen to the water, it will take you back to them. They are with us still."

Lenac knew the story well; their cetacean lineage was ingrained early, the most important part of their education, part of their way of life. She had frequently accompanied her family on the village's annual pilgrimage to the sea in their honor. Although dangerous, they con-tinued this transformational experience to swim with and touch the whales, to communicate directly with the giants of the ocean through their advanced echolocation. Lenac could have never imagined that as the enormous power of natural selection and ongoing evolution con-tinued, her descendants' generations from then on would lose the abil-ity to communicate with their ocean-bound predecessors. However, they had gained a telepathic type of communication, enabling them to communicate over great distances, including outer space.

After the terrodon attack, Lenac wondered why they had ever left the ocean at all. Lenac watched closely as Rana moved past the carvings of the waves, which joined one to the next, hanging on her every word.

"I bet you are thinking that this is just the same old story you have always heard. But it is not, Lenac. This is where the history we teach differs from the way the story actually went. We tend to take the migration to land for granted, and we like to water it down so that everyone feels comfortable. So that everyone can feel good about our past and how we evolved to be where we are today. But that is not the truth, Lenac. The reality is that we had to become warriors to survive on land.

"These ancient cousins of ours remained in the water for safety and sustenance. Millions of years later, we decided to come on shore. Having had years to develop in the ocean and evolve into intelligent beings, we had come as far we could. We instinctively knew that in order to continue advancement, we would need to migrate out of the water. We knew that the ocean was only one piece of the puzzle. And in order to advance, we were forced from our home forever; natural selection eventually divided us into a completely separate species."

Lenac knelt and touched the carvings one at a time; they outlined the sleek lines of the whale's tail as it disappeared and forked with each carving as her ancestors made their ascension to land.

"What happened next should have been avoided. It was a dark time with many dark days and much conflict. That is when the great divide occurred. When our tribe separated."

Rana continued as she came to stand behind Lenac, who was still on her knees at the base of the fountain. "There were others, four groups in total. Two no longer remain. They could not survive. It was our decision to do what was necessary in order to carry on; however, we refused to give up the reason we migrated in the first place. A love for Orbyss and a love for each other, a deep respect for knowledge and understanding so that we could help each other and make things better for the whole—this is why we left the sea in the first place, and it is the reason we are still here today. Because we want something better for those who will lead us in the future, for those who will continue long after we have gone."

Lenac rose up, her eyes meeting Rana's intense gaze. For the first time since her attack, she felt herself; she felt whole again. Rana seemed capable of passing her strength to others, so powerful was her composition both physical and emotional.

"How did we survive, then?" Lenac questioned. "Why did we succeed when the others failed?"

"It was our connection to each other, Lenac. Nothing is ever accomplished independently. Your first steps, your first words, the person you are today, it is all because of those who decided they would see you succeed instead of fail, the ones who selflessly made your progress possible. That was a choice, Lenac. They did not have to do that for you. They chose your success above their own desires, and that is why we, as a whole, survive. That is why we succeed where others fail. That is why nothing can break the bonds that tie us to each other, to the planet, to the heavens and beyond."

Rana continued, "That is why all the warriors you passed by when you came to me answered your call. They want the best for our collective future. To lose even one is one too many. And it is also important to recognize that losing one as strong and with such potential as yourself would have been a grave loss indeed. I see great potential in you, and I know that you will offer the gifts of strength and leadership of the highest caliber. Your questions are all the confirmation I need."

Lenac exhaled. Everything made sense to her now. She was no longer afraid; she was no longer afraid of anything. It was this newfound confidence she derived from Rana that inspired her to reveal the discovery of the unique plant she had found just moments prior to the attack. She described it in detail, as well as the high-pitched whistling of the thermal vents that, until that point in time, had gone undetected. Lenac had been raised to take an interest in and investigate the world around her. Their environment was of spectacular importance to them, and every effort was made to understand, appreciate, and coexist with all other life-forms on Pangea.

As Lenac led Rana and the warriors back into the forest, this time with anticipation and devoid of fear, she traced her exact path from two days prior. They proceeded tentatively, eager to hear the whistling Lenac had described.

The forest stood still; only the wind rustled through the leaves between the intermittent calls of the birds. Then, once again, everything went quiet, just for a moment, and the muffled hiss of the thermal vents turned their heads, drawing attention to what was hidden in plain sight. The plants consumed their gaze as the XYZs knelt down to explore the unique spiraled structure, in awe of the shoots and dum-founded that it had never been identified until now. As a species, they had painstakingly investigated every inch of their surroundings, log-ging every plant, animal, and organism encountered. Discovering a plant never before observed was monumental to a civilization whose most important function was the investigation of the world around them in order to facilitate a halcyon integration with their surround-ings for the betterment of all.

They were exquisitely careful while collecting a specimen, ensur-ing they didn't disturb the surrounding plant life yet digging down far enough to extract the root structure from deep within the forest floor. The location of the plant made retrieval difficult due to its proximity to the torrid thermal vents. The tangled roots, six times the length of the plant itself, were deeply entrenched in the soil. The strength of the plant's spiraled stock whispered its potential—although none of them could envision that these shoots would eventually enable them to grow carbon nanotubes into formations that would house, protect, and ulti-mately advance their entire civilization to levels unseen on the planet.

None of them had yet evolved the intellectual capacity to envision the significance of the plant that grew before them using a combina-tion of energy from the thermal vents and advanced photosynthesis. An incredible evolutionary singularity, never to be replicated, as these plants not only utilized carbon dioxide as an energy substrate but nitrogen in the atmosphere, as well. At the time, they could not have imagined a future in which they would strategically cultivate this plant so that, when heated, it turned to glass; and when adapted to their intellectual process, it could facilitate their way of life, their technol-ogy, their supercomputers; and when integrated in the development of a high-tech spacecraft, it would eventually make their escape from the planet possible.

It was named Lenacyth after the one who had discovered it, ensur-ing her legacy would never be forgotten. Legends and stories of her rule would be passed down through the ages. Leading her people after Rana passed was an honor she never bore lightly. She was everything Rana had been and more. Her influence continued for millions and millions of years after, because of her discovery of the spiral columns in the forest and how they would transform their world, their very

existence. The culture she created for her people, as close to the cetacean lineage as possible, carried on throughout their evolution; they
held steadfast to her vision generation after generation. One day her
legacy would inspire her 10^{600} grandson Herriden, as he prepared to
captain a starship in order to save the species.

CHAPTER 5

VASH

6.80 (Evening) / Orbyss / Ten Years
Before XYZ Evacuation Day

The D string on the suggestively curved, hand-carved instrument res-
onated throughout the square on the thinnest of carbon-fiber threads
in perfect pitch, a sound unmatched by any other to follow. The four
musicians intermittently closed their eyes as they played, in perfect
harmony. A number of bystanders gathered round, sporadically oscillating their attention between the expert quartet, with their jet-black
strings, and each other's lives. The piece was syncopated, its easy
cadence a carefree obrigado in appreciation that all was well, one that
lifted the spirits of the visitors to the square and suggested that everything might always stay this way, an existence engulfed in perpetual
bliss.

Vash, however, seemed immune to the performance as she passed
through the square, her long robes caressed by the unexpected breeze
that sporadically wound its way between the surrounding buildings,
sculptures, and patrons. As her garments floated around her, they

changed color either to match the surroundings, camouflaging her existence, or to enhance her profile based on the proximity to others and the pheromones she exuded as the clothing monitored her vitals by the millisecond. She was a typical member of her species in both appearance and size, not unlike her XYZ successors, save a few obvious differences. Natural selection, although perfect in its random ability to introduce new traits and characteristics to all living organisms, was dictated by the advantages these new mutations might ascribe given environmental influences. The most striking contrasts were in height and skin tone, ranging from dark grey to light brown and often mottled in complexion. Due to the stability of the warm climate, they had little need for hair on their bodies and had only developed hair on their heads in order to protect them from the sun.

Her civilization had continued to advance, not encumbered by war or competition, to the pinnacle of its existence. Great heights had been achieved, and breakthroughs had been made across all indicators of development. Alongside cultural advances, knowledge had developed spectacularly at an unparalleled rate tracked by a ten-hour clock resulting in twenty-hour days and a twenty-month year. It was a significantly more accurate measure of time captured in multiples of ten, instead of one reflecting the phases of the moon. They had no fears, no worries, no limits as to what they could achieve. The only caveat was the confines of their own imagination, or so it would seem. The purpose of absolutely everything had been amplified and perfected. Nothing had been left unconsidered. Everything was conceived of organic intelligence and worked to benefit not only each citizen but society as a whole, the planet, and everything that inhabited it.

They could not imagine an alternative to this world they had literally built for themselves, working within the laws of nature, the planet, and as they had also discovered, the universe. The actualization of self and appreciation for nature, the beauty of one's surroundings, the unending celebration of what a cherished and protected environment had bestowed upon them. They had achieved a quintessential civilization for the whole without sacrificing the potential of each individual. Without a struggle for resources, without the struggle to survive, their attention was turned to a collective fulfillment, creativity, and the expression of self in its truest form. A global experience of one another held them in a delicate balance. Through transmission, not only could they communicate their thoughts but also the associated physiological response that resulted from them—sadness, joy, as well as pain. It was as if they had been rewarded by the universe for never accepting less than the very best for each living thing they encountered, and the prize was a perfect existence in an everlasting equilibrium. But none of these amazements found a home in Vash's mind as she scanned the dense crowd scattered throughout the expansive square, her sole purpose to find her true love and best friend, Grynn.

As was typical here, in their favored meeting place, he would see her first, beckoned by the elaborate display of her gown. Garments were of utmost importance to them, not only in terms of expression but also, most significantly, function. Their clothing, composed of Lenacyth, was intelligent, detecting the natural rhythms, pulse, temperature, all other vitals, and the overall health of the body it protected. An advanced form of protection that had been specifically designed not only to shield them but also to optimize their comfort and health while reflecting their feelings. In Orbyss, what covered you literally had you covered. Clothing acted as your personal assistant, your physician, your councilor, and your guard. It would provide reminders or deliver required information as it received your thoughts. It provided the collected information of the whole to the individual as seamlessly as it read your mind.

"I hate to see this." Grynn came up behind her as usual, but today, instead of playing the universal game of "guess who," he noted her furrowed brow as he had been watching her from afar across the square, and instead, he whispered these words to her as his index and middle finger eased the pinched skin of her forehead directly between her eyes. She turned around to face him. His best efforts at literally wiping away her worries had little impact, in stark contrast to the impact she had on him, running through the square in an effort to find him.

"Look, we can still see your disoriented path in the square. You really were quite desperate to find me, weren't you?" Grynn spoke softly as he motioned beyond her to her still-glowing amber footprints on the jet-black surface—her path across the square, its inductive surface not only able to capture solar energy but the energy of any who traversed it.

"Our travel plans have become impossible," she murmured. Vash had spent nearly a year in Grynn's company. They were relatively young to have developed such deep feelings for each other. Being seventeen years of age left them independently dependent on their parents. They were inseparable; everyone knew this. A couple that drew a crowd. Together they exuded a sense of heightened awareness others found difficult to ignore. Today was no exception; all eyes were on them at the start of what would become a melancholy conversation laced with disappointment.

As many hominid parents would do, Vash's and Grynn's had eavesdropped on their children's plans to take a trip together instead of with their respective same-sex best friends. As part of their natural development, it took time to master the ability to transmit to only the intended recipients. Vash's and Grynn's immaturity was easily exploited, as their parents simply heard their thoughts by listening to their "confidential" transmissions to each other.

Their parents' fear was not about the danger of the journey itself; any one of them could transmit and locate each other in seconds. The issue was a collective desire for Grynn and Vash to be physically distanced until they were deemed "old enough" to manage a mature relationship. The protective measures of their parents were there to prevent the emotional consequences of young love gone wrong. The XYZ brain processed emotions in sophisticated and complex patterns, and thus their social cohesion reached a level unmatched by any other mammals, including humans. As a culture, they had developed a distributed sense of self, strongly connected to the feelings and behaviors of all group members. It made them act in a way that humans would never understand or, more importantly, never be capable of in their own right. Still, adolescent love is unbearably hard to impede. At the height of the disenchantment felt at their plans being thwarted, they could not have imagined that things were about to get much worse. That soon all travel and, in actuality, every single activity and pursuit was about to be channeled into one hope for the future, one hope for the species—the *HELIX*.

CHAPTER 6

ANAE

6.00 (Morning) / Orbyss / Ten Years
Before XYZ Evacuation Day

The ebony inductive caps at the top of the living, corrugated spiral structures, whose shape echoed the Lenacyth they had been fashioned from, contained the existence of a city of two million; they collected, stored, and distributed the energy required to sustain their own existence. It was ironic, almost cruel, that this bright and sunny day should be the one that would radically shatter their world hereafter.

Anae stepped away from the glass-like window connected seamlessly to the carbon-fiber panels attached to it. The top floor, as it were, housed the meetings of the Inoto Council, which was charged with determining the level of the potential threat that currently lay outside their solar system an estimated ten years away.

Her position—though viewed as an esteemed and sought-after role only the wisest and most knowledgeable amongst them achieved—offered little reward or pleasure, as it was and had always meant that she was burdened with the most difficult decisions. The ones required to ensure the future of Pangea. Her council was composed of the leaders from each region, a total of forty-six representatives. Each one focused on the direct impact to their territory, with only Anae to decide the fate of the whole.

Today they had been gathered in confidence, none of them fore-warned or prepared for the discussion she would lead them through. Her only allies, the physicists who had been her sole advisors for the past three years, had assisted her as they carefully tracked, monitored, and hoped that they could avoid what they now had no choice but to acknowledge.

Over time, Anae failed to recognize her own voice when it came to discussions of this tragedy. She now mimicked the scientists. Her language, previously trained to inspire and lead, now sounded foreign to her as it spouted facts, projections, and predictions regarding the estimated arrival of the pending terror.

"I am pained to deliver this news to you, my friends, advisors, col-leagues. I will not mince words, as we haven't the time. Unfortunately, our very worst fears have been realized. If there was a way to avoid the disaster that is making its way towards us as we speak, this would be a very different conversation. Please believe and trust that I—that we—have investigated every possibility; however, there will be no avoidance of the event that will destroy our planet, and if we remain here, all of us will be destroyed along with it. We have ten years grace, but we cannot waste this convincing ourselves that some outside force or fate will intervene. I wish we had this luxury. Instead, the ten years before an asteroid of epic proportion enters our atmosphere and destroys the planet must be used to prevent our own extinction. We have no choice but to leave if we are to survive. From this moment forward, all our resources, every thought, every word, every moment, must be strategi-cally channeled towards engineering our evacuation." Runaway tears trailed down Anae's cheeks as her voice failed her halfway through her last word, "evacuation."

The faces of the friends who had become family—seated around the beautiful jet-black table as it silently collected energy from its guests in order to power the information systems, lights, air, and heat that surrounded them—all stared back at her in disbelief. The reality of what she was saying would not sink in for some time. She realized this. She had expected as much; her own initial reaction had been that or worse.

Perhaps their acceptance would come more easily, as they would have each other to console and comfort. She hoped for as much as she made her final statement to the group, her colleagues and confidants for the past fifteen years. Her tenure as head of the council had been a harvest ripe with success and progress. As such, it had done little to prepare her for the secret she had kept these past three long years, and it pained her to have to be the one to break the news, especially to the individuals before her. She had suffered a physical price for keeping this secret, and more than one of them had inquired after her health as she aged before them at hyper-speed. What was once her sleek blond hair was now a short grey cap; her weary eyes had become sunken; and although her tall stature remained straight, her strong shoulders had begun to cave in slightly, a hint at the fight she had lost. She had always brought a message of innovation, progression, and encouragement. Of course, there had been obstacles to overcome, and she had prided herself on being able to win the council over when necessary and gain their trust in the process. Only, this time, there would be no winners.

"I urge you all to ask as many questions as you would like. We will stay here as long as necessary. Please know that you are not alone and I would never have brought you here to deliver this tragic news if there were any possibility it could be avoided." Anae's emotions got the better of her as she scanned the table and realized many of them were holding back their own tears. The days leading up to this had been long and the nights had been sleepless. She was only hominid, after all.

Their culture was not one of compliance; all opinions were respected, validated, and considered. As such, Anae would have been surprised and perhaps disappointed if they immediately accepted her explanation as the only truth.

"How was the asteroid discovered, and what are you using to determine the orbit? How can you possibly be tracking it ten years out?"

"How widespread will the damage be?"

"How are you determining the minimum orbit intersection distance?"

The questions came rapid fire. She had asked them all herself initially and was more than prepared and now qualified to answer them.

However, she had failed to give sufficient weight to those amongst them who were overcome emotionally by the shocking news she had just delivered, and she was forever grateful for Haur's exquisite timing as he came to her aid, especially as she had spent the last three years of her life unsuccessfully attempting to prove the lead astrophysicist wrong.

And so it began, day one of the plan to leave Orbyss. The knowledge slowly sunk in around the table, a gradual acceptance that a catastrophic event would take place. An asteroid five hundred kilometers in diameter would inevitably reach Orbyss in ten years, bury itself deep into the planet's core, and extinguish life as they knew it forever.

CHAPTER 7

GRYNN

4.85 (Early Evening) / Orbyss / Ten Years
Before XYZ Evacuation Day

Grynn paused at the upper galley of the sculpted staircase listening as the echoes climbed up the pie-shaped steps to meet him. The helical stairs were as beautiful as they were functional. Their acoustics amplified conversations in the foyer like an intercom system, making it possible for him to assess if he should stay hidden or race to the door, without having to make his presence known.

The design of the staircase reflected that of their home and the shape of the plant on which their fate would rely. It paid homage to the golden ratio, which accounted for so many beautiful things in nature. Beauty beyond even what they could have imagined.

Typically, when Grynn heard the melodic cadence of Vash's voice, he would race down; however, his mother had answered the door this evening, and when she did, he always waited, preferring to hear them laugh together before he joined them. Nothing gave him more pleasure than to listen to the shared laughter of the two females that meant the most to him. Today would unfortunately be the exception.

"Grynn, so glad you could join us." Vash's sarcastic tone was not lost on him. Evidently, she was wise to his strategic eavesdropping.

Grynn noticed his mother's weary expression and mistook it for regret at having invaded his privacy, and Vash's, as well. He had been consumed with embarrassment when Vash spoke of their respective parents' betrayal. In truth, it was conjecture; both teenagers were secretly comforted with the knowledge that their parents' love knew no bounds. However, the anticipation and excitement about their plans, now thwarted, took precedence in their teenage minds ripe with thoughts of separation and sovereignty.

Grynn took the seat beside Vash at his mother's suggestion and waited patiently for the anticipated apology and explanation that would surely follow due to their not-so-secret plans and the unavoidable action both sets of parents were now forced to take.

"I have something to explain to both of you, and I am going to start by saying I am truly very sorry." Her words were exactly as expected, but the tears in her eyes were perplexing to Grynn. His mother was a steadfast leader full of love for him but not typically one for emotion, especially if he were in the wrong. At the same moment, Grynn's father entered the room along with both of Vash's parents.

Grynn and Vash were both only children, as was the case in many XYZ families. The emotional bond between parent and child was the strongest of all mammals and not meant for separation. Many lived with or near their parents for the duration of their lives. As such, many chose to limit the number of offspring they had, preferring to invest themselves fully in only one or two at the most.

"Look, we are very sorry for this . . ." Grynn was horrified that all four parents would come together to lecture them as a group. He could not have anticipated anything like this or imagined that what was, in his mind, a small transgression would result in such a display.

"Please let me continue." Anae pressed on, determined not to let her emotions get the better of her, especially in front of Vash's parents.

"Although we do regret both the plans you had to deceive us and the unfortunate steps we felt necessary to take by way of invading your privacy, the reason we are all meeting here today is of much greater importance." Aricis had taken a seat next his wife, and Vash's parents took their places beside their daughter.

The silence in the room was deafening as Anae paused for a moment, determining how best to continue, choosing her words with the utmost of care, recognizing that what would come next was far beyond a lecture for a mere adolescent tryst.

"As you both know, you are most important and loved by us all, and we truly wish we were here today to open a discussion about adulthood, timing, and responsibility. But sadly, I have brought you here to tell you that from this moment forward, your lives—*all* our lives—will not be as we had imagined or hoped. The four of us wanted to tell you together out of respect for what are obviously the very deep feelings you have developed for each other, and due to the timing of the interception of your transmissions, we are all here because we could think of no better way to show support for the comfort you will undoubtedly require from each other. Our desire is to lessen the uncertainty and dismay you will have regarding the changes and sacrifices that will be required of you, of us all." It was difficult for Anae to take in the bewildered expressions of both teenagers, and her heart broke for the innocence that would be lost at her hands instead of their own during a clandestine trip presumably meant to solidify their bond.

She continued, "Later tonight I will be making an announcement to all of Orbyss that will outline the protocol that will be implemented immediately. It is absolutely imperative that all protocols are followed by each one of us. We will require all of our resources, our collective knowledge, skill, training, and technology if we are to survive. I wish this were not the case, and I am the last person who would ever want to have to tell you this, but please know I have fought hard to find a better solution. I have done everything in my power to spare you both and all of Orbyss from what we will have to endure. An event will occur approximately ten years from now. We will be struck by an asteroid so large that when it makes impact, it will destroy our world and everything that inhabits it. In order to survive, we will be forced to leave this planet and find a new home. We have exactly ten years to accomplish our plans for escape, and we do not have a moment to spare. I am heartbroken to deliver this news to you and may have to one day live with the regret that I did not tell you sooner—that I did not share this news with everyone sooner—however, I needed to be absolutely certain that there was no other way." It was so very difficult to continue amongst the tears of Vash's parents, her husband, and Grynn. It was only Vash who sat silently, seemingly unmoved by what Anae had just conveyed.

"I don't believe you," Vash retorted, anger creasing her fine features.

"Vash, please stop . . ." her father insisted.

"*No!* You are just making this up to punish us. Why do you want to ruin our happiness?" Tears of rage streamed down her cheeks as she stood up, shaking, fists clenched by her side. The beautiful face before them, now contorted in betrayal, reminded the adults of the tsunami of emotions adolescence carried with it. For Vash, Anae's words inflicted fear. But the emotional pain transmitted with it was unbearable to the hypersensitive XYZ. Communication between the species did not begin and end with conversations capable of sending adrenaline racing through veins and tears streaming down faces. XYZs actually felt the impact of physical pain alongside emotional trauma through transmission, and the younger they were, the stronger the impact was. It was not until well into adulthood that they could fully master the difficult skill of transmission. Grynn stood up next to Vash, his arm protectively placed around her trembling shoulders. He literally felt her pain, no more wanting to hear his mother's words than she wanted to say them, but knowing that every word she spoke to them was true.

"Far from here, ten years from now, I promise you we will build a new life, and we will survive, and you will become everything you were meant to be." Anae was on her feet, closing the distance between herself and the teens, desperate not to lose them, not to let them lose themselves. Her role was clear to her now as she stared into their young eyes filled with dread and anguish. She needed to take on the weight of this impending disaster and its outcome not just for her own family but for their entire species. It all depended on her ability to convince them they would be OK, that they would go on, that they would survive as individuals, and as a species. Even if she wasn't sure she would survive. Even though everyone in the room older than thirty-five knew that they were only ensuring a future for their children. Even if she didn't believe the words herself.

CHAPTER 8

GRYNN

9.85 (Approaching Midnight) / Orbyss / Nine
Years Before XYZ Evacuation Day

Grynn's footfalls were stealthy and hasty as he made his way along
the inside corridor, closest to the building's entry point. Entry points,
unlike doors, were fluid, invisible, and intelligent, opening only when
required and otherwise remaining imperceptible. There was no need
for a key to gain access; ownership was shared amongst them. No theft,
no greed—the concept of these human frailties was unknown to a species who lived in abundance and valued shared knowledge and emotional connection above all else.

The curfew had been in effect over the past year and a quarter. It
was one of the many restrictions Anae had reluctantly put in place
in an effort to ensure that all resources were allocated systematically
towards their escape plan. It was a huge ask of every citizen to deliver
what was required in order to make it possible. She could not ask
everything of them without providing the infrastructure and support
needed. While the young XYZ viewed it as a punishment, the curfew

was enacted to ensure that all members, including the youth, could function optimally and remain safe. However, Anae's best intentions backfired, and the curfew, especially, was wildly unpopular with her teenage son and his friends. It had been Grynn's idea initially to seek out a way to avoid it, and now he and Shal had become veterans. They had been meeting in an all-but-abandoned warehouse facility since shortly after the curfew had been implemented. In fact, tonight was the anniversary of an entire year spent in the company of his contemporaries during the hours he should have spent alone, asleep, and confined to his home.

The clandestine meetings had, at first, included only himself, Shal, Vash, and a handful of trusted friends. Now they rotated in order to avoid detection through a list of twenty-four "members," and it would have been more if said membership had been easier to attain.

Following Anae's announcement, the significant amount of time and attention parents would have normally allocated to their offspring became highjacked by the impending arrival of the asteroid. And now the plan for escape demanded almost all their time and energy. As a side effect of the draining hours spent fighting against the countdown, parents had begun to rely heavily upon the restrictions and guidelines put in place. They sought a reprieve from the demands and resulting stress of the task at hand, and, as such, they trusted that the measures were working for, instead of against, them. Forced to remain focused on the survival of the species, it became all too easy for disillusioned teens to plan their own escape from the curfew.

It was tragic; Anae had made her announcement, and the lives of their children, especially their teens, had been irrevocably altered, their adolescence lost. All resources, everything, everyone, were to be fully invested in the development of the required infrastructure, technology, and testing needed to get them off planet prior to the asteroid's arrival. Every vocation, position, and job was altered; even education became tailored to focus on subjects vital to accomplishing their exit. It was all hands on deck, as no time could be spared. Regardless of the circumstances, Grynn felt the shared weight of the news his mother delivered and could not bear to see all of their lives sacrificed this way. It was Grynn who first disobeyed curfew, desperate to make a difference, at least to try. Now a senior, he had been assigned to study under the lead engineer assigned to the *HELIX*'s interior. Something he disputed from the start. To him, it was little more than a design assignment, and he was disappointed if not a little insulted.

Shortly after the curfew was first imposed, he and Shal had gone on a reconnaissance mission of sorts, searching for the perfect hideaway, and they'd found the warehouse. It had been Shal who pointed it out first. Although, if Shal had the chance to do it over, he would have walked straight past the place.

"Grynn, why do we need to meet somewhere? We can just transmit to each other."

"And risk being found out? Not a chance. We need a place, our place, in order to achieve our own command." Grynn was through with obeying his mother, their leader, no matter how much he loved and respected her. Had Anae known that her announcement and the subsequent restrictions would create a break in the trust they all held with their children, she would have immediately retracted them. Her actions, her intentions, took their safety into consideration, and the restrictions were put in place out of love in order to protect them all. However, when she underestimated their need for time together and attention in favor of safety and control, she made a fatal error, one that would impact their society for years to come.

Grynn hated the bureaucracy surrounding their escape. The snail's pace at which the council moved forward on even the simplest of decisions. As if they debated this long enough, the asteroid might just change course and drift away. He watched his mother's anxiety over the push and pull of their arguments get the better of her, and something inside him could no longer continue to stand by, regardless of her and his father's best efforts to "protect" him. It was Grynn who decided that he would contribute at any cost, even if it meant deceiving his parents, night after night. To his advantage, they were genuinely too stressed and too busy to notice; it was definitely not that they did not care.

At first, he and Shal would meet for an hour or two. The warehouse was a large space inhabited by only a few benches, drawing boards, chairs, tables, and a water closet. It had been all but fully neglected, and a stale dampness filled the air. Even the warehouse intelligence had been set on autopilot. Minimal operation was functional, which made it the perfect choice. Only a dull amber glow lit the room from the east wall, a reminder of the luxuries they had traded and the surveillance, found in their respective homes, that they were now able to avoid. Shal did not care for it and had spoken his mind more than once. Although Grynn always nodded his agreement, the look in his eyes spoke his dissent, and Shal braced himself, knowing full well they would definitely be spending time here, potentially lots of it. Grynn implored Shal to agree with him that if their parents could not find a solution to the impending disaster, if their collective society could not save them, then why should they fully trust them any longer and just fall in line? Why should they adhere to rules put in place that were having little to no impact toward discovering a solution that could save their lives? If they were to be cast aside and left disillusioned only to witness their own destruction, then why not, at the very least, enjoy the time they had left? And if they could come up with their own solution, if they could plan their own escape, all the better.

Grynn liked to play games, and consequently, it began this way, a game, a club, and members had to be initiated. The intention was never to leave anyone out but to protect themselves from being found out. It was a difficult initiation. A test that even Shal and Grynn had only just achieved but not yet mastered. Adolescent transmission was frustrating; the skill was a work in progress, and their transmissions flickered until they fully figured it out. If you could transmit without detection, even under distress, then you were granted access. However, the circumstances of the test were exclusive, every time, so that the initiation exercise was always a surprise. The games were highly structured sporting events. A complex set of rules and scoring, and elaborate virtual playgrounds set in multi-dimensions, were constructed only to distract the opponent from the real test: whether or not they would forget themselves and transmit back to someone who interrupted them during the course of play, someone outside of their fellow players, when the game reached its climax or as they lost.

CHAPTER 9

VASH

9.96 (Approaching Midnight) / Orbyss / Nine Years Before XYZ Evacuation Day

The club's first members included Grynn, Shal, Vash, and their closest friends, Moda, Tac, and Rhys. The first meetings were nothing more than small parties, all of them giddy at having deceived their parents. Parents who were too overwhelmed by the responsibility of saving their children that they had no time left to contemplate, let alone manage, the impact the end of the world was having on them. It was Vash who had tired of the status quo and, after several months, devised a way to extend their two-hour escape till sunrise. Every two hours, each of their suits completed a full diagnostic report on the body the garment protected, and everything, including their location, was distributed to their family pod, i.e., their parents. The only exceptions were when the clothing was removed for sleep, sanitation, or sex, for the most part. One evening, high on their own variety of herbal mood enhancement, Vash announced that she would not be leaving anytime soon as the minutes crept steadily towards their inevitable departure time. She marched defiantly towards the back of the warehouse, freeing herself of her garments before she reached the end of the hall. Horror mixed with appreciation stole over the faces of her friends; then, overcome and inspired by her act of rebellion, all followed suit.

"Aren't you tired of this? Waiting for the end of the world? Isn't it obvious that no one is going to save us? That we are going to have to save ourselves? If we want to get something done, we are going to have to do it," Vash said.

Her questions hung in the air unanswered as the others struggled to free themselves of the clothing that constantly monitored them. Usually a comfort yet simultaneously a constraint, they were free, at last. The only required rule was they had to walk past the pile in order to signal their well-being to their cloth keeper at twenty-minute intervals. Fortunately, the garments would signal, by way of a reminder, their need for a status update, and as a sign of their appreciation, the suits would light up as their owner passed by. Hopeful puppies looking for a pat from their owners.

As the club grew in size, rumors spread about its unconventional ways. The truth was that as the numbers grew, the minimal ventilation of the "unused" facility made clothing almost unbearable—so the members' lack of attire, undergarments or nothing at all depending on their preference, was made more of a necessity than an act of liberty. True to her word, Vash was more interested in getting something done than anything else, and their "parties" quickly became planning sessions. They worked through most nights troubleshooting the physics required to overcome the flaws in the *HELIX*'s design outlined in the engineering log updates left on Vash's father's home office desk each day, which were all too easy to return before he left for work the next morning.

Vash was her father's daughter, and he felt pride and joy at all she had learned under his guidance. That was before he had been forced to work round the clock on a structure for their escape. Now their interactions had been reduced to a swift morning hello and a brief kiss good night. It had always been an unspoken truth between them that she would one day be the teacher and he the student. Her aptitude for mathematics and her intelligence were off the charts. Even if her emotions got the better of her and she was prone to outbursts and obstinate when challenged, there was no denying that she possessed ability far beyond her years.

Her father and Grynn's father worked closely together as the lead engineers responsible for the design, model, simulation, and testing of the craft that would hopefully carry them to safety off planet. Their hands were tied on so many occasions. The council debated even the most minute considerations, leaving them hanging for weeks at a time. However, in this forum, in an abandoned warehouse facility, in this club and company, limitations did not exist. They had been discarded as surely as the garments piled at the far end of the warehouse.

It was fateful, this league they had formed. They had all laughed together when they coined themselves the Blowholes in memory of their ancestors, as naked as their predecessors who were still inhabiting the sea. Perhaps it strengthened their bond. Had it not been for the stronghold the end of days had on their parents, on their society as a whole, things would have been different for the young XYZs. They would have enjoyed an effortless and easy existence on Orbyss that more closely resembled heaven. But fate had intervened in the form of a mammoth asteroid, and there would be no return to innocence. A sacred bond had been broken; their safety, their home, their birthright would be taken from them. And they wanted to fight for their future more than any other members of their society. Parents protecting their children's future was one thing, but to stand idly in the face of a stolen future was quite another. The anger, betrayal, and horror of an uncertain hereafter drove the kids' actions. The crippling fear of never seeing each other again gave them cause to find a solution. And the love they had received from not only their parents but from all XYZs gave them courage to find a solution not only for themselves, but for their entire species. This defiant, unabashed collection of rebels, intent on saving the day, would one day take command of the *HELIX*. And just like their whale ancestors had before them, it was they who would make the journey to a new world a reality.

CHAPTER 10

VASH

2.61 (Late Afternoon) / Orbyss / Eight
Years Before XYZ Evacuation Day

Vash was filled with constant unrest that quite often bordered on rage. Her emotions were a reflection of the growing divide between members of their species. Facing the destruction of the planet, XYZs began to experience mistrust, anger, and a lack of control, feelings previously foreign to them. Despite respect for Anae, many had become disillusioned by escape as the only path forward. True to their culture and their adherence to Percivious, the ultimate in altruism being at the center of their existence, it was easier for them to accept that escape, or an attempt at escape, was unnecessary. It wasn't that they fought the theories or the science required to leave the planet, it was just that it was so far reaching, so far beyond anything they had previously understood or experienced, that they found it difficult to subscribe to. For the growing majority, the means of escape had become just as frightening as the pending arrival of the asteroid. More and more, XYZ began to abandon it in favor of fortified shelters promised to protect against the asteroid, some built on land and some in the sea. It pained Anae to watch, but ultimately it was their choice. The bond shared by all XYZ was akin to the love parents have for their children. It was pure and it ran deep. They all wanted the very best existence for each other, and they supported each other so that each of them could achieve this end on their own terms. To reach their collective potential, they believed it could only be accomplished through acceptance and support, never through manipulation or coercion. While it troubled Anae to witness the disillusion of many XYZ, she also knew that as the numbers of those who wanted to escape fell, their endeavor would become more feasible. It was devastating but no less true that the less XYZ they had to save, the more likely they would be to succeed.

Vash would have liked to join those who refused to believe an asteroid would end their nearly perfect existence and had instead left the city to begin a new life on their own. She envied their righteous attitude, the stubborn belief that Orbyss would somehow protect them from the large ball of fire that would eventually destroy them. It was difficult not to envy them, living their lives in a state of bliss, unwilling to accept the truth. Enjoying the present instead of longing for the past and fearing the future. Despite these beliefs, she would have been horrified had she known that in the end, only 1 percent would escape the asteroid, that 99 percent of their species would perish.

Vash's extraordinary intelligence would not allow for irrational decisions or thinking. Her IQ hovered around 240 points, making it impossible to buy into their mirage. To be the daughter of the most celebrated aeronautical engineer amongst them, with the genetics to match, sealed her fate. It was her father, until today, upon whom all of their hopes for survival seemed to rely.

Vash had been a blessing but also, in some ways, a disappointment. This was, of course, never spoken out loud but instead was understood in the way family members accept the inevitable from each other. It was as if the additional IQ points had absorbed her patience as compensation, and she was prone to outbursts growing up, at times complete meltdowns and tantrums. These eventually subsided at the age of ten but were replaced by a despondent type of silence that left others wondering if she had heard them at all. She found it impossible, sometimes, to express her emotions and feel understood, even by her own parents. That was, until she'd met Grynn.

Grynn had loved her from the first moment they met. A cataclysmic bond was instantly formed, and they became inseparable. Their thoughts were fluid, like that of one person, and they raced through ideas and information at a speed few could keep pace with. It was Grynn who made her feel that she was the most beautiful creature alive, not just physically, which was obvious to everyone, but that she was unparalleled both inside and out. He revered her, fully accepting who she was to the point that even her flaws were endearing. He was always the first to celebrate her successes and mourn her failures.

They had big plans for each other, the two of them. Neither could bear to be without the other for long, and it was often Grynn who found excuses or devised circumstances where they could be in each other's company. In the absence of the trip they had planned together, the one their parents forbade, their daily excursions took on a rebellious twist, often led by Vash.

Vash was a driver, preferring to be the one behind the wheel. Their transportation required no operator; however, the controls could be accessed and transferred to the pilot should a system failure take place. Upon entering the vehicle, Vash would immediately disable self-drive, then usher Grynn to take the seat beside her. He had accepted his fate and resigned himself to the likelihood that he would perish from one of their "drives" together but that at least he would die happy in the company of the love of his life.

The vehicles were readily available to all who had been licensed to operate them and could be summoned on command in every variety of sizes determined by the number of passengers, which for Vash and Grynn meant the equivalent of a two-seater sports car. A pod, designed for a seamless travel experience, capable of infinitely more.

Transportation was multifaceted; vehicles could cover all terrain, were semi-submersive, and could hover in air. On a sunny day, such as this one, Vash would insist on the top being down. She loved the feeling of freedom as the wind rushed past her face and teased her long hair into hundreds of knots. Every inch of the car's carbon-fiber frame absorbed energy, enabling it to replace much of what it expended as it drove. Vash loved nothing more than to feel the warmth of the sun shining down upon her face as it pacified her mood and powered her ride.

The roads the vehicles travelled on were carbon fiber, the perfection of efficiency for speed, safety, and the capture of energy. They optimized travel without impacting the environment around them. The onyx-black pathways directed traffic through a sophisticated series of light indicators that were almost redundant, as all vehicles were self-driven, unless something went wrong or the driver chose, as Vash did, to be their own pilot. Grynn hated to see her this way, and it unnerved him that she would continually take control of the vehicle when there was no need. He forgave her this transgression only because he understood her need to control something, anything, even if it were just the function of their ride.

Her focus was a razor, and Grynn knew better than to interrupt. She lived for the moment when just prior to a potential collision, he would close his eyes and his fingers would turn white against the armrest. It was at this moment that she would steal a glance at him. Relishing his abandon to her. Today would be the exception.

Today she had decided they would head to the ocean. She wanted to swim. For her, it felt as if one day mirrored the next, trapped in an ever-spinning wheel, round and round, the same direction, the same mundane tasks. She needed to break the mold, because she was finding it impossible to solve the equation required to get them off the planet, the one they all depended upon to survive.

Day after day for the past year, "borrowing" her father's logs, beginning where he had left off in the calculations and ending still in the same place, was weighing on her. It had become repetitive, cyclical—formula after formula, calculation after calculation. Her efforts seemed in vain, but there was also no alternative. A species without warfare or the need for it had no reason to invest in military or arms. As such, the option of using missiles to obliterate the meteor was not even considered. Even if they had decided that, in this one case, they would make an exception, it would have been overruled. What if they missed, and their attempts somehow damaged the planet or any of its inhabitants? For them, leaving this planet in search of another was the only answer. In their defense, they had already identified potential options for hospitable planets with advanced telescopes on Orbyss and in space. But the problem was deciding which one, and they needed the answer required to make it possible.

These were the thoughts running through Vash's mind as the car she piloted took a sharp corner towards the cliffs overlooking the ocean below. They were all drawn to the ocean, the home of their ancestors, and Vash was not the only one who had decided to head for the water on this perfect sun-filled day. At the same time as she took the corner, a family, looking to take in the view at the top of the cliffs, headed across her trajectory, and she had no time to react due to the speed she had reached.

The vehicle immediately regained control, and they began their diversion away from the family and towards the cliff. The scraping of the top bar against the manicured pathway alternated center stage with the screeching of the brakes. Intervals of scraping and grinding composed their soundtrack as the vehicle rolled ever closer to the cliff's edge.

Extensions of their clothing immediately covered their faces and heads to protect them against potential impact. Grynn caught Vash's eye through the mesh carbon-fiber Lenacyth veil only briefly, as the car, now upside down, became momentarily airborne as it slid over the cliff's edge and plummeted down towards the water. For seconds, they were suspended in time hoping against hope that they would be saved, that they would survive. As adolescents, they could not imagine that these might be their last breaths. Despite his mantra, his resignation that he would eventually perish this way, Grynn was nowhere near ready for it, and if there were something that could be done to improve their chances and stop this death drop, he would have done it. As it were, they had no choice but to remain in their seats and try to hold to the knowledge that they had advanced themselves to a point where a crash like this would be easily survivable. In theory, they were protected, but there was really no place for speculation as you dropped from a 150-meter cliff into the rocks and churning water below; one only had time for panic.

The vehicle could sense the rocks before it hit the water and hovered to a position just clear of their glistening peaks. The force of impact against the cresting stone from a 150-meter drop would have compromised the bodies within the vehicle and left the teens entirely reliant on the clothes upon their backs. Therefore, it was imperative that when they hit the water, it should be just that—water, not rocks.

Grynn caught a glimpse of Vash's tear-streaked face as she transmitted to him that she loved him, that she could not be sorrier, that this was all her fault. He took her hand and raised it to his lips as the vehicle met the surface of the water with an impact that stole the air from their lungs. Unable to catch their breaths, they struggled in their seats as their garments injected a flow of oxygen from the carbon-fiber shrouds covering their faces. Now they were both passengers, along for the ride, as they should have been in the first place.

The vehicle corrected itself, flipping right side up in the water. It swirled in the waves, threatening to roll again, pitching its young passengers around in their seats. Then the seats automatically reclined and enveloped their bodies as the car transitioned from a land to a sea vessel in preparation for their dive in order to steer away from the rock face hidden beneath the water protruding below them.

Simultaneous diagnostics were run by the semi-submersive in order to access the vehicle's damage as well as the passengers' vitals. It shared information seamlessly with the armor-like garments both of them wore and then transferred the results directly to the predetermined emergency contact.

Seconds prior to the diagnostics completion, Vash turned to Grynn.

"Are we OK?"

"Yes, yes, I'm fine. Are you?"

She never answered but instead initiated the emergency shutdown sequence as the vehicle met with the sand on the shore.

"What are you doing, Vash? You need to be assessed."

"No, I'm fine. Please don't tell me what I need. The last thing *we* need is another parent-initiated meeting over at your place that will undoubtedly end in our driving privileges being revoked."

"Vash, please, come on. We . . . we have to at least get you home. It's getting dark, and soon it will be curfew."

"We are not going home. I have something I need to do." These were the words Vash chose to end the conversation with as she took back control of the vehicle and headed towards the warehouse.

Once they reached the warehouse, Vash marched past the others who had already arrived and assumed their positions, all of them now quite comfortable with skipping curfew. She headed straight towards *her* board without even acknowledging their presence. A two-by-three-meter interactive surface capable of running any calculations she annotated on it. They had been slowly retrofitting the vacant space to suit their needs, and the board was one of the first elements they had introduced. Not only was it interactive, it was also intelligent, communicating independently with its surroundings and, when necessary, tapping into their shared data storage. It was as alive as the plant from which it came, and its interface silently interacted with everything it came into contact with, as seamlessly as nature intended. The only thing it lacked was the ability to provide her the answer to the formula that she required. It was a problem they had yet to face, a field of study they had yet to discover. She was still shaking from the shock of the accident but was determined not to let the others see it, and after she stripped herself of the clothing that had just saved her life, she headed directly back to the board and started to map out the formula from scratch, again. The formula that consumed her days and haunted her nights.

They all knew better than to interrupt her when she became fixated like this. They conversed as if she weren't even there as Grynn recounted their near-fatal accident. They would have preferred to hear Vash's version of the tale as well, but she would have none of that, and the headset that covered her ears made the point abundantly clear that she would not be reliving it for their entertainment, no matter how terrifying albeit exciting it had been.

Grynn recounted the experience at least five times before they all had their fill. The last round of the tale even had them all laughing, the look on the face of the poor boy who, inches from impact, instinctively put up his hands to cover his face as his clothing engulfed him in a carbon-fiber cocoon. Grynn had had enough of it himself, was hungry and tired, but was mostly concerned about Vash. As she scrawled her equations at a feverish pace, they all stared at her in unison, now concerned about the impact the accident might have had upon her.

Sweat ran down the small of her back, and Grynn's touch startled her, causing a smudge through the end of her equation, jarring her out of her mathematical trance as he wiped the glistening fluid from her flawless skin.

She offered him a small smile and removed the headset. Listening to music calmed her and helped her to focus. She had not heard a word of his tales of the accident the others had shared in.

"Please stop this, love, or at least let us help you. You have run through this so many times and—"

"Yes, but we are missing something. I am missing something." Vash was obsessed. She needed, they all needed, to determine the gravitational force and velocity the spacecraft required to reach an unknown planet at some point in the future. It was exceedingly complex, and everything they were throwing at it just would not stick. She was coming up against the same predicament as her father. She had run through every potential solution, arguably gaining far more ground than he had been able to cover due to the constraints of the council and the boundaries imposed by his position and assigned responsibilities. If she could just solve this one problem for him, she could make up for all that had come before, all the arguments, all the outbursts. He would be so very proud of her; she would finally become the teacher, and she knew that through his acknowledgment would come the respect of all his peers.

"Look at this; your equation doesn't even make sense. You should have a G here." Grynn loved the opportunity to point out her errors, mostly because they almost never occurred.

"It is a G, just like the first letter in your own name. I am shocked you, of all people, would fail to recognize it." Vash lost her words as she looked back at the board where her smudged equation, due to Grynn's interruption, had resulted in a G being converted to what now closely resembled a K. She sat with it a moment, then a light flashed before her, goose bumps formed on her forearms, and she barely whispered these words to him.

"Grynn . . . it's not about gravity . . . it's about energy."

For hours, the group sat debating the idea. Energy was the missing link, and their fixation on gravity had made them overlook it. In order to successfully leave Orbyss's atmosphere, they would need to look beyond what they had already experienced in order to conquer the unknown, in order to conquer space. Unconventional thinking was a leap for a society that held tightly to the greater good, collective thinking, and problem-solving. It had tied the hands of her father despite his advanced understanding of physics, whereas his daughter, unencumbered, raw and unwilling to fail, had taken the leap.

"What if we looked at a very short time interval instead of the entire trip? So, we calculate the vector from the planet to the space-craft. Update its momentum, then update the position of the space-craft, and then finally update the time. It doesn't matter which way it's travelling as long as it starts with the same speed at the same distance; it does not even have to be at the same location, and you will still get exactly the same plot." Vash's excitement could not be contained, and it grew as she negated every argument they threw at her.

It was this discussion, this debate, in the bowels of an all-but-abandoned warehouse, by a group of teenagers, that delivered the work for what they required—the energy principle.

"Vash, this is brilliant! It doesn't depend on direction; the direction doesn't matter, and we can determine it at any point in the future. If we develop a craft that can leave the atmosphere and start and stop at a point we can measure, this will be all we need in order to find a new home." Grynn had tears in his eyes as he made the realization that their escape could now potentially become a reality.

CHAPTER 11

GRYNN

The drill had been perfected both in its design and its deployment. Grynn and Shal had become mechanically complacent as they retraced the steps of their daily mock evacuation. It was the final countdown. There was no discord, no questions, no second-guessing themselves at this point. It had all been decided long ago, but like rehearsal overkill, they kept practicing far more than what was required—to the point that the players wondered if opening night would seem fabricated, if it would lack the edge required to captivate the audience.

The two of them walked side by side, assuming a synchronized gait and comfortable banter that could only be perfected over years of familiarity facilitated by an almost patriotic friendship. Their relaxed stroll was out of place with what was to befall them only a handful of days away.

Grynn and Shal's friendship had stood the test of time, unlike Grynn's relationship with Vash. As is common with young love, it did not last. Vash had unleashed a new realm with her discovery. Her ability to focus on a problem at the cost of all else changed the course of history for the species. She had given birth to an entirely new field of study within astrophysics, enabling the advancements required for the incredible engineering that would make their escape possible. She was the first astronautical engineer amongst them; it was her calling, but one that left room for little, and no one, else.

Ironically, Grynn had gradually been replaced in a relationship he had treasured more than anything by his mother. Anae had by now almost exclusively given control of their collective future to Vash. Vash had saved them all, it seemed, and Anae held on to her like a lifeline, their greatest hope of survival. The two females were inseparable, each a mirror to the other's strength and weakness. Vash and Anae were yin and yang, and they balanced the equation required to leave the planet both physically and emotionally.

Grynn had suffered at first, cursing what he and Vash had once celebrated. Of course, he wanted to survive; of course, he wanted to build a new life, to inhabit a new planet. His desire for adventure, his wanderlust, was unparalleled. He just had not been prepared for the speed at which the ground had shifted underneath them all the moment Vash had solved *her* problem, invented *her* equation. He just wasn't quite ready for it. Like everyone else, he had not known it would be the beginning of the end.

Grynn was far from privileged; as a culture, it was a foreign concept to them. The choices they made were forged with love and driven by their desire to protect each other, above all else. That was why he had asked to be assigned to the very last elevator on the very last ascension to the *HELIX*. Today, as he looked up to the clouds above, he paused for a moment, scarcely able to believe he would likely never see them again.

The sun spilled down upon their mock survival march towards the fifty elevators that rose from Orbyss and disappeared beyond the sky into outer space. A beautifully macabre reminder that this was really going to happen. Vash's creation, perfect cylindrical links, arms reaching up from Orbyss through the atmosphere into space, into the unknown. Perfectly spiraled carbon-fiber tubes, her elevators, which defied containment and conquered the unknown, a reflection of their inventor. She had been born for this; it was through her fulfilled destiny that they would all succeed in leaving the planet.

Grynn had endured this turn of events with Vash during those formative years; however, it was not long before his needy heart would seek out another home. In young love, the winds of one's attention, even in the face of the most unbearable angst, could suddenly blow in a new direction. Grynn was not blind to the fact that Herra had loved him for as long as he could remember, despite her attempts to hide her true feelings. He was five years older, and she had admired him from afar, separated by age and its related interests. Through Herra's eyes, he appeared larger than life. To Herra, both Grynn and Vash seemed untouchable. They were a bright light, almost too bright, and when the crushing reality of the need to escape took over all of their lives, Grynn and Vash had paid the price.

While Herra could have easily been consumed with her task of transforming their garments into space suits, she instead became consumed with Grynn. The final inductee to the Blowholes, she did her best to contain her crush until she knew for sure her sentiment would be returned. Vash had left almost directly for the council following the acceptance of her equation. She was immediately absorbed by its members, their hope to turn her theory into reality. This left a gaping hole in the Blowholes, one that could not be replaced, and so they clung to each other in an effort to fill the void.

Grynn had put on a brave face at the time and spoke of nothing but the contribution that all of them had made. If not for their collective decision to break curfew, Vash's discovery may have never occurred. From Herra's perspective, Grynn's effort to hold them all together, to exalt Vash and, at the same time, inspire them all to continue in their respective roles, gave her hope but broke her heart, as well, as every time they spoke, she could feel how much pain Grynn was in after losing Vash.

Slowly, over time, their paths intertwined. The interior of the *HELIX* was directly linked to the design and development of their space suits, just as their garments were linked to their homes and surroundings. Grynn and Herra were charged with the synchronization of the individual and their surroundings. They were obsessed with creating something beautiful, an experience. They were both determined that the transition to the *HELIX* would lift their collective spirits. It was meant to surprise and invigorate the passengers from the moment they arrived in their assigned space elevator right up until they left the starship in order to inhabit their new homes on Orbyss II twenty years later. They vowed to create a thing of beauty, something that would not only offer comfort but also inspiration and peace to its inhabitants as it carried them through space and time itself.

As their two worlds collided, so did their work. They meshed seamlessly together as they developed the blueprints for the *HELIX*'s interior. It was innocent and organic, not manufactured or synthesized. Soon their plans took amazing leaps. They redesigned smaller accessory spacecraft for planetary exploration, enhanced architectural schematics, and space-suit thermodynamics, all controlled and regulated by the user and the ship simultaneously. As their vision for the *HELIX* came to life, so did their appreciation for each other.

When their joint ideas were presented, they would inspire tears from the council. This was a species in love with its home, terrified to leave, that wanted nothing more than to remain part of the beautiful planet they inhabited—never taking more than they gave. To see that a tribute to their home, Orbyss, could be possible in the vast, freezing, lethally cruel, hard vacuum of space gave them hope for the future that few had dared to wish for.

These were the thoughts that crossed Grynn's mind, with Shal at his side, seven days from departure. Clouds floated above them while spontaneous tears filled Grynn's eyes as he gazed up at the sky, burning its image in his memory so that one day he could describe it to his child, the child that he and Herra so eagerly awaited.

CHAPTER 12

VASH

2.72 (Late Afternoon) / The *HELIX* / Seven
Days Before XYZ Evacuation Day

Vash sat in the control pod on the *HELIX*, one of the first to have made the trip up to the spacecraft five years prior. Vash had remained aboard their temporary home ever since. The starship was required, in seven days, to function alone, without mission control from Orbyss, and therefore every moment of her existence had become devoted to its performance in space. Space had become her new residence; she had not returned home, even briefly, since boarding the ship. For her, the sky was black, scattered with beautiful stars, devoid of the warmth that had once enveloped her on Orbyss.

Anae provided her with everything she needed from the control center on the ground. The video link was useful because they could see each other's expressions, they could see each other's eyes, making it far more difficult to hide the truth. One could hardly believe that in one week, mission control would be shut down forever. It seemed surreal that they would all board the *HELIX* with no thought of return, at least not in their lifetime.

"Have you run the sequence again?" Anae had begun to observe a change in Vash; she had become either extremely focused or extremely distracted. It was difficult to tell, and Anae wished she were aboard the ship to see for herself.

"Yes, confirmed." Annoyance draped Vash's reply without her consent or recognition.

The truth was that Vash had a lot on her mind. Not only was the *HELIX* designed for planetary exploration, but in order for them to survive and flourish, it had to be capable of facilitating space colonization. She was exhausted, hadn't slept uninterrupted for days, as something would trigger her night terrors as she lived out her worst fears in her dreams. The *HELIX* had become a prison for her, as much as it was her home. She envied the passengers still on the ground, the luxury of the anticipation they would experience prior to boarding the ship.

Vash had little time to mourn her past life on Orbyss. She had given up what she once considered to be her birthright in exchange for her future, all of their futures. It weighed more heavily on her today than ever before. All the years she had sacrificed in order to build the *HELIX*, only to become a refugee forced to leave her home for good. It terrified her to think that almost anything could happen once the massive ship began its mission. She had managed a lifetime of learning in the last ten years, and yet their understanding of interstellar travel was basic at best, something only theoretical up to this point, something that would be put into practice in only a matter of days.

Overwhelmed by what lay ahead, she had found the best coping mechanism was to focus on what they knew for sure instead of the questions that remained unanswered. Currently they had two options; two proximal planets had been identified that could potentially sustain life. They had chosen between a moon-based planet, five light-years away orbiting a young star similar to Orbyss's, and a tidally locked planet, four light-years away beset by a red giant. The latter emerged the winner only because it was 20 percent closer, a five-year difference in time—five additional years on the *HELIX*, five more years of interstellar travel where anything conceivable or inconceivable could destroy the entire colony of Orbyss's soon-to-be last existing life-form.

Orbyss II was not meant to be a temporary substitute for Orbyss but a permanent relocation for their species. Unlike Orbyss, it had the potential to sustain life but only within its terminator zone, a five-hundred-kilometer strip at the center point of the planet. All of this information gleaned from the long-range telescopes demonstrated liquid water, an atmosphere containing oxygen along with an abundance of nitrogen, and a gravity of 0.93 to that of Orbyss. The lack of rotation due to its proximity to its red giant sun meant living in an eternal twilight, with day never ending and night never beginning.

It was only after their understanding of hypothetical astrophysics had been soundly verified that she traded her team of scientists for a new team made up of aeronautical and astronautical engineers she'd handpicked in order to build a ship that would be capable of making their theories a reality.

The ship was designed to house and transport up to 150,000 for its four-light-year journey. A distance both incredible and astounding. The nuclear fusion reactors, fueled by the endless capture of solar energy, enabled the *HELIX* to achieve an impressive 20 percent of the speed of light. Ergo, twenty-five years of interstellar travel would be necessary to reach Orbyss II.

The starship was built not only to transport them to Orbyss II but also to colonize the planet. It had been assembled outside of Orbyss's atmosphere in order to save the immense energy that would have been necessary to enable a fourteen-kilometer mega-ton structure to escape gravity. Lying in low orbit, each of its four million parts were sequentially carried beyond the atmosphere in one of its fifty space elevators, lifelines from one world to another. Seemingly sparsely connected, they formed perfect glass-like tubes. Their role was vital until the very end. The end of the beginning. Their final task to transport their passengers prior to the *HELIX* launch. Then, immediately afterwards, the elevators would take their final bow, released from the starship, as they fell back to Orbyss.

In the absence of contrived competition, the XYZs, able to extend inherent altruism beyond one's own family, developed a collective culture, a symbiosis that enabled incredible discoveries and propelled them beyond a technological adolescence, resulting in quantum inductive computing. Once Vash discovered the energy principle, it opened the floodgates for the rest of them. The council, under Anae's lead, embraced the theories that Vash and her father brought forward together and bolstered their position within the advisory team. It encouraged the rest of them to push the limits of their respective fields, and using Lenacyth, the cornerstone of their technology, they were able to advance quantum computing through organic induction and perfect their plans to leave the planet.

Therefore, much of their planning took into consideration problems that did not exist or were highly unlikely. It was troubleshooting, extrapolating in the future, in another dimension, where they were forced to prepare far beyond what any of them could conceive.

By way of comfort, the council had agreed that they would design and manufacture a ship that matched their home environment as closely as possible. The ship was a replica of their homes on Orbyss. This part of the design process was made easy, as the properties of Lenacyth were just as well suited for life in space as they were on Orbyss. The carbon-fiber nanotubes formed and protected the outer shell of the craft, collected its solar power, formed the connections of its quantum computers, and was capable of transitioning into a stand-alone habitat in the event Orbyss II was more hostile than anticipated.

The *HELIX* was built for speed, comfort, and colonization. Its blueprints outlined each of its compartments in detail. It expanded symmetrically from its nucleus, the control pod, the heart of the ship, which could function entirely on its own should the rest of the spacecraft need to be sacrificed or become compromised. It was a collection of mobile units, each capable of independent navigation and space travel should an emergency situation arise. Each familial pod was capable of keeping its inhabitants alive for the duration of the quintillion-kilometer voyage but also contained everything required to start life anew.

"Vash, did you hear me?" Anae was becoming more worried about Vash's state of mind by the second.

"No, I am so sorry, I am just distracted. Just a lot on my mind prior to departure. Could you please repeat what you said? I am listening now."

"Are you sure you are ready, Vash? I don't mean technically; all of us have complete confidence in you, the ship, and our plan. But do you *feel* ready for this? Please come back down, just one last time, to say goodbye."

"What is the point, Anae? I said my farewells a very long time ago. The *HELIX* is my home; I can't even remember life on Orbyss, nor do I want to."

"Then how will we recreate it on Orbyss II?"

"We won't, Anae. That would be impossible, and it cannot be my mandate; it should no longer be yours either. On Orbyss II, you will soon realize there will be no room for fantasy, no time for your fairy tale."

"I must go, Captain. The next time we speak, it will be in person. I look forward to seeing you and your entire crew on board. It's almost time for the next chapter to begin. We will begin again; we will all be reborn."

Anae managed a small smile at Vash in order to end the conference, but she worried about Vash more than she was able or willing to admit. It was then Anae decided that as soon as she was at the helm of the *HELIX*, with Vash at her side, she would set out to provide her with the support and comfort she seemed very much in need of and so greatly deserved.

CHAPTER 13

ANAE

3.11 (Early Morning) / Orbyss / One Day
Before XYZ Evacuation Day

A stillness had enveloped her space. Everything seemed to advance in slow motion for Anae during these last days, their last hours on Orbyss. She followed the plan as if sleepwalking. It had been carefully mapped out, day by day, hour by hour, minute by minute, then by the seconds once they ascended in the space elevators to board the *HELIX*.

The halcyon conditions had been a gift; it almost seemed as if the planet itself was doing everything it could in order to ensure their evacuation was a safe one. Anae had packed her most valued possessions and made her peace with their forced exit as best she could years ago. This had been necessary in order to keep her focus, now, in this last stage. She had become almost robotic in carrying out the final tasks required, deliberately numb in an attempt to leave emotion out of the equation in order to fulfill the given tasks required each day prior to their departure. Today would be no exception.

This was the very last day Anae would spend on Orbyss. Tomorrow she would find herself aboard the *HELIX*, and she wondered what it would be like to look down from the starship at the planet below, intact for the very last time.

In one way, it was monumental to spend her final day on the planet performing what was arguably the most important task of her existence thus far, and in another, it was morbid, almost tragic. Perhaps gathering with friends and loved ones, rotating through them as the hours slipped by, would have been more appropriate; however, that was not meant to be. The schedule and the plan had been decided long ago, and besides, she was anxious to set foot on the *HELIX* in order to evaluate Vash's state of mind rather than frivolously living out her final hours on Orbyss. In any case, this day would be monumental. Her mission, should it be successful, would counter the impact of the asteroid and ensure their story continued on Orbyss forever.

The water was calm, reflecting the sky above. The ship was laden with the equipment the divers required for their mission as they set out onto the waters of what would become known as the Baltic Sea. The caravan stopped at the predetermined entry point, only five meters from the shoreline. Anae's team was ready, the weight of their treasure was figurative, the capsule literally weighed no more than twenty-five kilograms, secured to the drilling unit of the submersive vessel required for its transportation deep in the ocean waters, its destination the ocean floor.

The divers adjusted their suits, which singularly contained all apparatus necessary for the journey. They escaped exposure to the ambient pressure with the assistance of their carbon-fiber wet suits and by individually slowing their own heart rates. The protective suits would provide ample oxygen in order to complete the dive to the floor of the ocean. Their submersive vehicle and specialized equipment was capable of drilling into the seabed through thousands and thousands of decades of accumulated sediment.

Anae laughed to herself. It suddenly occurred to her that she *was* actually spending her last hours in the most appropriate company; it was only the purpose that was anything but frivolous. Despite her initial request that Grynn not join the dive team, true to his nature, he had insisted, and now she could take comfort in the fact that she would be spending the day with both family and friends regardless.

Shal had designed the capsule, and as the lead for the team that would embed it, he had insisted that Grynn, his best friend, be at his side. Grynn was an excellent diver, and Anae eventually recanted, deciding that she would join them in order to ensure everything went as planned.

It felt good to be in the water; they were all soothed and calmed by the ocean, the waters from which they had come. It seemed fitting that this was where they would bury their last hope, beneath the ocean floor. In the distance, two giant Basilosaurus, ancestors of the Livyatans, could be spotted, curious as to the activity of the vessel and the capsule it contained.

The spot was chosen because it was the least compromised, clear of any faults or fractures below the ocean floor. They had completed a trial run twenty meters away, in order to test the drill and the composition of the ocean floor. It had all gone as planned: no indications or issues identified, nothing that might impede the insertion.

Their equipment would remove a ten-kilometer cylinder of sediment from the ocean floor, then immediately inject the capsule in its place. The DNA capsule was their plan B—should their plan A, to escape the asteroid and begin life anew on Orbyss II—fail. A self-contained message, the story of their species. Thousands of viral vectors—perfect tiny packages composed of their DNA, wound like an infinitely small ball of yarn, complete with the entire XYZ genome.

The rush of the water down into the hole would carry their precious cargo to its resting place ten kilometers beneath the surface of the ocean floor. The capsule's trip down would be like travelling through a straw until it came to rest in position, pushed down by the force of thousands of tons of ocean water, its predetermined resting spot deliberately selected to ensure an optimal position for its long sleep ahead.

They left the vessel one at a time. As Shal, Grynn, Moda, and Anae entered the water, they positioned themselves in preparation for the capsule submersion. A two-person submersible vehicle was required for the task. Tac and Rhys would pilot the submersive, which had the ability to drill out the core and inject the capsule into the well before the rush of the water would bury it deep into the core of the planet. It was a Blowhole reunion of sorts; the only difference was that Anae had taken the place of Vash.

As the hood of Anae's dive suit enclosed her head, she smiled at Grynn, grateful that she would share this experience with him. Mother and son would plant the secret code of their existence safe in the planet, in a place where nothing—not even an asteroid—could destroy it.

Tac and Rhys took their positions, checking that the capsule was secure and positioned for its descent. They would follow the others down to the floor in the submersive. Shal was the first to lead the way. Anticipation overcame him. This was his moment; he had been the one to design, develop, and orchestrate what they would carry out today. It should take no longer than an hour to complete, if all went to plan, and he was already celebrating the success of the mission in his head.

Grynn, Moda, and Anae followed closely behind him as he led their descent, the color and temperature of the ocean deepening and dropping as they made their way towards the floor. They would communicate exclusively through transmission during implantation. And the very first transmission would come from Grynn, an announcement to begin their race to the bottom.

The submersive would require more time to join them; Tac and Rhys constantly monitored its progress, ensuring that all variables remained within acceptable levels and that the stabilizing mechanisms, ensuring the safe containment of the capsule at the nose of the vehicle, were in alignment.

Grynn won the dive competition with ease and raised his arms high above his head as the victor, now standing in the freshly disturbed debris that comprised the ocean floor.

The silt and muck were knee-deep, and he found it hard to keep his balance in the ocean's quicksand. The others congratulated him as they joined him one by one at the bottom, all struggling to maintain position and balance on the shifting ground. Their combined weight disturbed the saturated powder around them, and they could barely see each other through the blanket of algae smoke they had created.

The lights from the submersive caught their attention from above. In synchronicity, they looked up at the capsule, taking in its perfect pill shape as it sunk closer and closer to them. It seemed out of place in this almost barren environment, an aquatic existence with no discernible signs of life, a wasteland, one that foreshadowed what was soon to come at the surface.

Tac shifted the submersive into a horizontal position as it balanced the capsule at its head. Next, he retracted its feet to secure its landing in order to begin the drill. Grynn and the other divers moved to safety, where they could congregate in sight of each other as well as the submersive. As the drilling commenced, unlike their test excursion, the silt that comprised the floor of the drill site created a giant explosion where neither the submersive nor the capsule could be seen through the algae fog.

"How is it going? Visibility is zero from where we are," Shal transmitted to Rhys, who controlled the drill.

"All readings are positive; the drilling is proceeding as planned, and the . . ." Then her transmission stopped.

"What's happened?" Shal's heart rate increased as he desperately tried to make out even the slightest indication of what was going on through the silt and haze.

"We've just hit something. The drill is not responding, even with an increase in power." Panic filled Rhys's voice.

Grynn approached Shal in time to grab his arm to prevent him from racing to the submersive. With zero visibility, Shal could easily compromise not only himself but the entire mission.

"Grynn, let me go, I need to help them. You know how important this is. We don't have a backup plan here; there is no second chance."

Just then, Rhys responded. "We are accelerating to full power now to see if we can continue." Following his transmission, a fresh explosion of debris filled the air, enveloping the divers ten meters away.

"It's moving. It's making progress now. But we will need to keep it at full power. Let's hope we will have enough to finish." Rhys was trying her best to complete the task; she knew just as well as any of them just how important this was.

The drilling continued as the divers looked on. Tac watched the progress reading, which had them at four kilometers . . . six kilometers . . . They were making strong progress once again. Each of them unnecessarily holding their breath as the drilling continued.

"Shal, we are approaching the seven-kilometer mark. The power readings are low; we won't make it to ten kilometers. Not with enough power left for the implantation and return to the surface."

"We have to try; continue at full power. Get as close as you can." Shal's response was frantic, his head throbbing and his stomach churning into knots. How could this be happening? The test drill had gone flawlessly.

The descent continued, 7.7 kilometers . . . 7.8 kilometers . . . and as they approached 8 kilometers, the drilling stalled again.

"It won't take any more, Shal. We need to stop here," Rhys said.

"Just five hundred meters more; please try." Shal knew better than any of them the risk of an implantation shy of the optimal depth. The impact of the meteor was only an extrapolation; they needed to leave room for error, and Shal needed to be sure the capsule would rest in safety.

The drilling created more clouds of debris; the submersive and the capsule floated in and out of visibility and then became completely disguised by the sediment.

"Shal, it's no use." Rhys's transmission was desperate. "The submersive now does not have the power to return to the surface; I'm not sure it will even manage the implant."

Anae took over the joint transmission. "How far did you get?"

"We are at eight and a half kilometers," Rhys replied.

"That will have to do," she responded.

Shal felt sick. He felt responsible for this; it was his error. He should have considered the possibility that the floor might not be the same as the test site they had drilled just twenty meters away.

"Shal, we need to implant the capsule, we need to do it now." Anae's transmission interrupted his thoughts.

"Yes, please proceed." Shal's heart sank in his chest as he gave the command.

Tac started the sequence, and the suction unit repelled five meters into the hole. It would temporarily replace the drill and hold back tons of surrounding water so that the capsule could be inserted.

"We are in position, Shal" was Tac's transmission.

"Yes, go ahead."

The submersive transferred the capsule in slow motion, drawing on the very last of its power. There was no option to replenish its supply. There was no sunlight at this depth. The only light was a dim glow from the submersive and the halos of light that emitted from each of their suits.

"The capsule is in position, Shal."

"Yes, go ahead. Prepare for insertion."

Tac entered the sequence for implantation. He entered it again. He switched to manual. Nothing.

"It's no use Shal; it's out of power."

"We need to bury this capsule. There is no other way. We have to finish this." Shal was desperate. His worst nightmare realized.

"Shal, there must be a manual override for this; we must be able to initiate it from outside the submersive." Grynn felt his best friend's distress as if it were his own.

"That's insane, Grynn; you cannot stand beneath a thousand tons of rushing water and not be dragged into that hole along with it."

"Well, we will have to try."

"Grynn!"

Both divers raced towards the submersive with the rest following close behind.

"Grynn, let me," Shal insisted. "I cannot let you do this!"

"You won't be able to manage this alone, Shal. We need at least one diver on each side of the insertion controls."

"Grynn, move back! There is no way I will allow the two of you to disappear down that well forever. Besides, you will need me to guide the capsule into position." Anae's transmission was unmistakable. She was the first to catch up with them, signaling to Moda that she should stay put, determined to complete this mission without any casualties.

"No, let us do this!" Fear washed over Grynn as his mother came up behind him. He suddenly realized he had more to worry about than just his fool-headed best friend.

"Listen, we need to use everyone we have down here. You know we cannot fail with this, son."

The three of them searched each other's eyes, forging a plan, synchronizing their thoughts as one.

"Now, get into position, and we will release the capsule. I will give you the cue to begin." Anae floated up to where the capsule awaited its descent.

Shal and Grynn watched Anae as she manually guided the capsule into position with the help of Rhys and Tac, now outside the submersive.

They would drop the capsule and then release the water to fill in its grave.

"Now!" Anae shouted to the divers and crew as the capsule gently dropped towards the hole.

The capsule's descent was unsupported by the submersive, and it shifted without guidance from the implantation apparatus. It floated towards the hole, then shifted to the left, balancing on the edge of the opening.

"Shal, Grynn, release the water," came Anae's command. She left the others and quickly dove down towards the capsule. From where Shal and Grynn were positioned, they could not see her and were left only to trust in her transmission.

Tac and Rhys realized too late what Anae was doing as they watched her pull the capsule towards her chest with all her strength as the force of the water Shal and Grynn had just released, like pressurized water exploding from the nozzle of an eager tap, pushed them both eight and a half kilometers beneath the base of the ocean floor.

Shal and Grynn were moments behind the others, encouraged as the suction device retracted and there was no sign of the capsule or the hole itself, replaced only by the eerie fog of the debris.

Grynn took in the other divers, then his eyes searched for Anae.

Her transmission came to him as clearly as if she were standing beside him.

"I am so very proud of you, my son. Remember, at every step, that I am with you, that you are never alone. I have already said goodbye to your father. He will be waiting for you . . ."

"No! No!" Grynn visibly trembled inside his suit, now kneeling chest deep in the disturbed ocean floor trying in vain to claw his way to his mother below it.

Her transmission cut through his despair. "Please do not make this harder, my sweet boy. I have been lucky to see you become a man.

You will become everything your father and I had ever hoped for and more."

"No! No! You don't understand; we need you, all of us. We were waiting, saving a surprise for you once we all boarded the *HELIX*. Herra, she . . . is expecting . . ." Grynn's voice cracked at the thought of his bride and their unborn child who would never meet their grandmother. He could barely finish the transmission.

Anae paused a moment as she choked on the knowledge that she would never meet her grandchild. "Oh, Grynn, I am so very happy, so very happy for you both. You will promise to tell this precious little one all about me; you will promise to share our past, all of our stories. But listen now, son, you need to return to the surface. This mission was a success. It will ensure that our species will survive even if we do not."

"I will not leave you; I cannot!" Behind the veil of his suit, tears streamed down Grynn's face, down all their faces. They could not hear the transmission between mother and son, but they did not have to.

"Goodbye, my precious boy. I have loved you more than I ever thought possible. I always will." Anae's last transmission hung between them as she deflated her suit, which had been holding back the weight of the capsule and thousands of tons of water from crushing her to death. She knew that her son would never leave her alive down there and that she would have to go, in order for him to return to the surface.

"Mother . . . Mom!" His desperate transmission received no reply. He somehow knew, he always knew, that she would be the one to save him, as she always had.

The divers held Grynn as he shook with grief. They supported his limp body as they all floated back to the surface. An oxymoron to the ocean, as it became lighter and its pressure reduced; their return to the surface was composed of dark sorrow and heavy regret.

CHAPTER 14

VASH

3.12 (Early Morning) / The *HELIX* / XYZ Evacuation Day

Today was the day. Vash pulled herself from the bed that had been an evil accomplice to the fitful unrest she had suffered that night. She had refused the sleep aid the ship's physician, Dexl, had recommended, just in case an emergency surfaced that would require her to be sharp. In her head, she knew there were others capable, potentially more capable, of dealing with a potential emergency that might arise; however, she could never convince herself that they would make the required connections between what presented itself as a crisis and seemingly extraneous factors that might, in actuality, be the root of the problem. It was the Vash factor, as her colleagues referred to it; she could see ten steps ahead and apply everything at the present moment from ten steps behind simultaneously. An almost infinite decision tree, always changing, ever in flux.

As it turned out, there were no emergencies. Nothing she needed to lose sleep over anyway, just her own unfounded worries that had started creeping her towards paranoia. She was tired but snapped herself out of it. Adrenaline was a potent cure for grogginess. And it coursed through her veins as she took her seat at the helm of the control pod only to realize that none of her messages to Anae had been answered from the day before. From Vash's perspective, this in itself was emergency enough.

There was not one but two control pods situated at the core, or the heart, of the *HELIX*. In the event Anae made the call to initiate colonization of the new planet, the pods would leave the ship; one control pod would remain, and the other control pod would become the brain of the ship. This was also true in case of emergency; the pods could escape from their formation, and the base of the *HELIX* would become an emergency craft, able to carry on alone if necessary, or to reassemble the pods once the danger had passed.

The controls of the *HELIX* appeared to be nonexistent; however, the intelligent ship had no need for buttons, gadgets, or even a steering wheel. It was capable of self-navigation through voice activation, transmission, or, if necessary, the thoughts of its captain and/or any member of the crew. The ship held its own seat at the table; the opinion of the *HELIX* was one of the most valued, as it had constant eyes on not only the interior of the ship's every inch and all of its passengers and crew but also the exterior of the ship in order to assist navigation to Orbyss II with the utmost efficiency and safety.

What the control pod lacked in bells and whistles, it made up for with state-of-the-art astronomy and quantum computing. It was a high-end safe room that Vash had built together with Anae, where nothing was left to chance.

From the captain's seat, surrounded by twenty-five advisors, Vash reluctantly took Anae's position so that she could safely transport the last XYZ aboard the *HELIX*, not least of which would be Anae herself.

She counted to three before she began her transmission to the captain. She needed to remain calm and in control and not jump to the worst possible conclusion; however, a thousand scenarios rushed at her, a waterfall of unclaimed fears. She took a moment to steady herself, then methodically began the transmission directly to Anae, one that would be received by her ear alone. Vash's message was simple: "Please advise that all is in order for final transport. We are ready to receive the last group, the remaining passengers to board the ship, including yourself." Perhaps Anae was avoiding her on purpose. Vash had made one last request, an additional check on the location of the asteroid. Perhaps Anae had decided she'd suffered the last of Vash's compulsive inquiries. They were all leaving today; there was really no reason to second-guess anything, as nothing had been left to chance or negligible coincidence. Vash's calculations had been exact on everything, exact to the millisecond.

Twenty thousand were to join the *HELIX* per day over a five-day period. That meant eight trips per day for each of the space elevators that took exactly fifteen minutes and four seconds to leave Orbyss's surface and transport their fifty respective passengers. Vash had insisted on the staggered entry pattern; she needed to ensure the numbers were manageable so she could control for anything unforeseen. The arrivals had to be briefed and oriented to the new world they would inhabit for the next four light-years at a minimum, and she felt strongly that she needed to be there in person in order to greet each group. She had decided upon eight trips per day; this was optimal regarding the ship and number of passengers but, most importantly, herself. It was exhausting managing the questions, concerns, and fears of twenty thousand excitedly anxious XYZ per day who looked upon her, correctly, as the prodigy who had theorized, engineered, and brought to fruition the surrogate home they were to inhabit for the next twenty years. She had become an involuntary diplomat, and by the end of the tour, they all left for their respective pods with their spirits transformed, so spectacular was the architecture of the *HELIX* and the living legend who had sacrificed everything to build it.

The starship was the XYZs' most accomplished creation. While the interior reflected their home on Orbyss in terms of aesthetic, the exterior, which most of them would not see until they colonized their new home planet, was built to withstand the harsh environment of outer space and interstellar travel. The shell of the *HELIX* could not only protect against the elements of extreme temperature fluctuations but could also independently detect and deflect potential threats to its superstructure from cosmic radiation, abhorrent photons, and even neutron storms. Every element of the *HELIX* acted independently, akin to a sentient being, coordinating with other subsystems to maintain self-preservation without harming its occupants.

Lenac, their ancestor, had discovered the plant, growing on an undisturbed forest bed, that would become the nucleus of their infrastructure on Orbyss and now, most importantly, in space. Its carbon-fiber nanostructure performed flawlessly. The Lenacyth's composition, multiple times stronger than steel and resilient in temperatures approaching absolute zero through to the heat emitted on the surface of stars, would enable a safe "theoretical" passage to Orbyss II. Spawned from Orbyss's magnificent garden in ideal growing conditions, Lenacyth was a plant capable of not only energy transfer but also the transfer of information. Much like the process of photosynthesis, it could collect and transmit information through induction, and because of this property, it was also the ideal material for the *HELIX*'s quantum computing required to navigate and travel through space. Elegant, sophisticated, strong, flexible, but most importantly, versatile—it would protect them completely while they journeyed to Orbyss II, and beyond, if need be.

The air lock that received the passengers upon exit from their respective space elevators was ascetically disappointing but a necessary entry to the ship. It was utilitarian, equipped with the required decontamination and medical equipment should any breach or unforeseen condition arise that could compromise their safety. It was a holding area devoid of any signs of life, color, or potential for escape—that was, until the passengers were evaluated and the security doors opened.

Once the air lock opened, the beauty, symmetry, and scale of the ship were instantaneously displayed. It was the same every time; a synchronized, audible sigh of relief surged through each cohort. It never failed to impact her, and for a moment, Vash could take solace in their exhale, a welcome distraction from Anae's ongoing silence.

The ceiling of the vessel soared thirty meters above their heads, creating the illusion that they had travelled up the elevator only to step right back on Orbyss, instead of a ship hovering in low Orbyss orbit. The galley's dome reflected the weather patterns, colors, and shifting of clouds in the "sky" above, instead of the unending darkness of space. Large areas customized for gathering, recreation, solitude, medical attention, education, and vocation were interspersed with family pods. Everything had been tailored and customized to meet every need and preference. Unfortunately, it was a forced façade; the reality was a twenty-year prison sentence, in a jail cell, with a cloud-covered ceiling at best.

The *HELIX* was their new *home away from home*—or, at least, this is how Vash introduced the ship upon each elevator's arrival. As she set out to greet the first group of twenty-five hundred new arrivals on their last day of boarding, Vash surveyed the surroundings with a mixture of pride and precaution. Suddenly she was flooded by the realization that she would never fully be at ease on the *HELIX*, not until the mission was completed, not until they were all safe on their new home, Orbyss II.

As the doors to the holding area closed behind her, thoughts of Anae once again filled her mind. After the tour, she promised herself that she would head straight back to the control pod in order to make another attempt to reach her. It was very odd that Anae would not have replied to her request, no matter how obsessive she thought it to be.

"Welcome to the *HELIX*!" was Vash's greeting as fifty doors simultaneously opened, her voice betraying only the slightest hint of the unease that grew within her in the absence of a response from the ship's captain, her captain, and her surrogate mother, Anae.

Hours later with no response, Vash sat at the helm in mission control, her chair for the last five years, trying in vain to transmit to Anae, the seat's rightful owner. Concern morphed into dismay and was now verging on panic. Mission control was operational, and everything seemed to be running smoothly, but where was Anae? Vash started to doubt herself; in actuality, they had not discussed the final transfer to the *HELIX*; Vash had just assumed Anae would be online as she had been every other day prior. It was conceivable that there were numerous tasks to be accomplished in order to shut down fully; they just never discussed them, and in the absence of specifics, Vash tended towards panic instead of thinking positively.

She thought better than to transmit her worries to the crew at mission control—better that she should stew alone up here than to alert an entire team still left on the ground. They would be on the final ride up soon enough. There were only two more full transports left in order to complete the *HELIX*'s full capacity.

She couldn't stand it any longer, and she started to pace the room. She had a full twenty minutes left prior to greeting the second-to-last group of twenty-five hundred, and she had no one to turn to. Where the hell was Anae? She stared at the video conference silently begging it to chime so that she could accept the invitation from her captain, but it was in vain. Seconds passed like an eternity as she marched the length of the control pod. It was with tears in their eyes that the crew at mission control observed her distress from Orbyss, having been instructed not to disclose that Anae had been lost during the capsule implantation. A mission neither Vash, nor any of the others already aboard the ship, were ever supposed to have learned about in the first place.

A sick feeling had begun to form in Vash's stomach. She was now unable to concentrate during the second-to-last tour, which had gone off course in terms of time and topic. Something was wrong. She could feel it. As she led the group up to the grand finale of the tour, the observation deck, she was almost too distracted to remember to tell them of its ability to not only observe the solar system but also to chart planets and stars up close in a way never possible from Orbyss. She was staring pensively at the room's monitor, desperately waiting for a signal from Anae, when a young girl pulled at her arm in order to gain her attention.

"The stars are so beautiful up this close, I feel that I could reach out and touch them." Vash tried in vain to concentrate on the child's fascination until she continued with: "Especially that big one, as it moves so quickly through the black sky."

The terror on Vash's face alarmed the child along with all the others who had witnessed their exchange in the observation room. It was her worst nightmare coming to life. All this time, her worries about Anae's whereabouts were compounding, when she should have been worrying about the asteroid. How could she have been so stupid? How could she have possibly missed this? Now it was too late . . . but she had to try. The sensitive young child was left standing in tears, wondering what she had said to offend the ship's second mate, as Vash raced to the control pod to warn the others still left on the ground.

"Emergency . . . I repeat, Emergency . . ." Vash screamed into the transmission device. She had completely lost track of time in her distress over Anae and now realized that she had no way of reaching her or any of the others who had already boarded the elevators.

How could this be happening? But it was real. She saw it now. In these final hours, the asteroid, which had followed the exact course she had determined it would take more than nine years ago, suddenly accelerated on a new path heading directly towards them.

She had not a second to waste. It was at this moment that she ordered the speed of the elevators to be increased. Then she began a transmission message from the *HELIX* to each passenger, simultaneously explaining the terrifying news that the asteroid was travelling at an accelerated speed and they could not predict its impact now, nor guarantee their safe transport.

To Vash, it was impossible; they had run the numbers so many times to ensure the asteroid would arrive after the *HELIX* had left, a full two days from now. Vash frantically charted the asteroid's new course in haste. She identified that its orbit had been altered, as the progression of Saturn's orbit was in resonance with its own, and as a result, its course had been impacted and its speed had been accelerated to thirty kilometers per second.

They all sat watching from the control pod, Vash at the helm of the ship in the company of *most* of the flight crew. All of them helplessly waiting to witness whether the asteroid would spare them or if it would push them all back down to Orbyss while on board the *HELIX*, only to be obliterated on the planet they had spent the last ten years attempting to escape.

Vash's mind was racing; she longed to navigate the craft away from the asteroid's path. The starship could reach speeds thousands of times faster than the giant asteroid, but with twenty-five hundred passengers tethered to it, trapped within fifty space elevators, she had no choice but to remain in place.

As they watched the giant space rock approach through the windows of the control pod, they desperately continued to run the calculations, as extinction headed closer and closer towards them.

"Vash, from what we can tell, it will bypass the ship by fifty-four meters. But with its accelerated speed, the space elevators won't dock in time. As you know, we have tried to reach Anae without success. You need to make the call."

"I will not sacrifice twenty-five hundred."

"Vash, they will be dead anyway."

As the asteroid approached the ship, screams could be heard from the observation deck. The massive space rock dwarfed the spacecraft, and from the passengers' position in the dome, it looked as if it would crash into the *HELIX*.

"How long till the elevators reach the air lock?"

"3.2 seconds."

"You need to make them go faster—increase the speed!"

"We already have, Vash; they're already at max."

". . . 2.2 seconds."

And then it began, the blinding light that announced the mighty asteroid's arrival as it hit the surface of Orbyss. One by one, like dominos, the space elevators fell, destroyed immediately, incinerating their passengers as blazing heat and fire absorbed the elegant structures still tethered to the ground.

On the control pod monitor, the indicator for the final elevator lit up. It surged into position and was now safe within the *HELIX*.

Vash raced to the air lock, desperate, her heart pounding. Her mind began an invocation . . . *At least one, please let there be at least one that I have saved.*

As the last elevator rose into position, tears streamed down her face. A crowd had gathered in the galley outside the air lock, desperately hoping against hope that their loved ones had made it.

They made way for Vash so that she could stand as the head of their anxious assembly. She would be the first to greet them, as she had every elevator that boarded the ship. The first to greet whatever awaited her on the other side of the elevator door.

It labored to open, suffering damage from the speed of its arrival. She had no idea what she would be facing when the doors finally opened and the lethal mix of hope and fear that battled within made shreds of her soul.

It happened in slow motion, the door sliding open, left to right, revealing passengers huddled on the elevator floor, the sounds of moaning and cries of pain, and then Grynn emerged, the first passenger of the last elevator to set foot safely aboard the *HELIX*.

It was the only elevator of the last group to make it. All fifty, save this one, had been consumed by the fire and eventual chaos that would rain down upon Orbyss for millennia to come as the mammoth asteroid plunged deep into Pangea. An intrusive, abhorrent guest intent on making an impact long after they were gone. The space elevator shook violently, its base still tethered to Orbyss. Its passengers cried out, clinging desperately to each other as they made their way through the open door. Despite the seismic oscillation, the crew knew they were safe; being a hundred kilometers from Pangea's surface afforded them a few much-needed nanoseconds to offload the final elevator and start their epic journey, a journey of equally mammoth proportions.

As the air lock doors opened to the galley, the screams of the passengers already aboard the *HELIX* who had witnessed the event sounded like whispers. Grynn went cold with shock as the crowd consumed them, eager to embrace them all. He felt Vash's arms wrapped around him for the first time in years. The adolescent crush he had tried in vain to forget, the first love he never could. They clung to each other, both orphaned in their own way, now and forever.

As the *HELIX* departed from Orbyss's gravitational pull, passengers horrified and filled with grief watched the once-aquamarine planet turn red with fire burning beneath them. Now there was no way to turn back, and nothing to turn back for.

CHAPTER 15

HERRA

5.49 (Morning) / The *HELIX* / Day One of Intrastellar Travel

Home is where the heart is, or at least that was what Orbyss's early hominids told themselves as the *HELIX* commenced its journey towards what they believed would become their new home. Until then, the ship would be their surrogate. A ship so closely resembling home, it was easy to forget that they were not still on Orbyss, so long as they stopped themselves from looking out the windows.

Herra had taken special care since the elevator disaster to ensure that the habitation pod she shared with Grynn and their unborn child would comfort him. Perhaps one day, as his grief began to lift, he could recover from the pain of entering the *HELIX* an orphan, having lost both his parents within twenty hours, a single day of unparalleled misery that would haunt him forever. It was a nightmare no one deserved. He left his mother below the ocean floor in a solitary grave, unmarked, to be lost in time, and then lost his father seconds from escaping into the vast nothingness they endlessly travelled through. Herra's attempts were unfortunately in vain, as Grynn was overwhelmed with guilt as he replayed over and over his father's best attempts to raise his spirits in spite of having just lost his wife, Grynn's mother, the love of his life, only hours before.

Immediately following boarding the *HELIX* and seeking solace in Vash's embrace, Grynn sought out Herra and demanded that, together, they make their way to his parents' pod. He illogically and irrationally believed they would be there, waiting for him, as they always had—as they always promised. He fell to the floor as they entered the pod, and he saw the portraits of him and his parents throughout his childhood, perfectly positioned to be admired, perfectly obsolete now that they were gone.

Unlike Grynn, who had the comfort of Herra, Vash would find no such reprieve. In Anae's absence, she was the captain, and the *HELIX* needed its new captain urgently. The shock, grief, and loss of her mentor and surrogate mother for the past ten years would need to be pushed aside. The full weight of the mission fell squarely on her shoulders now. No more would she have Anae to lean on; no more would she have Anae to steady her, to fill her with confidence and confirm her course.

She wasn't sure how she would manage, and she desperately longed to seek out Grynn for support. But instead, she pushed aside all thoughts that perhaps they could console each other, because her place was at the helm of a giant ship transporting Orbyss's last survivors through space. The realization left her breathless. It filled her with anxiety and a crushing fear, but to look at her was to witness only steel composure. No one could have guessed at the storm that swirled within her, threatening to consume her by the second.

Herra's heart broke to witness Grynn's gradual decline, consumed not only by grief but also by guilt. He had stopped eating and had withdrawn from everyone, and she would catch him awake in the middle of the night, literally staring out into space from the pod windows. He refused to leave his parents' pod; he and Herra had all but moved into the space, leaving behind their own pod Herra had prepared so lovingly for their upcoming time as a trio.

Herra would never say the words, but it quietly broke her heart that she and their future child were not enough to give Grynn hope for their collective future. As days bled into weeks, her sympathy and understanding slowly became twisted with tiny strands of fear and resentment. She struggled without Grynn—the old Grynn—at her side. Suffering in silence amidst a flood of raging hormones, she desperately tried to believe everyone who told her to be patient. They looked at her with such pity and sadness in their eyes, but in the end, there was nothing anyone could do; they were all reeling, attempting to adjust to their own loss and a new way of life.

It is a universal truth that *everyone* has *someone* they need. Sadly, it is not always who we want it to be. That one person in life that makes everything OK. The person key to our capacity to carry on. As it turned out, Grynn was that someone for Herra, but the same was not true for Grynn. All of them had secretly come to realize this unfortunate truth . . . all of them, save Grynn.

CHAPTER 16

TIRUS

1.14 (Afternoon) / The *HELIX* / Week
Three of Intrastellar Travel

The *HELIX* was the ultimate playground if you had an inclination for
mischief, a savage imagination, and an insatiable sense of adventure.
For the ship's youngest passengers, safe with the knowledge that their
parents were somewhere, it was far better than anything they had ever
known on Orbyss. For them, the *HELIX* was a giant pirate ship floating through space, headed for a world all their own, and they fancied
themselves the true captains, the ones who would find the treasure,
the ones who would save the day.

Tirus (Shal and Moda's firstborn) had been a handful, even in the
womb. When Moda wasn't suffering from morning sickness, she was
being kicked to death from the inside out. Tirus was her very own
little alien, first taking over her body, then eventually her heart. He
was a whirlwind and could be maddening, amusing, then endearing
all within the blink of an eye. Boarding the *HELIX* with Tirus and a
newborn baby in their arms, losing Anae, and now suffering alongside

Grynn was about all Shal and Moda (a second romance forged in the Blowholes' warehouse hideout) could manage. And when all the weary parents realized that their youngsters were more or less captured on the *HELIX*, the ultimate babysitter, they quickly left them free to explore the massive ship . . . and explore they did.

When you are five years and eighteen days old, desperate to be six, nothing is quite as it seems. To Tirus and his mates, every moment outside of ship school (as they referred to their education aboard the *HELIX*) was dedicated to their not-so-silent coup, their ultimate goal (according to their magical thinking) of taking control of the ship.

In less than a week, the youngsters had constructed their own mind maps of the starship, all its hiding places, secret rooms, and private corridors. Their screams, secret signals, and never-ending laughter filled the ship with normalcy the adults were reluctant to relinquish. And so, it continued, the stealth takeover by a crew with an equal number of males to females spanning the ages of four years and 57 days to eight years and 208 days.

"What do you think is up there?" Tirus was fascinated with the closed-off space above the dome of the observatory.

"It's where we make the sacrifices to the aliens in order to appease them so that we can safely inhabit our new planet. I heard you are next on the list." Rahl, the oldest and the unofficial leader of the crew, loved to tease them, especially Tirus, who became enraged so easily.

"Stop it, Rahl! You'll scare him," said Geel, the peacekeeper, who stuck with the group as much for the fun of it as she did to keep an eye out that their escapades didn't get completely out of control. Old beyond her years, she hated to miss out on anything but also had a deep-rooted sense of responsibility, especially to the younger ones.

"I'm not the one who's scared. I'm the one who's going to find out what's really up there instead of standing around making up stories. You are the one who is too scared to actually go up there," Tirus retorted. He was not about to let anyone, especially Rahl, get the better of him; no one put Tirus in the corner.

Rahl laughed in reply. "And how do you think you are going to get up there? Just use the stairs?" His sarcasm was not lost on Tirus, who looked up in vain.

The attic directly above the observation dome appeared to have no access. However, it was obvious that an entry did exist, as it contained a visible cockpit complete with seats and control screens. It was designed as the final escape of twenty-five passengers should the *HELIX* be destroyed and also provided a shield from the space storms and debris where it mattered most, at the very tip of the starship.

"Tirus, I have been looking for you for over an hour." Moda collected her son from the entry of the observation area. She was tired from the never-ending sleepless nights with her newborn, Eelaa, and had lost patience with this never-ending game of hide-and-seek. The young boy was an aficionado of ignoring his parents' transmissions.

Moda walked over to him, taking his arm in her hand to ensure there would be no escape. The look Tirus shot at Rahl as he was dragged from the room spoke volumes, and Tirus transmitted to the older XYZ, "This isn't over." And so, it began . . . the quest for the occupation of the secret pod above the observation deck.

CHAPTER 17

VASH

1.35 (Early Hours) / The *HELIX* / Week
Four of Intrastellar Travel

It had been three nights of the same dream. Vash awoke each time startled by Anae's face hovering just above her, diligently making her request . . . each night a little louder.

Vash's night terrors and subsequent insomnia had started to get the better of her. She knew that avoiding Grynn could not be maintained indefinitely, especially now that her dreams were being haunted by his mother.

Her anxiety over being at the helm of the *HELIX* had worked itself into something potentially much worse. She was now fully consumed by the functioning of the ship. It had become an elixir to her fear and her pain at losing Anae. It had also become the remedy for her worries. As long as she was focused on the ship, everything would be OK.

All things being equal, she would have preferred to wait until Grynn sought her out instead; however, this wish was not to be granted. The *HELIX*, as usual, demanded she take the lead. Even after the starship had almost fully consumed her, it was still not enough; Grynn was needed to mitigate a number of design issues, issues that eluded detection until a hundred thousand habitants had come aboard.

"I know you don't want us to disturb *him*, but the position of the venting in the ship entry air lock needs a work-around. Sure, it looks better aesthetically, but that counts for very little when the lack of airflow is preventing the water vapor from escaping and the entire space is sweating. Soon the seals will malfunction, and if he doesn't let us know how he wants the vents rerouted, then we will implement the optimal and most direct route possible to ensure this doesn't happen again." Vash could no longer put off Arnik, the lead *HELIX* mechanical engineer. She was all about function and had little appreciation for appearance. So, if Vash didn't reach out to Grynn soon, the stunning foyer he had created as the entry to the ship, the first impression of the *HELIX*, would be spoiled by two massive air vents billowing O_2 directly at anyone who dared set foot in the space.

"Yes, yes, I will go find him. Please hold off until you hear from me." Vash, reluctant to leave the safety of the control pod, which had become her personal panic room, was now forced to venture out, and the prospect terrified her.

She had been told that Grynn refused to relocate to the pod he shared with Herra, and instead, they were both still holed up in his parents' pod. Undoubtedly an attempt to preserve what Grynn could of the past. Vash could hardly blame him, but it did cross her mind that living in her dead in-laws' pod with a new baby on the way would be a nightmare for Herra.

She thought it best to transmit a warning as she neared the final corridor to Anae's family pod. As she walked past the rows of pods, she took in their stunning design. They were as beautiful from the outside as they were on the inside. The pods adjusted their lighting automatically, continually reflecting the time of day or night, a never-changing twenty-hour cycle, as it had been experienced on Orbyss. A subtle but important feature that kept them all on a familiar schedule of day and night that would have otherwise been abandoned in space. Just as each of their homes on Orbyss had an essence or personality, so, too, did each family pod on the *HELIX*. Each of them unique but similar, a reflection of the occupants that also paid homage to a collective representation of their species. One particular pod, the most popular by far, contained a single shelf that protruded enticingly into its corridor carrying with it the scent of the head chef's trial delicacies, long after the starship's kitchen had officially closed. It was the best-kept secret amongst the starship's late-night snackers. And it wasn't by coincidence that the inhabitants of the neighboring pods were the best fed aboard the ship. All that was expected in return was an honest opinion on the new culinary creations.

"Grynn, I need to speak with you . . . ten steps away . . . not taking excuses. I need your help . . . now," Vash transmitted directly and exclusively to him. She didn't want to have some emotional display. She had neither the time nor the inclination, and therefore she decided to set the tone from the corridor as she marched towards what would have been Anae and Aricis's home.

The pod sensed Vash's presence, and, in reply, the exterior seamlessly parted to grant her access. Grynn had not managed to respond to her transmission, and instead, it was Herra who greeted her at the entry. She looked worse than Vash had imagined, ravaged by morning sickness and what one could only imagine to be despair at the situation.

Vash was taken aback; Herra and Grynn should have never been left like this. She berated herself for Herra's anguish . . . Anae would have never let this go on. Vash should have been checking on the two of them. It was the least she could have done out of respect for Anae's memory, the woman, the mentor, who had been like a mother to her, as well. Perhaps her recurring dream had been more of a premonition, a last request from her captain while Vash slept, or tried to.

Vash embraced Herra, less out of instinct and more in keeping with what she imagined Anae would do. It seemed that she would be filling Anae's massive footprints in more than one capacity.

Herra, emotional, exhausted, and frail, fell limply into her arms. The gasping sobs she emitted were what induced Grynn's entry into the room.

"What did you say to upset her?" Grynn growled at Vash from across the room, barely recognizable in his unkempt uniform of grief.

Herra sobbed more loudly, desperately trying to control herself and failing miserably.

"Nothing, Grynn, she just got here. I assume she needs you," Herra replied as she wiped at her gigantic tears, mustering all she could to contain them and compose herself, for Grynn's sake.

Well, Vash would have none of it. Her heart broke for his losses, but it would do him no good if she allowed him to succumb to his grief. She felt for him, of course, she did, but seeing him this way also left her with resentment. His grief carried on without end, attaching itself to him permanently, despite the promise of a child on the way. She had lost Anae just as he had, a loss equal to his in her estimation, potentially worse. If she could manage to continue on without Anae, then so could he. He was a husband, about to become a father. What could he be thinking? Not only did he have Herra and a new little one to think of now but she needed him too. Vash needed him to at least fix his own mess on this ship, and she was not about to take no for an answer. This had gone on long enough—far too long, in her opinion.

"Grynn, you are a disgrace, look at you. What would your father say? What would Anae say?"

Her words cut through him, and tears pooled in his eyes, acting as concave magnifiers and making his already large aqua-blue irises appear even larger.

"If I had known this was going on, I would have come much sooner, but nevertheless, I'm here now, so this is all over. You will leave this pod immediately and move into your own." Vash attempted to channel Anae, to speak the words Anae would have spoken.

"You can't just come in here and order us around!" Anger was clearly boiling in Grynn behind his tears.

"I can and I just did—I am your captain, and more importantly, I am your friend. Grynn, look at her! Look at Herra! Look at yourself!" Vash, interfacing via a transmission with the entire east wall of the pod, effortlessly transformed it into reflective glass, a mirror for him to inspect what he had become. Only she and Anae had the clearance to communicate and override any and all aspects of the *HELIX*. It was a safety measure Vash had insisted on early in its construction in order to respond to unanticipated events at a moment's notice. The transition of the dark wall forced Grynn to look at himself, something he had avoided for days, for weeks.

As Grynn sunk to the floor, Vash rushed to embrace Herra, who seemed to go weak with what Vash sincerely hoped was relief. Vash wasn't finished with Grynn, not by a long shot.

"Herra, do you think you can go pack, or shall I summon someone to help you? Take only what you need immediately; I will have the rest sent up."

Herra left the room and quickly started packing. Vash and Grynn could hear her continuing sobs from the adjoining room. She was obviously desperate to leave the pod, one that had become a tomb, a shrine. It reeked of death and sadness and seemed to want Grynn as its victim too, Grynn and Herra both.

"How could you do this, Grynn? You offend the memory of your parents. Worse than that, you must know you cannot become a father yourself, not like this. What were you hoping to find here? Perhaps you thought it was just a bad dream, that they would be here waiting for you? Maybe if you stayed here long enough, they would reappear? You need to steady yourself; they raised you better than this, better than what I see here before me. You are better than this Grynn, much, much better!" She had come to join him on the floor; he had to understand there would be no escape from her, not this time, not ever again.

Grynn grabbed at her suit, desperate for her to stop, and in return, she pushed back against his chest, then pulled him close to her, and they rocked back and forth on the floor of his parents' pod, tears streaming down both of their faces.

"I can't . . . I can't do it, Vash! Please, I need more time."

"What about me, Grynn, what about the time I needed? I lost not only Anae but you, as well. I have been holding everything together on my own. I thought if I were patient, you would come around in time. I need you, Grynn, we all do."

His entire body shook beyond his control. He buried his face in his hands; then suddenly he stopped, looked up, and his eyes, red-rimmed from his tears, met Vash's.

"She loved you, Vash. She loved me too, but she loved you like the daughter she never had. She never told you, I know, but she worried about you night and day. I know it was her plan to come aboard and give you all the credit you deserved; she was so proud of you, so incredibly proud of everything you have accomplished. I know she never told you this, but she should have; instead, she told me—*I can't wait for the day she realizes how good she is.*" The last of Grynn's words were a transmission, one that Herra was omitted from, as she stood in the doorway fully packed and ready to leave.

Both of them rose from the floor, feeling awkward to be caught in an unexpected exchange. The once young lovers, reunited in an intimate embrace.

Herra hardly noticed, so complete was her relief to finally be leaving. If it took Vash to bring Grynn to his senses, so be it.

Duty prevailed, and Vash suddenly remembered her place. "Grynn, the venting in the air lock is the problem. It's creating condensation, and Arnik needs it rerouted to the galley."

"She wants it vented through the foyer? There is nothing wrong with that venting; she doesn't have the pressurization or the humidification allocated properly. You should have told me about this earlier!"

Grynn was now in a rage. The anger he had suppressed with grief and solitude had suddenly found its own vent. Now he, like Vash, could see a light at the end of the tunnel in the mission itself and the demands of the *HELIX*. The science that Vash discovered and the ship they had conceived, built, and would now command together.

CHAPTER 18

TIRUS

3.63 (Late Afternoon) / The *HELIX* / The Next Day

Without fail, in the late afternoon, just as all the young XYZs were summoned home in preparation for their evening meal, Tirus—never one to comply with his parents' call—would instead head to the most prized meeting area aboard the *HELIX*. An area unlike any other on the ship, it had been designed to facilitate comfort and collaboration with modular furnishings, ample refreshments, and a spectacular view of the stars. It was here that his grandfather would wait for him, with an ancient game already assembled, one which taught him strategy, sequence, and endurance.

There was no queen, no king, not even any pawns. The similarity to chess could only be observed in the tactics and each opponent's ability to thwart the other's advancement.

It was obvious, even to Tirus, that his grandfather dearly loved him. The boy was a replica of his grandfather Sond at that age, full of mischief and questions, too smart for his own good, not smart enough to realize it. Sond had "coached" Tirus since three years of age, the initial lesson . . . that Papa could tell if you were transmitting the lay of the pieces and "secretly" requesting assistance from your mother.

The pair inspired smiles from fellow patrons and passersby alike. To witness the players, generations apart, was to witness the continuation of their kind as they voyaged through the dark abyss of space.

"You will not beat me today. I will warn you before we even begin." Tirus had a new plan up his sleeve. He had been practicing with Shal and was positive this new play would secure his victory.

A smile creased the old XYZ's face in response. It was clear he enjoyed this time of day more than any other, and that the game was only a distraction he used in order to capture the young boy's attention. It facilitated his true agenda: to pass along the lessons and values of his experience to his grandson.

"Yes, well, please take a seat. I have been waiting for you. Let's see this new plan of yours." Their eyes twinkled in unison, genetics highlighting their similarities in terms of physical appearance in equal measure to personality. High cheekbones, wide-set eyes, and a determined set of the jaw left no doubt they were family.

Tirus was Sond's first grandchild, a novelty and treasure to him. He took it upon himself to ensure that Tirus received all the attention he deserved, especially with the recent addition of a new sister to his family.

Sond's wife, Lival, had passed years ago. He missed her terribly, but for her sake, Sond was grateful that she did not have to make the trip. She was a gentle creature, and her strength had been derived from her ability to embrace all those around her with compassion and love. But the weight of such empathy had seemed to take its toll, and while he had wanted to fight against her illness, she, in opposition, had seemed to embrace it, like everything and everyone who touched her. She had been either unable or unwilling to waste a moment that could be spent helping another.

A shadow crossed Sond's face at the thought of his love. A moment that was destined not to consume him, not while Tirus was in the room.

"It's your turn, Grandfather. *I have already stumped you!*" Tirus was overcome with excitement as Sond looked up, perplexed, as Tirus rarely, if ever, referred to him as Grandfather. Papa was the boy's nickname of choice for his best friend. It was obvious Tirus was all too eager to show off his newfound knowledge.

His exuberance was infectious, and Sond had no choice but to rise to the occasion. Tirus was not to be ignored.

"Yes, this is a difficult position. It seems that you have not only cornered me but now you stand to overtake my greatest defense. What shall I do now?" Wide-eyed, Tirus watched Sond sit back in mock dismay. He had no idea just how much his grandfather loved to take in his grandson's reactions and tried his best to instill confidence in his abilities.

"You will not beat me, not this time!" Tirus transmitted the threat, determined to scare his long-time opponent.

"So, Tirus, you let me think about my next move for a while. Why don't you tell me what it has been like for you on the ship. How are you and your friends making out at your new school? Have you found anything to amuse yourselves aboard the *HELIX*?"

Tirus was accustomed to these pauses his grandfather required in order to contemplate his next move. Each time it happened, it worried young Tirus. He had begun to hope that he would not end up like his grandfather one day, needing such a great deal of time to formulate his play.

"Yes, we are all very happy with ship school and have explored the *HELIX* from top to bottom!" He contemplated confessing that his "crew" had devised their own plans for a takeover of the ship's controls. However, he decided against it. Undoubtedly Sond would disapprove. Tirus was highly aware of his grandfather's position when it came to anything dangerous or naughty.

Unbeknownst to Tirus, Sond had spotted them, on more than one occasion, and had witnessed their affinity for congregating in the observation deck.

"Yes, a ship well worth exploring. Myself, I love the telescopes hidden in the observation area."

"Telescopes?"

"Yes! Now, Tirus, you should know that there is a code required to access them. However, I would be willing to share it with you if you were to do something for me?"

Tirus looked up at his grandfather with wide eyes, eager to hear what Sond's request might be.

"I want you to promise that we will only use them together. I have many things to explain to you about the solar system and the position of the stars."

"Of course, of course, I will." Tirus was overcome with excitement, almost turning over the game as he jumped up and ran to the window.

"Can we go to the observation deck now?"

"Tirus, you know it is dinnertime. How long has it been since your father called you?" When Shal and Moda sent out the transmission to Tirus, it had been sent out to Sond in unison. He seldom accepted, instead feeling it was important that the couple have their own family time together, especially with their new addition. Nevertheless, they always extended the invitation.

"Oh, I may have found something . . . this just might work. Look at this!" Sond leaned forward, dramatically taking in the pieces on the board. "If I move on the diagonal, and take the position behind your player 2.7, then I can advance beyond your defense."

Tirus's face fell. Not again! As it stood, his grandfather did not believe in losing for the young XYZ's enjoyment. Sond felt that it would not serve Tirus well to be coddled or placated, and as such, he forced the young XYZ to accept defeat. He learned as much confidence from losing as winning from Papa, a trait that would serve him well in the years to come.

"Papa, how did you do that?"

"Here, let me show you. It is a brilliant play you have here, Tirus, with only one flaw."

"I want to be the best. Can you help me? How can I win?"

"Tirus, it is about placing yourself outside the game. Position yourself as an observer. Like you are floating . . . even floating outside the *HELIX*. Then you can consider every move. You can see it before it happens."

Tirus looked at his grandfather with such admiration that it brought tears to Sond's eyes. His grandfather, seemingly all-knowing, had not only foreseen his deepest desire but also planted in him the means to achieve it.

CHAPTER 19

GRYNN

3.75 (Early Morning) / The *HELIX* /
Week Five of Intrastellar Travel

The onyx flooring of the grand foyer glistened as it reflected the artificial light the *HELIX* shone down upon it—the ship's best attempt to mimic a sunny day on Orbyss. The black carbon-fiber surface was ready to begin another day of inductive charging from all the footsteps that passed over it. As always, there would be too many to count, as the foyer had become a destination point due to the grandeur of the space. A close replica that paid homage to the large square on Orbyss, one of the most beloved landmarks of their former home.

Today its first contributor would be Grynn, as he briskly paced its length, his footprints slowly fading behind him. He was on his way to inspect the air lock while there was still time. Time to save this beautiful space he had designed from becoming a wind tunnel, should Arnik have her way.

Vash's words still haunted him: *You must know you cannot become a father, not like this.* Grynn was embarrassed now, humiliated at having become entirely self-absorbed in his own grief. How could he have become so completely consumed? Herra was due any day now. He vowed to make it up to her, to be the father and husband she and their unborn child deserved. It pained him to think that it would take Vash, of all people, to wake him out of his indulgent trance. He would never let it happen again.

"Well . . . look who's here? You seem very pleased with yourself. You know I remember contributing to the initial drawings long ago, way back when we were the Blowholes. You shouldn't be standing here alone with that look on your face, taking all the credit . . ." Shal embraced Grynn first with his words, then with his arms. He could not have been more relieved to see that his best friend had finally left his parents' pod.

Grynn could not help but laugh back at him, even though tears stung his eyes and blurred Shal's figure as he stood before him. How could he have stayed away from Shal for so long?

Shal could see Grynn needed a moment to collect himself, and so he continued, "How is Herra? She must be ready for the new arrival. I think Moda is more anxious for your little one to make a debut than either of you. I know that she could definitely use some company. Someone other than little Eelaa to entertain her. I have been too busy with the ship to pay much attention to either one of them."

After completing the mission to bury the DNA time capsule, Shal had taken over as lead aerospace engineer, overseeing the *HELIX*'s nuclear fusion engines. He was up early despite being exhausted because Vash had him triple-checking everything prior to their activation in just twenty-two days. The activation of the engines would allow the starship to transition from intrastellar to interstellar travel, which simply meant that they would be picking up some serious speed in order to reach their new home on Orbyss II in the time allotted. It was a well-kept secret that these propulsion engines had never been fully tested; their sheer size and capabilities precluded prototypical examination on Orbyss. Vash's compulsion, this time, was well prescribed.

"I am so sorry, Shal; I've been a terrible friend. I'm heartbroken over how I have treated you all, especially Herra. It was—"

"No . . . stop. You have no need to explain yourself. Not to me. Not to anyone. Just know we are all here for you, and we can't wait to celebrate the arrival of your child."

They embraced again, standing locked in each other's arms, in the space they had imagined together, years before, when they were young and nothing bad was ever going to happen to them. They were the very first members of the Blowholes, and they had survived. All that was left were their memories and a small capsule of their DNA buried safe within Orbyss's core, the only evidence they had ever been there at all.

CHAPTER 20

TIRUS

5.14 (Morning) / The *HELIX* / The Next Day

"Yes, that one is also a star . . ." Sond explained to Tirus.

He was captivated, standing in the observatory, taking turns with his Papa to look through the telescope, investigating a new sky. Not only could they identify the stars, they could also witness them forming the colorful mass of dust and gas that surrounded them. Gravity, the ultimate power in the universe, coalescing energy from the randomness. Other stars, having exhausted all of their atomic fuel, either flaming out in a spectacular nebula or collapsing into a black hole. The clusters were magnificent, and the pair had been mesmerized by the activity for over an hour.

"Look at that one, Papa!" Tirus, standing and staring intently through his telescope, identified a runaway star that exhibited a brilliant cascade of colors, photons created from the surrounding gas and dust that stretched to eternity, for only a moment.

"Come see this, Tirus! See how it illuminates the dense clouds encompassing it? The stars, this new young star, not unlike yourself, is proof of our very existence. You see, we are all connected atomically to all the planets, all of the universe; we have all come from the dust of stars."

Tirus's awe and enthusiasm were infectious, and it was difficult to tell which one was enjoying themselves more.

"Do you know what I want to be when I grow up?"

Sond looked intently down at Tirus, anticipating how his grandson might answer.

"I want to be the captain of this ship. I will relieve Vash of her duties, and then I will be the one who will take us all to new planets. We will travel to every planet in the universe!" After observing the stars, Tirus was more determined than ever to be at the helm of the giant ship.

"Well, my, that is ambitious! You have much to learn, Tirus. Perhaps Vash will show you the control pod if you were to ask her. Would you like to see it?"

"Would I? Do you think she would show me now, Papa! Please can we go now?"

"No. It would be unfair to interrupt her. But you leave it with me, and I will see if I can set something up. Your father is working closely with her, so perhaps he can arrange something." Sond was impressed with the boy's interest in the ship, space, and the stars they had just identified. While he was a little taken aback by Tirus's ambition, he chalked it up to the young XYZ's exuberance and did not feel it necessary to correct his thinking.

"Did I hear someone mention they would like a tour of the control pod?" Shal had been observing them from the doorway for some time. It warmed his heart to see both his father and his son quite obviously enjoying each other's company.

"Dada! I missed you!" Tirus made quick work of the space between them and embraced his father with a mighty hug. Sond joined up with them, and all three were locked in a circle for a moment. It had been the first time they had done this together since boarding the *HELIX*.

It only lasted a moment, but it was one all three would remember throughout the days to come. The youngest amongst them was the first to break free.

"Come see what we found, Dada!" Tirus was excited to have Shal join in their fun and pulled him towards the waiting telescope.

Shal played along, although he was secretly reluctant as he had already had his fill of the stars and would gladly trade them all for clouds, wind, and rain.

"Have you spoken with Grynn?" Sond asked about his son's best friend nearly every day. He had watched the pair grow up together, and Grynn felt like a second son to him.

"For once, I have good news!" Shal replied to his father from behind the lens of the telescope.

"Excellent! So glad to hear it! I have been waiting for you to tell me this for weeks. Herra must be due any moment now!" Sond could not have been more relieved. Sond had considered stepping in to help many times. In the absence of Shal's declaration today, he had planned to seek out Grynn himself in order to offer his assistance if he could.

"Yes, she is overdue three days. I am not sure who is more anxious, Herra or Moda. She is looking forward to the camaraderie, someone who can better relate to her own circumstances. They have always been close, so we are all very excited for both her and Grynn to have their new little one."

"Yes, it will be such a blessing and a wonderful diversion. They both deserve to have their lives back, ones that will be changed forever by the impending addition." The irony of change is that it's inherent to the fabric of life, difficult to accept, yet unending in its intrusion, and Sond could finally relax knowing that Grynn had turned a corner and was now finding a way to cope with his unfair circumstances.

"What do you mean changed forever?" Tirus was a master at following bits of conversation least intended for him.

"Never you mind, Tirus. One day you, too, will see how much a child can change your life when you have your own son or daughter," Shal said.

"Never! That will never happen; I will be far too busy as captain of this ship."

Shal and Sond filled the room with laughter in response. Laughter that seemed to announce the new guests entering the observatory.

"Tirus! What is that?" On all the occasions Rahl had investigated the observatory, he had never discovered that it contained hidden telescopes.

The reflective telescopes merged seamlessly into the infrastructure of the observatory, only presenting themselves for the appropriate user, with the appropriate code. The state-of-the-art astrological equipment was fitted with mirrors of the highest resolution. Replacing them was an arduous task, not one the crew had any inclination to repeat multiple times due to mishandling by XYZ minors.

Tirus was bursting with pride, not only because he had discovered something Rahl had failed to but because he had done so in the company of his father and grandfather, two of the most respected XYZs aboard the ship.

Tirus was happy to let Rahl and the rest of his friends examine the stars alongside him. His papa stood by with pride as Tirus explained the formations word for word as Sond had explained them to Tirus just an hour prior.

After delivering his fifth star lesson, the group became disenchanted, partially because they had less interest in the celestial bodies than Tirus did and, in Rahl's case, because he did not appreciate Tirus's telescope advantage.

"Let's check out the waterfall! Have you seen it change colors?" Rahl was anxious to take back control of the group, and the waterfall was the only thing he could think of that would outshine the telescopes and convince the rest of the group to follow him out of the observatory, and away from Tirus.

"Don't you want to go along with your friends, Tirus?" Shal noticed that his son hung back even after his friends had all decided to move on. He hoped that the boy had not done so out of obligation to him and his father.

Before Tirus could answer, Moda bolted through the observatory entryway.

"Shal, it's Herra! She's gone into labor!" Moda screamed her words, a mixture of distress and joy.

Relief and excitement washed over Shal and Sond. They rushed after Moda, all but forgetting Tirus. After all, he ran free exploring the

HELIX most of the time. He definitely knew his way around, and there were only so many places he could go.

For Tirus, this was a most fortuitous event. He could not have been more excited. In the absence of his grandfather's watchful eye, he could turn the powerful telescope undetected towards the space directly above the observatory. Tirus was no longer searching the stars; instead, he was searching for the entry point to the secret room at the top of the observation dome.

CHAPTER 21

HERRA

5.14 (Morning) / The *HELIX* / The Same Day

The pain was excruciating. It was like nothing she had ever experienced before. Herra imagined it was what a shark attack would feel like as her labor ate away at her from the inside.

It was foreign and at the same time familiar. The agony she had felt watching Grynn in his grief without being able to comfort him came close. The only difference was that this took hold of her physically and the other emotionally.

It was completely illogical. Pragmatically she knew her child would not be harmed by the external circumstances, but as a mother, she had worried about her state of mind through the last weeks of the pregnancy. She wondered if this new life about to join them had felt her distress, had been impacted by her sorrow. Had her grief shaped this little one within her, as the child had, in turn, shaped her?

Another contraction took hold, and her train of lucid thought was promptly derailed as she screamed out in pain. This was her greeting to the new faces in the doorway.

Moda, Shal, and Sond had made quick work of the corridors leading to the medical pod, eager to see for themselves how Herra was managing in order to help in any way possible.

"It won't be long now, you're almost there." Having gone through the same thing twice, Moda was well versed in the stages of labor and was relieved to see that it would be over very soon for Herra.

Dexl entered the room to witness Herra's subsequent scream and commented, "Looks like everything is going well."

His humor, meant to reassure them, was not well received by Herra and Moda. The ship's doctor was well known for his jocose manner, which was generally appreciated, regardless of how poor his timing could sometimes be.

As he took in Herra's vitals, a frown creased his brow. The delivery room within the medical pod was state of the art; it monitored the heart rates of both mother and unborn child by the millisecond.

"Herra, everything is fine, we just need to hurry this along." The result of his words caused her heart to race, and although Dexl regretted the comment, he knew that it could not be avoided or retracted. The fetal heart rate had started to decelerate slightly due to the stress of her labor, and he did not want to compromise a safe delivery.

The XYZs shared a similar reproductive system with their cetacean cousins. Like other mammals, female reproductive organs consisted of ovaries, a uterus, a vagina, and, during gestation, a placenta. However, unlike humans, the uterus was bicornuate, consisting of two uterine horns, only one of them housing the fetus.

Herra had been monitored regularly, and her pregnancy was normal. It was not until now, at the onset of labor, that Dexl could identify that her cervix had become obstructed by the cervix of the second uterine horn. It was an abnormality that the second horn had also begun dilating during labor. Due to the complication, it was now very unlikely that Herra could deliver the baby safely if he did not intervene. Not only did they stand to lose the child but they could potentially lose her, as well.

He administered a drug to accelerate her labor and waited for the violent contractions to occur that would indicate it had taken effect. It seemed an unkind thing to do, but he needed her to push; he needed her to push quickly.

The concern on the faces of Herra's parents was unmistakable despite their best attempts to appear optimistic. A ripple of fear for the life of both Herra and her child travelled quickly through them all as Dexl ushered everyone out of the delivery pod save for Grynn.

"Please tell me it's going to be OK! Please tell me my baby will be fine!" Herra begged Dexl to make her the promise all of them knew he could not, and the only thing that saved him from having to respond to her was Herra's next contraction.

It had now become obvious that the baby could not make its way through the birth canal unaided, and this was ultimately causing the infant's heart rate to decrease. Dexl changed his course and quickly located the necessary equipment so that he could position a vacuum to deliver the baby as quickly as possible.

He knew the emotions ran high for this delivery to be a success for both mother and child. They had all suffered the loss of both Anae and Aricis, and Dexl was determined that there would be no further loss, not on his watch. Not if he had anything to do with it.

Dexl inserted his hand into Herra in order to identify the baby's posterior fontanel, then moved his index finger several centimeters along the sagittal suture towards the anterior fontanel. From there, he could feel the tip of the baby's metacarpophalangeal joint with his middle finger so he could calculate the optimal cup insertion distance.

Herra felt helpless; she was desperate for this child within her to survive. A child she had loved from the moment she'd known of their existence, as if she had known them her entire life. Despite the discomfort and the pain she suffered, contraction after contraction, she did the only thing she could think of; she transmitted to the fetus within her: "I am your mother, and I love you. I will always be with you, and we are going to be together very soon."

The sophisticated medical pod, intelligently connected to all the delivery equipment, was constantly monitoring the baby. Herra's transmission triggered the infant's heart rate to increase enough for the *HELIX* to continue with the procedure. Had the baby's heart rate failed to increase, they would have had to perform an emergency C-section, which may have taken too long. The pod interface with the *HELIX* was able to assist Dexl in guiding the cup. Detecting by X-ray the exact position of the baby within Herra, it was able to identify the optimal position for insertion as long as Dexl did his part to ensure that no maternal tissue was trapped underneath it.

Dexl carefully checked the anterior and lateral portions of the cup multiple times. He knew that they had no time to spare but was determined that no error be made on his part. He knew all too well the potential dangers of this procedure: dystocia, scalp wounds, bleeding within the skull, even potential fracture. But now, as the *HELIX* monitored the baby's heart rate, it started to plummet again, and he knew he had to hurry.

Dexl worked quickly and efficiently under the bright lights of the delivery pod, waiting for the moment the interface would confirm his position and the suction would begin. Every second felt like an hour as they held their breaths in unison. It was a countdown of sorts, just as their race to leave Orbyss had been. All of them tied together to survive against all odds, Dexl determined to have this first delivery, this first new life born aboard the *HELIX*, be Grynn and Herra's daughter or son.

An unmistakable hiss from the vacuum began, to Dexl's relief, and he shouted, "OK, Herra, now push!"

She pushed against the tsunami of pain, not knowing if she would ever surface after the waves engulfed her. She had no strength left to scream and knew it would make no difference if she tried. She lost consciousness as the baby left her body, her heart racing and blood ringing in her ears.

The baby was blue, so very blue. Dexl's heart raced alongside Grynn's. They immediately transferred the newborn to the examination table. As Dexl checked the baby's vitals, he suppressed his own thoughts. *Do not die, little one, you have to survive* were the words that played in his head.

He swept the child's mouth and waited. The *HELIX* interface constantly monitored the vitals of the infant, and Dexl did everything he could to encourage the baby to breathe.

Then a cry echoed through the room, a cry that was not Herra's . . . not this time.

The tiny XYZ howled in Dexl's arms at exactly 7.12 on the forty-eighth day of intrastellar travel. Kicking and screaming, offended at the bright lights that surrounded them all, in stark contrast to the dark, warm, watery womb where life had begun.

Dexl carefully brought the infant to Herra with Grynn at her side. With tears in his eyes, he passed baby to mother, and asked her a single question with a hint of the humor he was so well known for. It was his effort to make up for the panic that had filled the space only moments prior.

"What will you name him?" he asked Herra with a candor unfitting to what they had all just witnessed. As if it had been the most uneventful delivery he had ever performed.

She began to answer that they would name him Aricis after Grynn's late father, which had always been her clandestine plan. It was her wish that the little one would own the name of either one of Grynn's late parents, depending upon the sex. However, Grynn stopped her before she could speak a word; he had guessed at her selfless intention long before this moment.

"The child's name will be Herriden," he announced, with a voice choked by pride, wonder, and tears. "His name will be Herriden— named after his remarkable mother."

There was not a dry eye in the pod as Grynn and Herra cried alongside the others who had joined them in order to welcome the child. Now parents, Herra and Grynn wept with relief and joy to be holding the first child of the *HELIX* in their arms.

CHAPTER 22

VASH

4.33 (Morning) / The *HELIX* / Week
Seven of Intrastellar Travel

The hem of her suit fluttered around her ankles in tandem with the dust that swirled around the stars that were clearly visible through the glass walkway that led to the control pod. Step after step, a rhythm had been perfected over the years, taking her exactly 3.4 minutes to make it from end to end. It was a space walk of sorts, within the safe embrace of the *HELIX*.

Her dreams of Anae had ceased, and reports that Grynn had become a father filled her with relief, joy, and something else she hadn't anticipated. Regret was new to her. She had experienced many emotions during her twenty-two years on Orbyss, and many more in the five years she had spent aboard the *HELIX*; however, regret had not been part of the repertoire—not until now.

Of course, she was grateful Grynn had managed to find a way back to them all, and she could not be happier that his and Herra's child was the first to be born aboard the ship. Herriden had increased their numbers after they had been reduced to an even 100,000 following the loss of Anae and the multiple casualties during the last trip of space elevators to the *HELIX* in the wake of the asteroid striking Orbyss. Now they were 100,001.

Despite this celebration, a sorrowful weight had formed at the base of her abdomen, one that seemed to be gnawing away at her heart. It made no sense, but she could not help but wish somehow that the child had been hers—hers and Grynn's, to be exact. Although she would never admit it and fought hard to ignore the longing within her, it continued to haunt her, a splinter that seemed like it should be so easy to remove yet was forever burrowing its way deeper into her soul. Fortunately, the *HELIX* provided a plethora of distractions for her as they made the necessary preparations required to pick up some serious speed.

Vash had a grueling list to run through; everything had to be perfect, and she alone shouldered that burden. The only item left to chance was unfortunately the most significant. One they were all counting on. The ship's nuclear fusion engines had never been fully tested—it had been impossible to test the enormous engines on Orbyss. A scale model and Vash's extrapolations had had to suffice.

She had spent so many years worrying about it that now she could not decide if she were relieved or terrified that the moment had almost arrived. She would never forget the hours she and Shal had spent testing smaller versions of the engine in a simulation environment. Perfecting each fusion reaction with various elements in order to capture the most energy required to propel the twelve-kilometer-long ship.

Alone at the helm of the *HELIX*, it was humorous now to think back on the testing disasters they had experienced and how many iterations of the model engines they had run through in an effort to perfect the performance. Together they had survived multiple flights, failures, and fires trying to successfully complete the design. Now she was immeasurably grateful Shal was the one in charge of the engines that would propel them at 20 percent the speed of light to Orbyss II. He had more patience than she did, and there wasn't a square millimeter of the engines that he hadn't built, taken apart, and reassembled. If it were anyone other than Shal, she would have never even agreed to attempt this. However, Shal's competence did not change the fact that they were depending on engines that worked very well, on a much smaller scale, during simulation.

Suddenly her thoughts were interrupted by a small hand on her shoulder. "Vash, will you show me around the control pod . . . please?"

"Tirus, I told you to wait patiently while I ask her." Sond was quick to apologize for Tirus's exuberance.

Vash spun around in her carbon-fiber-encased captain's chair, which—along with her suit—collected energy as it monitored her vitals and ensured that she remained at the most comfortable temperature and optimal ergonomic position.

Sond was allowed entrance to the control pod, as were all members of Shal's family as a safety precaution, should Shal require assistance. Sond was also one of the most respected XYZs for his work in developing the plans for colonization based on his years of study in the field of botany, specifically the compounds vital for terraforming a new planet. As such, he was granted clearance regardless of Shal's contributions. His access, as well as that of his young guest, went unquestioned and was always welcome.

"Of course, I will," she replied directly to Tirus, meeting him nose to nose as she sat in her chair.

It was easy to observe Vash's love of the highly sophisticated and intelligent function that the control pod provided the ship. Every second of the voyage was monitored and controlled from this one pod. Every inch of both the interior and exterior of the ship was continually assessed to ensure optimal homeostasis, as was every biological assessment and bodily function imaginable for each passenger aboard the *HELIX*.

Not only did the largest pod on the ship monitor everything related to and contained within the *HELIX*, and all functions of mission control, but everything Anae previously monitored on Orbyss was incumbent upon the control pod, as well. Without the eyes and ears of mission control back on Orbyss, the starship was dependent upon the assistance of more than five hundred satellites that had been deployed along the proposed trajectory of the *HELIX* over the last ten years in order to monitor everything from meteor showers, planet orbits, and solar winds or flares. Ten such satellites maintained a constant vigil on Orbyss and would relay information regarding the planet to the *HELIX* on an annual basis, affectionately called the O2O (Orbyss 2 Orbyss) satellites.

Tirus was completely transfixed by the rows upon rows of indicator lights that corresponded to the assigned monitors visible above them, all feeding into the main monitor at the center of the room. He was so absorbed that he didn't even notice when Vash went quiet while describing how the control pod monitored the vitals of each passenger, recalling the moment she had been notified of the time of Herriden's birth. Her pause escaped Tirus but was not lost on Sond.

"You seem preoccupied, Vash. Is something troubling you? Please let an old-yet-wise man share some advice with you, if I may. Distraction over purpose is a poor choice and a dangerous pastime. None of us know how long we have, how many days we will live in each other's company. Better not to waste a single one." Sond knew that Vash was their only hope; they all depended upon her, and it was an unfair burden, a hero's burden. He could only imagine the potential theoretical complications that she obsessed over. He was hoping that the short snippet of advice he gave her would be enough to help. If not by completely overcoming the distraction, then at least by cautioning her not to let it get the better of her.

Vash smiled back at Sond. "Yes, I do have a lot on my mind, given that we will be initializing the nuclear fusion engines in just twenty-one days' time. Perhaps the engine room is the next logical field trip for Tirus. And who would be better than your son to take over that show-and-tell?"

Vash led grandfather and grandson towards the control pod exit and watched them walk hand in hand down the windowed walkway as Sond pointed out the star constellations to Tirus.

From what Vash had translated from Sond's advice, he wanted her to keep her distance from Grynn, despite the fact that she had been the one to get him to leave his parents' pod for the first time since their deaths. Sond was clearly dedicated to the happiness of his family, a family that from his perspective, had always included Grynn, and now would extend to include Herra and their newborn son, Herriden. It was irrationally clear to Vash that Sond was looking out for his family and he had all the best intentions to preserve the happiness his family had recently acquired, which made her feel even more alone.

It was a sad truth that as their old world crumbled, their new world aboard the *HELIX* was only in its infancy. The focus had always been and, from Vash's perspective, remained on the safety and function of the ship. They were 100,001 in number now, significant but not enough to guarantee their survival. It was not inconceivable that something as arbitrary as an uncontained water contamination could wipe them out, let alone an attempt to colonize a new, unexplored planet. With this thought in mind, Vash made a conscious effort to appeal to Tirus and his overly protective grandfather in the future. It struck Vash how their voyage into space had further defined the meaning of Percivious, the ultimate example of altruism. Self-sacrifice in order to benefit others with no regard to reward or reciprocity. Not only were they reliant on each other for survival but they were definitively bound by each individual's action at any given moment, in all circumstances, at all times. Percivious protected them not only from the challenges they faced collectively but it also protected them from themselves and their individual reactions. If there was one thing that Anae had taught her it was this: *Compassion is what determines our success in any given situation. Percivious will always supersede intelligence because it is the ultimate in compassion, unconditional love, and trust in one another.*

CHAPTER 23

HERRA

10.00 (Midnight) / The *HELIX* / Week
Seven of Intrastellar Travel

What began as a soft and melodic coo soon increased in volume and intensity. Herriden's cries roused something within Herra; it was almost as if he were still within her. She had a physical response when he called for her, one that she could not ignore.

Herra had seamlessly adjusted to motherhood following what had been a harrowing delivery. The emotional sentiments and genuine support she had received still brought tears to her eyes and made the somber weeks she had endured in her in-laws' pod a distant memory. She loved her new son more than she could have imagined and fully believed the child had returned Grynn to her, returned Grynn to his own life, one they had planned together. It seemed that nothing could dampen Herra's hormone-induced happiness as she breastfed her child for the first time that day.

Herra relished these moments, feeling the infant's skin next to her own. His delicate features, his tiny hands and feet, his perfectly formed small body . . . he was a gift she could never imagine would bring her such fulfillment. It was in this state of maternal bliss that she would plan their collective futures and imagine the wonderful new world the three of them would inhabit together.

In Herra's mind, Orbyss II was a celestial paradise, a planet more beautiful than Orbyss could ever be, one that would raise their species to new heights, a world worthy of the beautiful boy at her breast. She believed their new home would welcome them and let them begin anew. These thoughts triggered her to travel back in time to when she and Grynn had been drawn to each other while working on plans for the *HELIX*.

Grynn had been everything to Herra; only now, with the birth of her son, could she imagine loving another as completely as she loved Grynn. She would happily die for either one of them; they meant everything to her, and she was fiercely protective of them both. She knew they needed her, and she believed that she alone was the strength of the family, the only one who could hold them all together.

Herriden, finally satisfied, breathed deeply in her arms. She loved to sit and hold him for hours on end. He slept so peacefully in her embrace. It was as if nothing could interrupt the beautiful moments she spent like this. She never wanted it to end, and she could not wait to have another. She wanted to fill the ship with her and Grynn's offspring. She could imagine nothing that would make her happier.

"What are you smiling about? Has our son whispered something wildly amusing to you in his sleep?" Grynn, still groggy from his slumber, could barely make out Herra's expression in the dim lighting the family pod had selected on their behalf for Herriden's midnight snack.

"Just thinking how lucky we are. He is beautiful, and I was contemplating how beautiful it would be if we were lucky enough to have more."

"Yes, I was just thinking that myself; perhaps we should start on that right now?" A devilish grin took hold of Grynn's face.

Herra, usually reluctant to give up the sleeping boy, gladly placed him in his cradle, which immediately replicated her body temperature, the rhythm of her breathing, and her smell in order to make his transition as peaceful as possible.

Grynn's eyes had now adjusted to the dim lighting, and as he examined Herra's shape, desire overtook him. It would be the first time they would be reunited following Herriden's birth, and Grynn was passionate about the prospect.

"How long do you think we have until he gets hungry again?"

"One never knows, you'll just have to be fast . . ." she teased.

"Oh, that is not the issue; I just want to make sure this is enjoyable for you. You deserve it, after everything you have been through." Grynn's meaning encompassed not only the terrifying delivery but also the weeks spent in his parents' pod. He wanted to make it up to her, in every way possible.

As had always been the case, Grynn's excitement soon became Herra's, and as they made their way to the bed, she quickly shed the garments that had been covering her. It felt new and different as Grynn touched her body that had undergone such an incredible transformation in order to deliver their child.

He seemed to sense her hesitation and pulled back as a result; however, her insistent hands and mouth would not allow the separation to occur.

Herriden's cooperation was appreciated; he did not cry or stir till the artificial morning light began to slowly seep into their family pod. Life had returned to normal, or as close to normal as a giant starship charting a course to a new planet could possibly provide.

CHAPTER 24

GRYNN

2.61 (Early Morning) / The *HELIX* / One Day
Prior to Initiation of Nuclear Fusion Engines

Grynn's favorite time had become "daybreak." He loved to witness the ship leave its slumber as its passengers slowly started another day. In some ways, time had become arbitrary. Without the *HELIX*'s artificial rotation of Orbyss creating the illusion that the sun was still making its way across the sky each day, it was difficult to believe that time had passed at all. If not for the birth of his son, the deeper wrinkles on his face, and the simulated lighting of the *HELIX*, he could have been convinced that no time had passed at all.

Grynn left Herriden sleeping soundly in Herra's arms. Both in deep slumber, their breathing synchronized, he could not bring himself to wake them, even to say goodbye. Herra amazed him. He could not imagine a more attentive and devoted mother or wife. A tenderness spilled through him as he touched her arm. As he took in their combined profile, it was as if the two were one. They were the most precious beings in existence, and he was overcome with the love he felt for them both.

Although leaving them was difficult, he was also looking forward to meeting Shal this morning. It was like old times for the two best friends. Grynn had been assisting Shal in preparation for the *HELIX*'s propulsion engines to make their debut.

In actuality, it was even more like old times than the reconciliation of the two best friends. Vash, quite obviously obsessing over the performance of the engines, was with them constantly. One could easily believe that she and Shal had permanently moved into the engine hull, as Grynn could not recall a time he had entered the space without finding them both there during the last four weeks.

The starship's mechanical quarters were the largest pods on the entire ship. Spanning five thousand meters, they housed the solar power units, engines, propulsion systems, exploration vehicle parts and equipment, as well as the structural material and corresponding infrastructure required for colonization. The rooms were managed day and night by a team of fifty engineers in rotating shifts, working round the clock.

As Grynn neared the engine room, he could already eavesdrop on the "discussion" between Vash and Shal. "So you have really no idea what the optimal cruising speed will actually be. How can you possibly think between 0.1 and 0.3 of light speed is even helpful? That isn't a range; that is a universe apart, and it leaves me with little to no confidence that these engines will perform at all. This was never what we discussed; you always had plausible figures within the realm of reality," Vash quipped.

Shal was beyond relieved to see Grynn approach. He was grateful to have any excuse to escape Vash. The fact that it was Grynn was a bonus. "Grynn, so glad you are here. We were just discussing how . . ."

Grynn knew this scenario all too well. It had repeated itself throughout his formative years and well into adulthood. Shal and Vash were a conundrum, polar opposites and two peas in a pod all at the same time. Both of them shared incredible EQs with IQs to match; however, that is where their commonalities began and ended. They spoke the same language but could not agree on a dictionary. What meant one thing to Vash could mean something completely different to Shal.

Shal was the absentminded professor. He carried on living his life while he worked out a problem in his head. Shal never worried about the solution; instead, he would allow his subconscious to take over and figure it out for him . . . all in good time. Conversely, Vash would fixate on the problem, even if she had already discovered the solution, because maybe—just maybe—in one of a hundred thousand iterations she had run in her magnificent mind, she may have overlooked an infinitesimal detail. And so, their dance continued and would not conclude until the *HELIX* commenced nuclear fusion propulsion or destroyed them all trying.

"So, you see, Vash, you should be thrilled with this 'range.' Yes, the potential of the *HELIX* is untested, but it is also unlimited at this moment. I guarantee it will be a safe ride; I just haven't been able to contemplate how fast the ride will actually be." Grynn hardly listened to Shal's rant. It was easy enough to take in that they would potentially be travelling faster than anticipated . . . which always sounded good to Grynn.

"Not good enough, Shal! If you can't project something as basic as the speed—"

"I did! You just don't care for the 'range,' Vash."

Grynn could see now that he had no choice but to step in. "OK, listen. I know that you two have been at this forever, and there is nothing that is going to change between now and tomorrow at 3.00, so let's just trust each other. You are both the best we have, and if you two can't figure out the exact speed these engines can safely cruise at, then no one can. So, let's just see how it goes tomorrow. Vash, I know this is driving you crazy, but what if Shal agrees to let you have exclusive control of the—"

"I am the captain; I already have that. I don't care how fast we go; I am more worried that once we fire these engines up, they will obliterate all life aboard this ship along with any potentially undiscovered life in the galaxy."

"Never going to happen," Shal said.

"How can you guarantee that?"

Grynn had heard enough. "Vash, he can't. But if you don't let him try, then I can guarantee that not only will we fail to make the trip to Orbyss II in twenty-five years or so, as planned, but we will inevitably fail to get there . . . ever."

"I just can't leave this much to chance!" Vash was sick with worry, not for herself or even the ship but for the one hundred thousand innocent passengers on board, all oblivious to the unimaginable danger they were exposed to aboard the *HELIX*—an undesirable necessity required to make it to their new home.

"You're not. You are leaving it up to Shal. A great deal better than chance, from my experience," Grynn replied, punctuating the comment with an exaggerated wink towards his best friend.

Grynn had greatly missed these exchanges; it felt good to be needed again. It was obvious that if he had not stepped in, this argument could have easily escalated to something much worse. They all needed each other right now, and it became very clear to Grynn that their lives, as well as the lives of all the passengers, depended heavily upon the three of them. He had been selfishly protected from this during the time he was sequestered in his parents' pod. It had been for the best, as he could not have managed the weight of this realization at that time. But to look at Shal and, especially, Vash, and to consider the immense pressure and sacrifice they had assumed on behalf of them all left him feeling that he had betrayed them, betrayed their friendship, and he was desperate to make up for it.

"What can I do to help? I am here for you both, you know that, but what can I do to make things go smoothly tomorrow?"

"You can be with the crew in the control pod. You can help run interference between me and Shal. He needs to be here in the engine room, and I can't leave the control pod, so you can go back and forth."

"You don't need me for that, Vash; you have an intelligent ship and the ability to transmit directly to him at any given moment." Grynn knew what she was driving at, but he wanted to hear her say it, to say that she needed him.

"That's not what she is asking for, Grynn." Shal laughed at him. "She is asking you to translate the situation in a way that will keep us from killing each other."

Grynn couldn't help but laugh back at him while nodding. The truth was that he was reluctant not to be at Herra's and his son's side for the ship's countdown. However, taking in his friends' searching expressions, it was obvious they were desperate for his cooperation. How could he possibly deny them?

"Of course, I will be your translator. How could I say no to the two most stupidly smart people aboard this ship?" Grynn couldn't help but tease them as they left the hull. The relief on his friends' faces was immeasurable, and Grynn, for one, was glad to be back on the side of saver versus saved.

CHAPTER 25

TIRUS

2.19 (Afternoon) / The *HELIX* / Eighty-One Minutes
Prior to Initiation of Nuclear Fusion Engines

It was a picture he held in his mind. An image, one in a million, that impossible shot achieved. The result of a plethora of prior photographic attempts, until the one photo that achieved perfection. This was how Tirus pictured himself as he stood in the center of the space above the observation dome with all his friends and family gazing up at him with wonder and admiration. Especially Rahl.

Tirus had been piecing together the puzzle for months now. There had been times when he thought that it might be too difficult and he had considered giving up. However, the lights of the exploration pod above the observation dome would not allow it. When they called his name, he could think of little else.

In the days leading up to the deployment of the nuclear engines, Shal's focus, as well as that of all the crew, had understandably been dictated by the launch preparations. Their distraction had been key in order for Tirus to fulfill his imagined destiny. More than once, they could have squashed his plans, but they had been too busy to notice what had caught his attention and too consumed by the launch to draw the required links between the questions he had been asking and what his secret project might be.

Therefore, it was not surprising that as Tirus set out towards the air lock of the ship, determined to put his plan in motion, no one knew where he was at that moment. No one had given it a thought.

CHAPTER 26

VASH

2.37 (Eighteen Minutes Later) / The *HELIX* / Sixty-Three Minutes Prior to Initiation of Nuclear Fusion Engines

Vash had stopped registering the star formations suspended in front of her from the captain's seat at the helm of the control pod. It was like looking at a green screen, or a backdrop. If you asked her, she would have had a hard time recollecting that there had been stars in front of her at all.

The only thing she had time for were equations. At times like these, mathematics was her touching stone. The only thing she could safely hold on to. The only thing that allowed her to believe they would all be OK, that they would make it to Orbyss II. That they would survive.

"Captain, we are three minutes from initiating the launch. All systems are optimal, and launch commands have been pre-sequenced so that when you give the signal, the countdown will automatically begin."

"Thank you, Rhys. Is everything in place?"

Rhys, Vash's first mate, was accustomed to her compulsions. She had understood them before most of the others back in the Blowholes' warehouse hideout, and today they neither surprised nor alarmed her. In fact, she would have thought it odd if Vash had not questioned her despite the fact that Vash herself had triple-checked already that everything was in place throughout the course of the day. A triple check was what Rhys had actually witnessed, but the true number was quite likely much higher.

"Can you please watch my seat? I need to speak with Shal about something."

Rhys suppressed a roll of her eyes until her captain had left for the engine room. Perhaps she had become immune to Vash's never-ending scrutiny or perhaps she had been lulled into a false sense of security by the burden Vash seemed to effortlessly lift off all of their shoulders. But for whatever reason, she missed the red light on her right that continued to blink as she discussed their well-laid plans for Orbyss II with the rest of the crew.

Upon her return, Vash sought out Rhys immediately. "All good?"

"All good! How about with Shal?"

"Yes, all good. Are we ready?"

In response, Rhys calmly smiled back to Vash and nodded. To her relief, Vash struggled towards a small smile in return before she began her transmission to all passengers aboard the *HELIX*. Simultaneously she initiated the launch command, and the blinking red light, hidden from Vash's sight by the sleeve of Rhys's right arm as she leaned over Vash in a protective stance, was overridden.

"Could I have everyone's attention please . . ."

CHAPTER 27

MODA

Moda wasn't easily shaken, nor was she one to worry. Therefore, she had loitered well into the countdown before seeking out Tirus in order to ensure they were all in position, safe within their respective family pods prior to the launch of the engines. It was not like Shal would be with them anyway, as he was to remain in the engine room while they deployed. He would likely be there long after the launch, probably until they reached optimal cruising speed.

"Sond, have you seen Tirus?" Moda thought she would stop and ask her father-in-law just in case he knew something of Tirus's whereabouts.

"I thought he was with you. Why don't you check the observation deck?"

"Yes, I was just headed there. You know what I am finding, Sond?"

"What is that?"

"While I didn't care for his name at first, now I find that 'Tirus' suits him perfectly. He never ceases to 'tire us' out . . ."

Sond could not help but laugh at Moda's exasperation. He decided to join her in order to assist in collecting his delinquent grandson and making sure he was safely returned to his pod where he belonged prior to the deployment of the engines.

As they walked the long stretch of the corridor, it seemed that they were not the only ones still loitering.

"Herra, you and Herriden should be back in your pod!" Moda, true to her nature, was more worried about others than herself, or even her own family. Having Shal in control of what powered the ship gave her all the security she needed to determine whether or not to follow the rules. She quite easily depended on her own compass for guidance as well as the knowledge that Shal and Vash were at the wheel.

"I was just waiting on Grynn, seems that he is running interference between Vash and Shal."

"Well, then, you should definitely head back to your pod; I can only assume he won't be finished with that anytime soon."

Herra cast a knowing smile towards her best friend and nodded in agreement. Herriden had just fallen asleep in her arms, and he was getting heavy. She was ready to put her little one down so he could enjoy a proper nap.

As Herra continued down the hall, she heard a low, moaning scream echoed by a second higher-pitched shriek of terror that jolted her in her tracks and caused her to wake the infant sleeping in her arms. Instinctively, she raced towards the cries that had morphed into transmissions for help to all passengers on board.

As Herra entered the dome, her blood ran cold at the sight just outside the observation room windows. At first, she shook her head in denial, but the sight of Tirus clinging to the *HELIX* solar shield from outside the ship crushed her insides and simultaneously compelled her to take action. Moda hysterically transmitted for anyone to help as she clawed at the window in vain, attempting to tear through the starship in order to get to him as Sond held her by the shoulders, not knowing whether to pull her away or stand by and embrace her for what looked to be the last time she would see her son.

"Take him and please stop transmitting," Herra screamed at Moda as she thrust Herriden into Sond's arms and bolted from the observation deck straight for the air lock.

Herra ran as fast as she could with not a second to spare, working out in her head the time she would have to retrieve Tirus from his space walk before the *HELIX* burned him alive.

It was Herra who knew the interior functions of the ship better than anyone, save Grynn. Every word, every conversation with him, was tattooed in her memory. Countless ideas, including the overall interior design of the ship, had been seamlessly incorporated into many of the features for their suits.

Herra knew that Grynn had probably disabled the air lock safety feature put in place for the engine propulsion sequence when he rerouted the venting. There was no other way Tirus could have made it off the ship otherwise. But why hadn't they been notified in the control room? The ship must have sensed him from the exterior. That did not make sense.

She summoned her suit to switch into its exterior mode. Her garment immediately covered her face and extremities, providing her with the required protection against radiation, the lack of gravity, and the temperatures just above absolute zero outside the *HELIX* air lock. Herra quickly grabbed an emergency kit prior to exiting the ship that contained a carbon-fiber tether, various repair tools and materials, as well as an axe for dislodging any refuse. As she summoned the opening and left the ship, she transmitted: "Vash, Grynn! You have to stop! Tirus is outside the *HELIX*! I am going after him."

She knew if she did so before she left the ship that Grynn and Vash would have stopped her from rescuing him. But it had to be her. She could not live with herself otherwise. She had designed and created these suits to protect them, to protect them all. She had fashioned them into an invincible sheath. But the children's garments were not the same as the adults'. They sacrificed exterior functionality in favor of mobility, monitoring, and physical protection. They provided safety, absolutely—of course, all of them wanted their most precious cargo kept safe. That was why the children were never meant to leave the ship until they reached Orbyss II. That was why the children's suits had never been designed for it.

"Herra! What are you talking about? We are literally in the last minutes of the countdown. There are exactly 1.89 minutes left before the propulsion engines deploy. It's too late. I can't reverse it. *We can't stop them!*" Vash shouted her reply aloud. A sick panic shuddered through the *HELIX* captain, causing the rest of her crew to crowd around her in alarm. The nuclear engines could not be contained at this point. They were a bomb about to detonate with no off button, not once the sequence began.

Grynn did not bother to respond; he raced to the air lock from the engine room with Shal staring after him in dismay.

Herra raced towards the dome, navigating the slow spin of the pods that composed the ship's behemoth helix formation, which had inspired its name. Her success would now be determined by how she spent each second. If she could not reach the boy prior to the engines being deployed, then they would both be casualties. Adrenaline sharpened her senses. As it rushed through her veins, her suit began an attempt to restrict her activity, which she immediately overrode. Herra scrambled along the length of the ship, desperate to reach Tirus and bring him to safety. Once she had passed over to the front spiral of the starship, she could make out his small frame as he clung desperately to the tip of the leaf-shaped solar surface intended to collect solar energy and simultaneously shield the ship.

Herra's suit contained an acceleration device as well as a magnetic attachment to the *HELIX*. Outside the ship, she had no need to be tethered, not in an adult suit. As she caught up with Tirus, she could see that his suit had indeed reached its limitations. While she knew that the thin, flexible layers of his suit were predominantly designed to offer comfort and monitor vitals aboard the starship and would also protect him for a short time from the radiation, she knew that it was not designed to withstand the harsh temperature for more than five minutes max, nor was it tethered to the *HELIX*. This was something Tirus had undoubtedly discovered for himself as he held on for dear life to the multipurpose solar surface/shield on the exterior of the ship, to the left and behind the observation dome pod.

As she closed the gap between them, his faint attempts at transmission brought tears to her eyes. She could acutely feel his terror and panic. She felt his pounding heart, her throat tightened along with his, and she began to tremble and shake in empathy for the boy. The ship's solar shield had never been designed as a last resort, a lifeline before a passenger was lost to space; however, it was Tirus's last hope, and he clung to it for dear life. For Tirus, it was a pointed fang belonging to the dark mouth of the abyss, and once he let go, he would be swallowed by space.

"Tirus, can you hear me? It's Herra."

He nodded slightly in response, unable to scream, barely able to respond, as he held fast to the ship's exterior structure not daring to look up at her. Even if he had, his vision was obscured, as his suit had been compromised and clouds of quickly freezing oxygen billowed across his face from behind the protective veil of his hood, freezing the tears that flowed down his small cheeks almost immediately. His mouth was full of his own blood, as he had initially started sucking his bottom lip in order to self-soothe, but as fear set in, he had gnawed through the flesh in a continued effort to pacify himself. It was achingly clear to Herra that there was no way Tirus could make it back to the ship in his own suit.

"Can you still breathe?"

He nodded back to her; however, she could see from the shallow, labored rise and fall of his chest that she did not have a moment to spare. If his suit failed entirely, he risked the bends, and his blood would start to boil despite the subzero temperatures that surrounded them. Just as the countdown for the deployment of the engines had commenced, the countdown for Tirus had also been initiated. In that second, as Herra watched the steamy air drift across his small face, she made her decision. She pried him from the shield because he refused to take her hand or assist her in any way. His terror had reached a point where he was just able to cling to the shield. Herra knew she had little time left. She wanted to scream; her instincts begged her to race back to the *HELIX*, to Grynn and their new baby boy. She fought against crying out in fear because the anticipation of dying had seized her and she had begun to panic. But instead, she inhaled deeply and steadied herself. She took Tirus in her arms and transmitted directly to him as tears stung her eyes and streamed down her face behind her veil. She knew very well that her suit would shut down with the weight of them both. She needed to ensure that it performed without fail—this last test she would demand of it.

"Will you promise me something, Tirus?"

He nodded.

"Will you promise me that you will always look after my boy? That you will always watch out for Herriden? That you will make sure he is protected and that you will never leave him?"

Tirus nodded as he shook against her chest, now clinging to Herra as tightly as he had the shield.

"It will all be just fine. Trust me, Tirus, you will see. Please tell Herriden just how much I loved him. Can you do that for me?"

Another nod from the small figure. She had made the choice to secure her son's future with this young boy who would undoubtedly be his friend and protector for life. She blocked the frantic transmissions from Grynn in order to do it. There was no time to tell him how much she loved him. It didn't matter; by now, he must know she loved him more than life itself. Instead, she transmitted her last goodbye directly to Herriden, through the lullaby that always calmed him and put him to sleep while he was still growing inside her.

Now it was time. Herra smiled down at Tirus as she pulled him close. She placed the safety kit in front of him in order to achieve the required weight; discarded her own suit while simultaneously wrapping it around him; looked him in the eyes, imagining what her son would look like in five years; and, sacrificing herself, sent him back to the ship.

Grynn entered the air lock just as the entry closed safely behind Tirus. He grabbed the boy in his arms just as the engines deployed, and they wept together surrounded by Herra's scent, which still lingered on her suit.

CHAPTER 28

VASH

3.43 (Early Afternoon) / The *HELIX* / Forty-Three
Minutes Following Initiation of Nuclear Fusion Engines

Vash turned the corner to find Tirus locked tightly in Grynn's arms, both of them shaking. She didn't have to ask what had happened. The chaotic transmissions from them both were painfully obvious. As she knelt down to meet them on the floor, her garment cascaded from behind her as it wrapped itself around all three of them in an effort to read their vitals and provide warmth against the shock. Vash wept at losing a soul aboard the *HELIX*. Especially a new mother. Especially Grynn's love. Especially on her watch. She would never forgive herself. Not ever. How was she going to save Grynn this time? How could he possibly recover?

A small hand came up against her cheek. Surely the trauma of today would leave its mark. She looked into Tirus's eyes, so like his father's, and whispered that everything would be OK. That he was safe now, that none of this was his fault. The truth was that it was hers. It was all her fault. How could she have missed this? How could this have even been possible? But as soon as Vash asked the questions, her impatient mind immediately delivered the answers. A random alignment, like a star constellation, had occurred; it began with Tirus's investigation of the ship and the control pod, then the countdown for the deployment of the fusion engines began, which involved a temporary pause in exterior monitoring as an outer shield was activated for the protection of the passengers as an extra precaution during the deployment of the engines.

Worse yet, if she reduced the situation in order to identify the immediate cause, it was Grynn. She would have gladly saved him from himself had she known what to look for. It was his failure to reactivate the safety feature in the air lock, preventing access to the exterior of the ship while the engines deployed. His oversight was what allowed Tirus to escape beyond the safety of the ship. And Vash was aware that Grynn knew this all too well. She could tell by the way his eyes refused to register a single thought. He had disappeared into a coma of grief, just floating within his own physicality, despite the fact that Tirus was still clinging to him for dear life.

"Tirus, oh, Tirus . . ." Shal joined them, and the sound of his father's voice calling out to him was enough for Tirus to break away and seek shelter in his father's embrace. In Vash's estimation, this was a good sign. Tirus was strong and young, and he would eventually bounce back. It was Grynn she worried about.

Moda, not far behind Shal, joined them, with Herriden in her arms. For someone so full of life, someone so sure of her own as well as their collective resilience, suddenly she looked helpless with the new baby crying in her arms.

Vash did the only thing she could think of in that moment that may have had the slightest chance of reaching Grynn. It broke her heart to do it, but everything within her told her she had to try.

She looked over at him, longing to hold him, to take all of this away from him. She wanted to spare him the pain he had thought was finally behind him—only to be replaced with something infinitely worse.

Instead, she held back her own tears and gave him a sharp command in place of compassion. "Take your son, he needs you."

Her voice sounded distant and cold, and she could feel them all tense at what seemed like a heartless demand in the face of tragedy.

Something far beyond what they stood for as a species. Far beyond their evolution. For Grynn, it was like being slapped in the face, and his eyes narrowed in response to it, unaware that, in actuality, Vash was extending the ultimate form of compassion, trying to save him from himself.

Herriden cooperated with her seemingly callous request and cried out for comfort. As Grynn rose to his feet, he gathered the screaming infant from Moda's weakened arms, cradled the child against his shoulder, and left the air lock for his pod without comment—without looking back.

Moda, Shal, and Tirus followed soon after. They headed back to their own pod huddled together, casting an outline from a distance as they moved together in unison, one that morphed them into a single being.

And there she stood, alone, left to carry the full, now obese, weight of the *HELIX* on her shoulders once again. None of it was Vash's fault; however, she would pay the ultimate price.

It is very curious the way life unfolds. How none of us exists in a vacuum. It is not fate or destiny, per se, but the impact of each choice we make and how it flows through not just our own lives but all lives connected to it.

The death of Grynn's parents, an accidental oversight, the guiding hand of a grandfather, the precociousness of a young boy. None of it right, none of it wrong, but altogether, it created tragic circumstances, ones unforeseen and irreversible.

CHAPTER 29

VASH

6.17 (Morning) / The *HELIX* / Week One of Interstellar Travel

"What does this one do?" Tirus's young voice full of questions during his tour of the control pod twenty-one days before the engines were deployed would not leave Vash's mind.

It haunted her as she sat at the helm of the pod and surveyed the control panel. How had she missed the indicator light? Flashing brilliant red to let them know an object had been identified on the exterior of the ship. The one that could have prevented all of this. Even more disturbing was her memory of Tirus during the tour. She had shared with him all of the details of the impressive control pod features and the attached rooms necessary to house the giant quantum computers, as well as the instrumentation, sensors, orbital elements, control, and life-preservation systems. Now she recalled all the questions he had asked, well beyond what should have been expected at his age. Now she understood the reason for his fascination about what each key on the control pad would do. Now she was certain that he had engineered his space walk, his escape.

In a way, she had forgotten that all the passengers were entities unto themselves, with their own thoughts, interests, and agendas. She reflected upon them as individuals instead of numbers as she looked down at her weekly stats report, which, amongst all relevant information, indicated that the passenger count was once again at 100,000. Despite the deaths and births that had occurred over the past five years, their numbers had remained constant so that Herra's death stood out like a sore thumb. Just because Vash saw the passengers as precious cargo she needed to protect did not mean that they remained static awaiting her instructions. She wished she would have paid more attention before and vowed nothing like this would ever be allowed to occur again.

It had taken a full week for the *HELIX* to reach its optimal cruising speed. Or rather, for Vash and Shal to determine what the speed would actually be. As it was, Shal had been correct . . . outrageously so. The range he had provided was accurate. If anything, he could have skewed his estimate even higher than the maximum speed he had predicted. As it stood, the time required to reach their new home would be less than originally projected. Much, much less.

The power of the nuclear fusion engines made quick work of the space between the current position of the *HELIX* and Orbyss II. What was originally estimated to be forty years of travel had now been reduced to twenty-five years. What should have been celebrated, Vash and Shal's monumental achievement, was instead completely ignored as a result of the tragedy that ensued the moment the engines were deployed.

"Vash, I am going to leave. Do you need anything?" Rhys was overcome thinking that it might have been her fault the indicator light had been missed. Therefore, Vash had lied to her, falsely suggesting that it had been a malfunction. The truth was that once the deployment had begun, exterior communication had been shut down with it due to the shield. So that by the time the indicator light had been overridden, it was too late to reverse the countdown. Regardless, Vash was not about to lose Rhys to a spiral of guilt, as well. They could not afford to lose anyone else at this point.

Vash performed her ceremony each evening. She would leave for her own pod in mock compliance, only to return exactly one hour later in order to continue her vigil from the optimal vantage point of the *HELIX*. She suffered from her own self-inflicted insomnia, intensified even more by the recent turn of events.

Vash would no longer leave her seat, refusing to miss a moment. She would scrutinize every detail, eavesdrop on every conversation, and second-guess every answer to each of the hundreds of questions she fired at the crew daily. In Vash's mind, Herra's death had upped the ante, and if she died strapped in her seat in order to protect them all, so be it.

CHAPTER 30

TIRUS

Tirus's night terrors would not cease. Neither Shal nor Moda had slept through the night since Herra's death. Despite their joint attempts to counsel him through the terrifying ordeal, Tirus could not seem to overcome it, and was tortured each night, forcing them all to relive the nightmare alongside him.

Over and over, it always began with his excitement in leaving the air lock and setting out towards the observation dome. Thoughts of sharing the tale of his adventure with his friends kept him company as he battled his fear while floating between the threadlike passage-ways connecting one area of the *HELIX* to another. Its spiraled forma-tion continued to rotate in order to provide the ship with the required centrifugal force necessary to achieve similar gravity to what they had known on Orbyss.

It was like running an obstacle course, at least at first, until he realized that it was nothing like what his father described. He did not "stick" to the *HELIX* as Shal had suggested he would, a reference to the adult suit that Tirus assumed was identical to his own, only larger. How could he have known that his suit did not contain the same engineering as his father's? By the time he discovered this for himself, he had drifted over all but one of the *HELIX*'s solar structures/braking flaps. Reacting with precision and commanding rationale in the face of mortal danger way beyond his years, he saved his own life by grabbing on.

He had never been more terrified as when his air supply thinned and his lightweight suit sent chills through his body as it was unable to adequately protect his skin from the harsh cold of space. It was at this exact moment during the night terrors, when he was alone hanging off of the ship, cognizant that no one even knew where he was, that his cries would begin. Moda and Shal had learned that this was their cue to wake him, unless they wanted to live through the screams and thrashing that would ensue moments after. During his terrors, he never made it back. Herra never showed up to rescue him. The vast, cold clutches of space tore through his suit and forced him to let go of the leaf-shaped shield. In his terrors, space devoured him fully. In the final moment before he met his end, he locked eyes with his mother, staring helplessly from inside the observation deck.

CHAPTER 31

MODA

10.07 (Just After Midnight) / The *HELIX* / The Next Night

After calming Tirus, Moda set out for Grynn's pod, leaving Shal to face a potential follow-up terror on his own. She had been feeding both infants, Eelaa as well as Herriden, since Herra's death. Coupled with Tirus's nightly terrors, Moda was exhausted, but refused to let it influence her commitment to the son Herra had left behind in order to save her own.

Grynn was always awake; he never slept. Despondent, he would stare out the window of the pod. She imagined he might be expecting to see Herra, or even his parents. Perhaps in his mind, they were all still with him. Perhaps for him, this was all a bad dream, amongst many bad dreams.

Ultimately, she was relieved, though. They had all worried that he might repeat his isolation just as he had after losing his parents, excommunicating himself from everyone now that Herra was gone. Herriden seemed to be a miracle for him, the reason for him to carry on.

"Grynn, how is he?" Moda startled him out of his reprieve.

"Fast asleep. You should get some yourself, you look exhausted. We can make it through the night now, Moda. You can wait until morning. He is gaining weight; if anything, he is getting heavy for me." Grynn gave her a half-hearted smile, attempting to ease her mind.

As if he could sense the potential of her loving embrace, Herriden awoke. Grynn retrieved the crying infant from his cradle and placed him in Moda's waiting arms so that she could feed him.

"Do you mind if I leave you both?" Grynn asked her.

Moda nodded, just glad to be of help to both of them and too exhausted to consider what might need taking care of this late at night.

CHAPTER 32

GRYNN

10.85 (Early Hours) / The *HELIX* / That Night

The waterfall's resonance called Grynn to action but lulled him into a trancelike state as he watched the water continually cascade, perpetually in motion, never ending yet never beginning. It was considered the most impressive feature of the starship: a waterfall that gradually spread itself through an eighty-meter pool towards the artificial beach composed of Orbyss's borrowed sand. It soothed him as much as it saddened him to think that he and Herra had designed the space together. It was the most romantic spot he had ever known on Orbyss and one he could not bear to leave behind.

The water pooled around his ankles, softly lapping across his feet as he stared across the lagoon into the depths of the waterfall before his eyes. It was difficult to discern between his own tears and the water raging from the fall. He wasn't sure which was which, but it did not matter at this point. None of it did. He had made the decision not to feel any more of the pain. Herriden was in good hands with Shal and Moda, much better than his own. He had failed both of his parents and now his precious wife, and he could not forgive himself. He could not sleep because she would come to him in his dreams, her face searching his own. It was too much for him to bear.

It had taken all his strength to continually convince the others he was fine. Forcing food into his grieving stomach, smiling when his face felt as if it may break the same way as his heart.

Grynn loved his son, and for this reason, he had worked out in his grief-stricken mind that the best thing was to leave him. Bad things inevitably happened to the people he loved, especially the ones who loved him back. So, it was necessary to do this now rather than later, once the child began to know and love him as his father.

Grynn took another step into the water and felt relief wash over him. He would finally be at peace; he would finally leave this all behind. The water rose to his waist as his feet sunk into the sand that made up the floor of the basin. Sand they had carefully collected from Orbyss. A tranquil space he had designed himself. He had designed it for comfort, never imagining the macabre purpose it was now about to provide.

The water felt cool against his body as it rose up the length of his chest. He struggled to remain standing as it reached his neck, and instead of taking a few more steps until it covered his face, he gave in to the swell and became buoyant, floating on top of the pool, looking out the skylight into space and its stars.

How beautiful they had once been to him. Filled with magic and wonder. He thought back to all the evenings the Blowholes had spent, how they had all become a family for him. Then thoughts of Vash made their way into his mind, and anger surfaced as he floated on the *HELIX* lagoon.

It angered him to think that she would be his last thought. Why Vash at this moment? He would not allow her to win this time. It seemed he would have pain right up until the very end, thoughts of his first love invading his mind, when his plan was to leave this life with only thoughts of Herra.

Determined that the time had come, he floated out to the middle of the small lake. He could feel the spray of the waterfall against his face as he let the air leave his lungs and he sank to the bottom of the pool. He tried not to think of the pain as he let water replace air. It took all his strength to fight against his survival instinct to rise to the surface for a breath. A breath of air—that had always kept him alive. Slowly he started to fade, and as he lost consciousness, a dark shadow took hold of his vision.

At first, Vash could not believe her eyes as the indicator light for the aqua pod flashed red. As she brought up the security screen to observe the area in real time, nothing looked amiss. However, the underwater indicator told a different story, and when she quickly sped through the data specific to the pool, it indicated that not only was there a body in the water, even though the area had been off-limits for hours, but also that the body had stopped breathing and its vital signs were now compromised.

Vash raced from the control pod, desperate not to lose another life aboard the *HELIX*, too desperate to even bother transmitting for help. Her first thought would have been to transmit to Grynn, as he had designed the lagoon and knew all its details, but he was barely managing with Herriden and she needed him to recover as soon as possible. She needed him to pull through his grief a second time.

Vash ran the length of the beach leading up to the water. She dove in, her suit instantly released from her body, floating on the water at her entry point in order not to encumber her descent to the bottom of the pool. She summoned the underwater lights to come to life so that she could see who was below her, and as they illuminated, a gasp of air left her body as she realized it was Grynn.

She dove deeper, despite the loss of oxygen at the shock of seeing him. Vash refused to lose a single second that could be spent saving him. As she reached his unconscious figure, she grabbed his torso and immediately began pulling him to the surface. Desperately, she kicked against his weight, determined to bring his body to the shore.

Once on the sand, she pummeled his chest and breathed air into his mouth, frantic for a sign that he might still be alive.

Again, and again, she continued. She would not let him go; she would never let him go. She would continue with this ceremony forever if need be, because she would rather die alongside him trying rather than accept his suicide and give up.

A gurgle morphed into a cough. At first, she wasn't sure if it came from Grynn or herself, but as the water slowly dislodged from his mouth, she realized it was him. She turned him on his side as he coughed up the remaining liquid and began gasping for air.

"Stop—get away from me! What have you done?" Grynn wasn't sure if he was alive or dreaming until he registered Vash's face and realized she had once again saved him from himself.

"What have *I* done? What in the world do you think you are doing? How could you do this to Herriden? How could you do this to me?" Anger coursed through them both, dripping wet from their almost tragic midnight swim.

Their collective energy had few options for release, as anger and betrayal grew within them both. Not only were they attached by the literal physical proximity of the first aid Vash had administered, but now Herra, tragically so, no longer stood between them.

They held each other, the thunder of the waterfall loosening their tears as they were overcome. The prospect of potentially never holding each other again, which had been unconsidered until this moment, was too much. They instinctually made their way back to the pool. Instinctual that they would be drawn back to the water for comfort and refuge. It had not been the first time Grynn and Vash had sought out water as a place for intimacy. Just as she had many years ago, Vash reached out for Grynn and pulled him close. They gently fell beneath the waves, in a dive the two of them had perfected many years before. Their heart rates slowed as they made their descent into the lagoon. It was like their first time together. Grynn, saved from what had been his form of escape, clung to Vash as they now found escape in each other. Neither wanted it to end. They remained wrapped around each other, desperate to extinguish the pain they had both suffered.

Vash would later describe to him the weight of actualizing the *HELIX*, how she had never wanted to leave him. The responsibility she felt, the pressure, and how it had consumed and changed her all those years ago. She needed him to see how much she would have given for a second chance to do it all differently.

Grynn would confess that her dedication to the *HELIX*, which he admired and ultimately supported, had also left him feeling abandoned and betrayed by her and what they had built together.

All these things were theirs to share, but for the moment, with only the waterfall as witness, something new to them both would begin. A new life—a life conceived from despair, pain, grief, and love—only, this time, aboard a starship, millions of parsecs from home.

CHAPTER 33

VASH

Saving Grynn had been a reflex for Vash. They shared a bond; they were each other's firsts. It had begun as a friendship because they grew up together as family friends. Countless days and hours spent in each other's company had formed a familiarity between them, especially as they were both only children. Their time spent together was consistent and had been a brother-sister relationship until the day they no longer looked at each other as a brother and sister would. It crept slowly into their consciousness and was perceptible to both sets of parents long before their children were aware. They began to communicate differently. Grynn became protective of Vash. Planned evenings shared by the families now began with a flurry of preparation by both teens. Suddenly, their time spent together was of the highest importance, and they soon found excuses to be alone in each other's company deliberately away from their parents and peers. Both families celebrated what was obviously a blooming romance. It would have been a lie to say that all four parents had not hoped for the match since Vash and Grynn were toddlers. However, the depth of their children's feelings for each other came swift and harsh, and despite their parents' collective advice to take things slowly, the teens were unable to censor the deep feelings that had taken hold of them, both in equal measure. She would never forget the moment she fell. His words would stay with her always.

"I am embarrassed to admit this, but I am jealous of the air that surrounds your skin—you should only be mine."

At that moment, her suit had reflected colors that corresponded to her heartbeat and moved in a way that reflected the response of her body. It told Grynn without a word that she felt the same. Their love became an entity unto itself, with Vash and Grynn helplessly at its disposal. With Grynn, Vash was stronger and bolder than she had been before him. She knew that Grynn was helpless to her suggestion, and that was why she had insisted they go away together, their plans soon thwarted by their parents. It was of little consequence; nothing could keep them apart. Nothing other than the arrival of an asteroid on a path to destroy their planet. And when Vash left for the council, feeling it was necessary to focus on their plans for escape, it broke her heart to learn that Grynn had replaced her. She loved Herra—they had all been very close—but something in her broke when she learned that Grynn and Herra were a couple, and she filled the ache with the *HELIX*. Or at least she tried to. Her mission, their escape, consumed her as much by necessity as by choice. She used it as a diversion to forget about Grynn and the past they had shared, especially since working closely with Anae was a constant reminder of her son. When Grynn lost his parents, it was all she could do not to go to him; however, he was a husband and a father, and she could not seem to breach the contract she had made with herself to turn away from him and never look back. However, it appeared that fate had other plans for them. It would seem that nothing could supersede what they had shared, that was, until Vash became a mother to Herriden.

Until that point, the *HELIX* was her life, her focus, her baby. She had poured all of herself and years of her life into the starship. Had anyone asked her if anything could ever replace her devotion to the *HELIX*, she would have laughed in reply. But that was before she had known and loved Grynn's son, the one Herra had been forced to leave behind.

Vash didn't think much about it; she simply needed to save Grynn. She hadn't even considered Herriden that fateful night beneath the waterfall. However, as early as the next morning, she was soon to realize just how profound her oversight had been. Children have a way of taking over one's life, and it seemed that even Vash would not be allowed an escape. Regardless of Grynn's attempts to shoulder the responsibility of his young son, Herriden would not have it.

Herriden slept more peacefully in her arms. His eyes lit up as soon as she entered the room. It was her voice he would follow no matter how engrossed he was in play. And as days became weeks and then months, Herriden taught Vash something no one else had been able to achieve. He passed along a gift to her, one she believed she would never receive, one that she had not felt worthy of. His love freed her from the chains of the *HELIX* that had bound her so tightly for so many years. The time she spent with Herriden allowed her to be exactly as she was meant to be. For the few short hours she was with him each day, she escaped into his world. Herriden's requests and announcements won her over each time.

"Mommy, *you* play with me."

"Mommy, I come with you."

"Mommy, I love *you* more."

They were soulmates in a land of his invention, and the precious time they shared collected like raindrops in the desert that had once buried her soul.

Grynn would catch them playing together, and seeing the interaction, a pure and innocent connection between mother and son, he would stop in his tracks. He witnessed something profound growing between the two of them, something that he was content to witness from the sidelines. It was their connection that freed him of his grief, his guilt, his regret over not only the circumstances out of his control but also those he had inflicted upon those around him, as well as himself. To see Herriden and Vash together was to witness peace. The light that surrounded them was almost visible, and it gave Grynn back the life he had almost lost.

Having Herriden seek out the attention only she could give him was addictive to Vash. He would do anything to please her, and her response was to teach him everything she knew. His capacity to learn and retain almost everything was not only satisfying for Vash but also endearing. It was as if she had been placed in his path for a reason—that their destinies were intertwined, as significantly as hers and Grynn's were.

If not for Herriden, Vash would have fallen prey to her own invention. The *HELIX* had threatened to consume her since she had given birth to it, and it was fitting that only another child, her child now, could possibly take its place. Initially, Vash had worried that she would not have capacity to extend herself beyond the demands of the ship and now also the demands of raising Herriden, only to discover that she would be a mother to Herriden and to another child soon, as well.

It was Herriden who prepared Vash for the life that grew inside her. A two-year gestation was ample time for him to train her on the finer points and requirements of a little one. Vash held to her promise "to die strapped in her seat if necessary" in order to protect them all, now more fiercely than ever. Not only had she vowed to die strapped to her seat, but she had also removed all other members of the crew from theirs as an additional measure of protection. Never again would she rely on Rhys or any other member of the crew. From now on, it would just be Vash in sole command of the *HELIX*.

Loving Herriden had made her realize that there was much more at stake now. She loved both Herriden and the new life that grew inside her more than she could have ever believed possible. They were the ones she would sacrifice everything for. She was more determined than ever before that Orbyss II would be a safe and sustainable home for her family, for her children.

To become the protector of the 100,000 passengers aboard the ship did not hold a candle to the responsibility she felt to Herriden. His was the life that needed guarding above all else. His well-being was what drove her, what kept her up at night, and what ultimately ruled her final calls on what was safe and not safe aboard the *HELIX* and beyond. It was Herriden she considered first and last through the course of every day and every decision, because she seemed to know, even in those early days, that it was Herriden who would one day be the captain of the *HELIX*.

CHAPTER 34

VANAE

9.49 (Almost Noon) / The *HELIX* / Five
Years of Interstellar Travel

Grynn and Vash's daughter, Vanae, had been mesmerized by the digital illumination just below the collarbone of each of their suits since she had opened her beautiful emerald-green eyes. The soft iridescent glow the color of amethyst had become synonymous with identifying her mother. It was like a night-light, even in the daytime—that color meant both she and Vash were safe and happy.

In reality, the hues of their suits were always in flux. Vash's "resting" color was an oscillating shade of amethyst, but depending upon the events of the minute, it ranged from magenta to wine, the color representing her overall state of being, dependent upon the circumstances.

The illumination was a digital indication at a moment in time, constantly being collected and then exhibited by the smart suits each of them wore. The suits displayed the date and time, they captured their owner's vitals, such as heart rate, temperature, respiratory rate, and blood pressure, and in addition, a fifth indicator represented mood or emotional well-being—derived from a scan of the limbic system. Ironically, this last indicator was the one all XYZs homed in on first, especially when greeting each other. It led their conversations and guided their interactions, so they could help each other. It had been Herra's idea, her design, and since her death, following Moda's lead, they had all begun initiating conversations with each other by briefly placing their hand against each other's emotional display upon first meeting, in memory of what she had sacrificed.

Vanae's illumination, like those of most children aboard the ship, glowed a vibrant purple, almost fluorescent, indicating her overall well-being and vitality. For Vash, this color meant, "I'm coming for you . . ." And while it gave her peace of mind, it also warned a barrage of demands would soon follow as Vanae, at three years of age, had become an expert at challenging her mother and stealing Vash's attention along with her heart.

Vanae had not forgotten her mother's promise made the night before. It had been Vanae's watchful curiosity that had led them both to this moment; she never missed a comment or conversation where Vash was concerned. She had become far too wise to be put off any longer with ridiculous explanations like these are "Mommy's important messages" or it's "Mommy's work." The more Vash tried to hide them, the more determined Vanae became to know their contents.

As Vanae approached, Vash risked a weary glance. Taking in Vanae's delicate features, so similar to her own, was like looking into a mirror, back in time. Pursed lips and a defiant jaw told her immediately that no, of course, Vanae had not forgotten her promise.

Vash was out of excuses. Today would unfortunately be the day. And she called in Herriden to join them.

"Can you tell us what a satellite is, Herriden?" *Her* five-year-old son was a quick study, and according to what he and the rest of his cohort had been exposed to, this should not be a difficult question for him.

As if reading from a textbook, he recited, "A satellite is an object that has been intentionally placed into orbit." He smiled at Vash's nod of approval, and his smile widened as Vanae looked up at him with wonder and excitement at finally being invited to share in something so important.

"Yes, very good, what you are referring to are artificial satellites, unlike natural satellites such as Orbyss's moon. The reason I have asked you to discuss this with me today is because, on Orbyss, we constructed artificial satellites and began deploying them prior to leaving the planet." Vash chose her words carefully as much for their benefit as her own. The better they understood her, the less questions they would ask afterwards, and judging by the way their eyes had both widened, there would already be an ocean of questions regardless.

She continued, "These satellites are of the greatest importance because they give us reports on everything that is going on behind us. In this way, we can be kept up to date on what is happening on Orbyss while travelling aboard the *HELIX*. It is like having ears and eyes behind us."

As the words left Vash's mouth, she had to laugh at herself. Perhaps nothing reflected her personality more so than the fleet of satellites she had unleashed. Vash hated being in the dark, and this was an army whose sole purpose was meant to prevent that.

"I want to see them! What are they saying?" It appeared that Vanae had already grasped the basics and was ready for more.

"Yes, yes, OK, my love. We will bring up the information collected from Orbyss. These are the messages and pictures we have collected from satellites millions of parsecs away over the past five years. You can clearly see the destruction caused by the asteroid hitting Orbyss's surface. Look at the fiery planet that was once our home. The Orbyss we inhabited was much different, as you both know. It was once a massive continent, green and lush, brimming with plant life, an incredible habitat for our species as well as thousands of others. It was an oasis, one that we have tried our best to recreate aboard the *HELIX*, one we all hope to enjoy again one day." Vash continued to describe their beloved Orbyss as she shared the remaining data with them both and explained the technical information the satellite relayed to the *HELIX* regarding weather patterns, temperature, and hundreds of other data points in order for Vash to accurately evaluate the impact of the asteroid. Hoping that life would return to Orbyss one day, they had purposely positioned the satellites within the asteroid belt, far enough away from Orbyss that they would remain undiscovered should life begin again.

"So, there you have it, Vanae and Herriden! Do you have any questions?" Both children nodded in unison, and at the mention of questions . . . began alternating, one question each, firing a steady stream of them at Vash, unwilling to restrain themselves even long enough to wait for a full explanation.

She answered the inquires with ease and pleasure, happy to share something in a way that would teach, inspire, and satisfy their curiosity, without placing them in harm's way.

CHAPTER 35

HERRIDEN

5.24 (Morning) / The *HELIX* / Ten Years of Interstellar Travel

Almost a teen, Herriden dreaded the days Vash was scheduled to "speak" to his class. It was a torturous version of show-and-tell for him, always the same object, always the same outcome.

It wasn't that he was embarrassed by Vash; quite the opposite was true. It was the stigma she inflicted upon him through his classmates and friends. Today he would suffer through yet another update from the control pod delivered by his mother. An interactive lecture where his classmates would undoubtedly try to impress her with their questions.

What Herriden did not realize was that *his mother* was the person solely responsible for his pain. His teacher, while appreciative for the break from center stage, had nothing to do with the frequency or timing of her visits. Long ago, Vash had realized that it was in the best interest of her children to be socialized and bonded with their peers aboard the ship. Refusing to give up what she deemed an education only she herself could provide, she instead aspired to teach not only her own children but all those who attended ship school.

She had begun to know them all quite well, those she had carefully selected for her unconventional meritocracy. To Vash, it was simple; the most brilliant rose to the top, and those were the ones she had already slotted in specific positions, the future crew of the *HELIX*. Vash was succession planning well before anyone had even bothered to consider it necessary, and what better way to train a team but from the very beginning? She would never be forced to select members from what was readily available, because she had built the future crew herself, just like this ship, now with a decade of captaining it behind her.

The population aboard the *HELIX* had grown to 104,000. While the growth was organic, it was greater than what they would have typically witnessed on Orbyss. They had not decided to actively encourage larger families; however, the close confines of the ship and its self-sufficient design required less of its passengers than had their existence on Orbyss. While on Orbyss, they had adopted the practice of having fewer children so that they could devote what was considered the appropriate and necessary attention to them while also fulfilling their roles and responsibilities in order to maintain the optimal function of their society.

With less demands put upon each passenger, more time was free to devote to their families, and as such, the family size had started to grow. Coupled with the knowledge that in approximately fifteen years' time, they would be colonizing a new planet and perhaps more hands would be a blessing.

In order to best teach the children with the available expertise, class size was limited to fifteen students maximum, ranging in a five-year span. So far, it had worked. The number was small enough to provide individual attention to each student, and the range of learning ability, aptitude, and experience was exploited to the benefit of all. The difference in age stretched the junior classmates while it provided an opportunity for the seniors to mentor them. They also cycled through age groups seamlessly enough. A fresh round of new juniors would fill the class as the seniors moved to the next level; however, Herriden and Vanae were usually within the same class, as they were just over two years apart, so Vash's work was made easy, as she could kill two birds with one stone, for the most part.

As Herriden entered the class, Tirus tapped the seat next to him. He loved when Vash was scheduled to update them, and although he was unaware that she was going to show up today, Herriden's expression was all the hint he required. The glum scowl on Herriden's otherwise happy-go-lucky face was as good as an advertisement for Vash's upcoming visit.

Herriden had become a younger brother to Tirus. True to his word, he had looked after Herriden, never forgetting his promise to Herra. What usually meant playing with someone five years his junior had also, at times, involved protection from roughhousing, explanations of the finer art of becoming a man, and lately, how to avoid, when possible, the seemingly ever-increasing demands of their parents. To say that Herriden and the other XYZ children were high functioning was an understatement. Tirus excelled both intellectually and emotionally, beyond what other XYZs could even fathom.

Regardless of whether they were on Orbyss or on the *HELIX* travelling through space at interstellar speed, the XYZs participated in a significant amount of social engagement. They were a highly social species. It was the mother's lineage that led the way, and this strong female core provided the collective history and knowledge to its new members, influencing their behavior and accelerating the learning curve of the young. To an even greater extent, evolution was responsible for their high function. As a species, they had evolved along a distinct neuroanatomical trajectory. This resulted in a unique arrangement of the areas of their brains responsible for social consciousness and complex emotion. They were considerably more vulnerable to stressors but could accomplish rapid intuitive choice in complex social situations and could feel greater empathy, which allowed them to develop a level of emotional sophistication never achieved before.

As the rest of the seats were soon filled and their teacher took to the head of class to introduce Vash's arrival, Herriden cast his eyes across the room, taking in the other students' expressions. As his mother appeared, it was like a wave of electricity entered the room alongside her, straightening postures, ending conversations, and widening eyes. Her presence was not to be ignored, and Herriden could not help but observe that his teacher seemed slightly envious of her command of the room.

Vash, per Herriden's request many years prior, made special care not to address him during these presentations unless he initiated the exchange. She held to this promise as long as he paid attention. That was their deal. And more than once, when he had failed to hold up his end of the bargain, she was quick to forgo hers. And so, it began, Vash at the head of his class, just as she was at the head of the ship and pretty much everything else that allowed them all to survive aboard the *HELIX*.

"What I am about to share with you today is something we have not discussed up to this point, and it is information that has not been shared with the rest of the passengers aboard the *HELIX*. It is private in nature, and before I share it with you, I will need your promise that you will not repeat it."

Despite the nods and murmurs of agreement, Vash knew better than to expect this lot to keep a never-ending secret. The information would be shared with all passengers later that afternoon; however, she knew the value of capturing their attention early on, and at this age, knowing something that no one else did was a potent promise.

She continued, "Now, you will recall that when we inhabited Orbyss, we could not have predicted that one day we would have to leave our planet in order to survive. But once we learned of the asteroid approaching Orbyss and that its trajectory would mean an unavoidable collision that would destroy the planet, we needed to devise a plan in order to escape. However, what I am excited to share with you that we have not shared up until now is the information that we have collected about our new home, Orbyss II."

Vash risked a look at Herriden, filled with relief at finally being able to share this with her son and his class. So many times, she had caught herself when their endless discussions would drift to a place where sharing it with him would have opened up their discussion to a whole new level. However, in order to protect him, she needed a plan first, and now she finally had one.

"Can anyone tell me what a tidally locked planet is?" Vash knew that Herriden would have the answer, but as he seemed to be paying close attention, sitting perched on the edge of his seat, she would avoid calling on him.

To her relief, Tirus volunteered. She hadn't decided if he was actually smarter than his father, but his aptitude for mathematics, physics, and engineering would suggest that he was at least as smart as Shal. The only difference she could see was Moda's burning desire to bring everyone together and her quick wit and humor, which also appeared to have been passed down to the boy.

"That's right, Tirus! Tidal locking, also known as synchronous rotation, occurs when an astronomical body always has the same face towards the object it is orbiting. For example, the same side of the moon always faces our previous home, Orbyss. This effect arises between two bodies when their gravitational interaction slows one object's rotation until it becomes tidally locked."

Vash continued despite the hands in the air indicating they had many questions for her. "Such is the case with our new home, Orbyss II. The gravitational pull from its dominant sun is strong enough to prevent its rotation, and as a result, it has very different characteristics than our previous home." It saddened her to continually reference a home many of these young minds, including Herriden, had never set foot upon. She constantly had to remind herself that a deep understanding of Orbyss was important for them not only to fully understand their history but also for them to access what life the universe was capable of supporting in order for them to fully manifest the finest future.

Again, many raised hands would indicate that they had numerous questions regarding what these differences might actually be. She ignored them, preferring to take them through this at her own pace, little by little.

"For instance, on Orbyss II, there will not be a night and day as we experienced on Orbyss. Near the midsection of the planet lies a strip most conducive to life." At that moment, she addressed the *HELIX* by transmission to display satellite photos of Orbyss II on the classroom's interactive display. It was the first time anyone outside herself, Grynn, and Shal had seen them, and it gave her goose bumps of excitement to witness the reaction of Herriden's class.

Not willing to lose them, she went on, "It is within the safe zone of this 480-kilometer strip that we will begin colonization. And when I chose the word 'safe,' I did not do so lightly. On the far side of the planet, temperatures reach lows of minus four hundred degrees, while on the opposite side, the heat from the sun can burn you alive in a matter of seconds."

At that point, the room erupted; no longer was the class willing to wait for Vash's acknowledgment of their questions. She did her best to answer them in the time they had been afforded, and at one point, she even caught Herriden's eye.

They shared a moment, despite his lack of interaction. In that second, his pride was obvious, safe from the invasive eyes of his classmates, who were much too enthralled by the photos of their new home. She was his mother and he loved her. There was no transmission between them, but an understanding managed to be formed regardless: from that day forward, their discussions would take on an entirely new focus. Without officially acknowledging the fact, it was obvious to him now that his mother had decided that he would one day take her place. All of the time she had invested in him, the detailed conversations she would entertain on any subject he brought forward, and the puzzles she would not so accidentally place in his path all made sense to him now. She had been grooming him for a very long time, and now she was giving him permission to take the lead in their future discussions based on the understanding that if he continued to meet her expectations, and if he wanted to sit at the helm of the *HELIX*, her seat would be his.

CHAPTER 36

VASH

5.33 (Evening) / The *HELIX* / Fifteen
Years of Interstellar Travel

Vash had discovered enough bruises on her children to know that whatever caused these fresh ones was no accident, despite the kids' denial.
It was Grynn who had noticed them first. When he inquired, Herriden
and Vanae exchanged a quick glance before reciting a rehearsed explanation that had obviously been prepared in advance. The only indicator
that something was definitely up following the conversation was that
they both began sporting longer sleeves in order to hide the bruises.

In response to their clandestine behavior, Vash became obsessed
with discovering their secret. She knew that this recent plague of teenage bruises extended beyond her two; Moda and Shal had noticed the
same marks on Tirus and Eelaa. And they exhibited the same secretive
behavior. It seemed that no one was ready to expose the monster . . . if
there was one.

All of them, as parents, were rightfully concerned; however, the
bruises seemed to be the only signs that something was off. They were

still the happy, well-adjusted teens all of them had raised. Their performance and attention were normal, perhaps even improved since the marks had begun to appear.

Unsatisfied until the truth be known, Vash set out on her mission. What if these bruises led to something worse? Endless potential disasters ran through her mind, and if need be, she would track them day and night in order to discover what was going on. In essence, that was her plan, and it would commence that very night.

The kids had been quiet for almost two weeks following Grynn's inquisition, and tonight there was something in the air. She could feel it. They seemed edgy, Vanae and Herriden ready to tempt providence. Well, she would save them. This was her kingdom, and saving was Vash's forte. Tonight, her children would be sitting safe at the top of the castle if she had anything to do with it.

Deliberately lying awake while Grynn slept, it was well past midnight when she decided to check in on them. Despite the fact that their suits reported them asleep in their rooms on the *HELIX*'s interface, they were nowhere to be found when Vash investigated their rooms. While suppressing her panic, she could not help being impressed by their ingenuity. The modifications made to the suits, albeit rudimentary, were no less impressive.

She walked on, as if in a dream, or perhaps nightmare, to the control room determined to track them the old-fashioned way. If she were a teen aboard the *HELIX*, where would she have gone? Then it occurred to her: Where *had* she gone? Remembering the Blowholes, so long ago, brought a slight smile to her lips. It was hard to believe she had been about their age, plotting an existence off planet from the confines of a warehouse hideout.

The *HELIX* was eerily quiet at this time of night, and as she made quick work of the corridors connecting her family pod to the control pod, all of the potential spots they could be hiding ran through her mind. She took solace in the fact that at least she knew they were not outside the ship. She had made sure no one would ever leave the *HELIX* without her knowledge again, especially her own children.

Once she arrived, she canvassed the control pod's three-hundred-some surveillance displays throughout the starship positioned at various angles. Nothing. Where would they be this late at night where she could not see them? It ate at her.

"Come on, Vash, you are better than this," she scolded herself aloud. Pushing back in her chair, she closed her eyes and then suddenly remembered something Shal had promised her long, long ago. And her skin went cold despite her suit's immediate effort to warm her.

As Vash neared the entry to the mechanical rooms, she paused, wondering if she should first transmit to Shal. Maybe he could ease her mind before she went on seeking out the worst. And then she heard it, and fear struck her heart. Perhaps she was already too late.

She summoned the entry and sprinted directly for the engine rooms. As a safety measure, the four giant nuclear fusion engines were housed in protective tunnels ten meters wide around each engine. The protective barriers were made of carbon-fiber casing eight meters thick in order to prevent potential exposure should an explosion or leak occur. They ran the full length of the engine, five hundred meters, with the addition of a reinforcement cap at the end of each casing closest to the body of the *HELIX*. Although Shal deemed this event an impossibility, the casings were installed at Vash's request, just in case. And due to the thickness of the containment structure, it was difficult for the ship's interface to permeate the enclosure, hence the absence of continuous surveillance; to see inside the casement tunnels, one had to go out of their way.

She couldn't run fast enough towards the humming sound that echoed in her head. She had no idea what the preview to a nuclear explosion sounded like, but the humming that had now transformed itself into an accelerating scream could not be far off in her mind. As she followed the cry around the corner, she summoned the entry to the containment tunnel emitting it, and the sight that met her eyes coerced a scream from her own lips.

The vehicles almost collided in an effort to avoid her. A near-deadly unwelcoming for the uninvited guest. They headed up the pipe accelerating to top speed in order to defeat gravity so that they could make it round to the opposite side of the engine they contained. The car-like vehicles, made of black carbon fiber, much like the structure of the *HELIX*, cried in unison. The speed and agility were like nothing

Vash had seen before, and the low-tenor humming of their fusion cell engines seemed reluctant to stop. They were built for speed.

Herriden and Vanae approached her, adrenaline still coursing through their veins, with Tirus, Eelaa, and Rahl in tow. They had parked their vehicles five meters away, refusing to fully expose the toys they had shaped for themselves. No matter; Vash would inspect them soon enough.

The rise and fall of Herriden's chest mimicked his pulse. A suit unlike any Vash had ever imagined, one containing the properties required to mimic glass, was pulled taut against Herriden's sweaty chest, and she almost did not recognize him as her own. Tirus ran a shaky hand through his tousled hair, almost an apology, as he approached. It was obvious that the vehicles were his design. But it was Vanae who took Vash's breath away with her look of defiance. It was like looking in a mirror, like travelling back in time. Back to an ideal childhood all too soon destroyed by the angst of her teenage years, amplified by the destructive path of an asteroid. She had been forced to grow up and become who she needed to be far too quickly, and she felt Vanae's anger as her own all those years before. It was a slow transition, trading disillusionment for determination. Responsibility, necessity, stability, altruism, all of the most important traits of their culture, its true fabric, were only perfected with age and time. She wished she could accelerate the process, especially for Vanae, who fought against it as she had herself. But because of her own experience, she knew better. This was something Vanae would come to in her own time; they all did, some finding themselves more easily than others. Because the XYZs were highly social and spent the majority of their time in each other's company, Vash could put her full faith in the process. And thanks to an endless supply of compassion, understanding, encouragement, love, and forgiveness from those around her, Vanae would eventually conquer the fear, anxiety, anger, and distrust she currently suffered from.

A solitary figure, Vash stood in front of them, phantomlike, demanding an explanation.

"Well, what do we have here?" she said, finally breaking the silence. Despite wanting to collapse in upon herself due to a mixture of relief and terror she had just swallowed, Vash was determined not to expose an inch of her true feelings to them. From what they would observe, she stood witness to unauthorized drag racing with unauthorized vehicles in unauthorized spaces aboard the *HELIX* on a daily basis. Nothing would throw her, not with this crew; she would not have it.

"None of you would like to explain this? Well, that is highly disappointing, considering what you have accomplished here. Any idea how quickly you would die upon exposure to the incredible heat from this engine? Anyone?"

"Between 0.001 and 0.002 minutes." It was Herriden's reply. *Now* was the moment he had chosen to break their code. It brought a sarcastic smile to Vash's face.

She walked deliberately close by Vanae as she made her way past her daughter over to where Herriden stood. Mother and son had stood eye to eye for the past three years. Looking down upon Herriden had been a thing of the past for a very long time.

She repeated the words she had spoken to herself aloud only twelve minutes prior, now to Herriden—only, this time, in a whisper. "You're better than this." And she chased it with, "Why didn't you come to me?"

"Who are you to decide what or who I am?" Herriden's pointed remark was clear. Vash knew his intent. She knew this day might eventually come. She would have preferred the absence of an audience, but she was not one to shy away from what needed to be said. Quite frankly, she had no time for it.

"No one. No one at all. If that is what you need to hear, hear it now. I set you free. You need not give yourself away for me, or anyone, for that matter, to claim. You are your own man now. That is quite obvious. One Herra would be very proud of. One I am very proud of. Make no mistake of that, Herriden."

It was not the answer he had expected. It was not the answer any of them had expected. This was her fault. She had been foolish to think that they would always adhere to her schedule. The bright, incredible souls who stood before her. The ones she had chosen. She had been very foolish indeed.

Despite the shock and the epiphany with Herriden, Vash now recalled that there were not one but a total of four sarcophaguses. "What's in the other three?" she addressed them all, dreading the response, while the looks of guilt they shot at each other confirmed her suspicion.

The second casing housed the lab for the new suits she had noticed first on Herriden. It was almost a relief for Vash, who, after the tragic loss of Herra, could not seem to commit herself to starting on the design of the suits they would all require for Orbyss II. It would seem this work had taken flight without her, and all signs pointed to Vanae being at the helm, based on the meticulous organization of the tools she'd laid out.

As Vash was given a tour through the last two casings, one used for testing the vehicles and the other, the suits, it was clear how the bruises came to be. It also became apparent that this was the most beloved part of the process. Testing how their inventions held up.

Upon Vash's inspection of the fourth and final casing, it was clear that Orbyss II would be theirs. Perhaps Vash had kept the *HELIX* from them, but she was not to rule their new home. She could see that now.

This casing was Vash's least favorite, a simulation of a space walk outside the *HELIX*. Herriden was all too happy to take credit for this. And as much as Vash tried to cover it up, it was clear the prospect terrified her.

"You do realize this design has no chance of holding up at the speed required for interstellar travel," she accused, her voice cracking slightly as she questioned him.

"Yes, but it will at intrastellar speed, and eventually we are going to need to get off this thing, Mom," was his earnest reply.

She smiled slightly at him in agreement. This had been an emotional revelation for her. She had been waiting for a sign that he was ready, and now he had given it to her. They all had. If this was not the sign she had been waiting for, then there never would be one.

"You know that you are all very bad liars. This is the only reason, other than your layers of bruises, that we had reason to suspect any of this. You are all very bad at lying, but I will not pretend that I am not impressed by what you have accomplished here. You are ready now. Ready to fulfill your own destiny on this ship and beyond. Ready to take on the roles I had hoped you would aboard the *HELIX* and on Orbyss II."

CHAPTER 37

TIRUS

5.44 (Morning) / The *HELIX* / Eighteen
Years of Interstellar Travel

It was as if Sond still stood next to Tirus in the observation dome, guiding his hand as he manipulated the angle of the high-power telescope to point directly at Orbyss II. Sond had died four years earlier, and Tirus would still catch himself wanting to seek him out with a question before the sad realization would take hold that his grandfather was actually gone. In the face of the tragedy that had followed Herra's sacrifice, Grynn's attempted suicide, and Tirus's never-ending night terrors, it was all Shal could do to try to keep up with Vash and ensure the ship stayed safely on course. Shal was with Tirus every day, but it was Sond who was actually present, guiding the boy through the worst of it, making him feel safe again.

Tirus was still the most frequent visitor to the observation dome. He would visit it daily. No other XYZ was more excited to set foot on their new home than he was. He had invested countless hours observing the tidally locked planet. Every day brought them that much closer to Orbyss II, and the more he could learn now, the better his modifications to the subterranean and overland vehicles would be once they landed. Truth be told, he also enjoyed being the one to update the others on what awaited them. Even the slightest piece of new information as to what they could expect when they touched down was valuable. Complete overhauls had already been necessary based on a new finding. He had to completely rebuild the vehicles due to the terrain they could now observe. Originally what they had imagined could be accomplished by a single vehicle now required three different models due to the extreme temperatures and terrain of the planet. While one vehicle could operate easily within the habitable zone, located at the midline of the planet, modifications had been necessary to explore the desolate polar regions covered in ice. The same was true for the opposite face of the planet, which Tirus currently viewed through the telescope—a goliath, rocky red-hot meteorite that appeared to somehow have fastened itself to a snowball. It was a stone oven he had scoured over through the lens of the telescope for the past hour, one set at a constant temperature of six hundred degrees.

Tirus, alongside Moda and Eelaa, had also labored intensively over the necessary alterations required for the Lenacyth to be genetically modified in order to stand up to the harsh conditions on either side of the planet, and he was keen to make sure any additional modifications would remain up to date, reluctant to redesign the entire structure, yet again, from the start.

As it stood, he was 95 percent confident that his designs would hold up from what he was looking at today. Besides honing the vehicles and perfecting the O2L (Orbyss II Lenacyth), his daily observations were a legitimate excuse to work more closely with Vanae on the design of the suits they would require. After all, the two went hand in hand: What good was a vehicle without its driver? How could they fully explore their new home without setting foot on it?

Tirus would make sure he was always in the observatory prior to Vash joining him. They had "run into one another" on at least a dozen occasions before she took his interest in the new planet to heart. He was obviously obsessed with their new home, perhaps even more than she was, and therefore, she had engaged him in helping her map out the new planet. They needed to plan exactly where to land, where to colonize, and how to begin the exploration of their new home.

Vash had a way of drawing others into her world, especially Tirus, who still had not completely abandoned the prospect of standing at the helm of the *HELIX* one day. Despite Herriden's obvious claim to the position, he had silently agreed to become Vash's apprentice of sorts.

He had also learned that the apple never falls far from the tree. It seemed to hold true: like mother, like daughter. Vash was unable to conceal her interest in the nuances of the new planet that he had been able to identify, details he had noticed before she had found them herself. This was the predominant reason he would consistently be the observatory's first visitor every morning, typically a full hour ahead of her. Today would be no exception.

She always began their morning observation with the same familiar opener, which had become affectionately overused.

"Well, Tirus! What a surprise to find you here!" It was comical. As the days had stretched to weeks and then years, she delivered the line with an ever-increasing level of sarcasm. Which they both managed to laugh at, every time. It was about as much humor as Vash was capable of.

The only difference was that today he had something special for her.

While most of the time Tirus spent at the telescope involved combing the terrain, he had noticed something outside his typical focus on the ground over the past few weeks. Something Sond had taught him to look for a long time ago. His grandfather had always gravitated towards the stars and was quick to focus Tirus's attention on them, so it was a reflex for him to take in their luster, or lack thereof.

"Perhaps I am mistaken . . ." Tirus was always careful not to make any assumptions where Vash was concerned. Her razor-sharp mind and flawless analysis had made him a fool on more than one occasion, and he preferred to avoid the prospect in its entirety. "However, I have been tracking the red dwarf that is the parent star of Orbyss II for the past several weeks, recording the ever-decreasing solar output. Now, it could be because of expected oscillation in the luminosity due to orbiting satellites/planets; however, it does not seem to follow any consistent pattern as one might expect."

He had definitely captured Vash's attention. She wasted no time taking her turn behind the telescope he had just pointed at Orbyss II's parent star. At first, she had expected disaster, but a close look at the star gave her relief. If there was reduced luminosity, it was essentially negligible.

"You may be right, Tirus," she addressed him with an air of superiority, hoping to put his mind at rest. "However, it is a very old star with likely only another two hundred million years of intrinsic fuel, and therefore, some oscillation might be expected."

He nodded back in agreement, having considered as much himself. Besides, his work had been accomplished. He had brought it to her attention more to impress than alarm her.

"Well, I will leave you to it. Until tomorrow, Captain!" He smiled at her with a dimpled grin no one seemed able to avoid answering.

She smiled back at him, then quickly returned her eye to the telescope. She was 99 percent sure that what she was looking at was an oscillation, but Vash was designed for 100 percent, and it was at that moment that she decided to ensure 99 percent became 100 percent prior to landing.

CHAPTER 38

VANAE

Vanae embodied the new planet they would all soon call home. She was Vash and Grynn in one soul. She possessed ice-cold logic and could compute even faster than her mother. On the flip side, she was emotional and hot-blooded, driven by feeling and passion. Her response in any given situation was a coin toss, heads or tails; no one was ever sure how she might respond, and while it repelled those more tender of heart, it seemed to attract those seeking adventure, most recently Tirus and Rahl.

In her mind, courting two of the most potent males aboard the ship was an accidental arrangement. This new dynamic had created a current of tension to begin flowing through their small group. They both seemed to have an obsession with her, for entirely different reasons. Tirus could not get enough of Vanae's mind, and while he was love drunk on her intellect, it had also not escaped him that she possessed a figure to match. Rahl, on the other hand, took Vanae's intelligence for granted, not that he failed to appreciate it. He just seemed to recognize her need to leave it behind on occasion, and he offered her the freedom. There was no one more charming than Rahl aboard the ship; he'd had an entourage since childhood, and his following continued to expand. More than one heart was breaking now that his compass had turned to point exclusively at Vanae.

The gravity that held the triangle in place was directed by Vanae. And she seemed determined to play hard with them both. For Vanae especially, and for her contemporaries, to a lesser extent, the *HELIX* had become a prison. In an attempt to entertain herself, she had resorted to tactics that she would likely have avoided if she had access to the plentiful physical space their species seemed to require for optimal function. She enjoyed the exhilaration she experienced at having them both vie for her attention and could not seem to bring herself to thwart their efforts to impress her, despite her older brother's comment that she should stop as nothing good could come of it. It was obvious to Vanae that Herriden wanted her help in maintaining an atmosphere of cooperation between the members of the future *HELIX* crew and that he opposed the way she was casually toying with his best friend and Rahl.

Vanae, along with all XYZ females, controlled conception. Her evolution maintained her ancestors' anatomy where reproduction was concerned. Her reproductive tract, consisting of a labyrinth of twists, corners, and folds, limited the advancement of semen and gave females command over reproduction. Vanae was fully equipped to solely decide when she would be open to offspring and with which mate. As such, she was also in control of the facets that drove the required relationship. This left XYZ males with no reason to compete with each other; their goal was to attract and hold the attention of the female. Vanae had no need to rely on a male for protection or security, as all her needs were provided for by the collective society. She had no obligation to choose the strongest mate, because size and strength were equal between the sexes, so she was absolutely free to select a mate based on her own genuine desires. Therefore, males had no choice but to follow the females' lead and invest a considerable amount of energy and time attracting a mate based entirely on her unique set of aspirations, preferences, and constitutions if they were to have a family. The same held true for males: all their needs were met, and females also required them as partners to have offspring. However, the element of competition was nonexistent because the XYZs did not have societal expectations or restrictions as to the shape of the partnership. As children were raised communally, how long the partnership endured was entirely up to the two XYZs involved. There was no judgment, and an insignificant amount of change, and therefore, there was minimal impact on the couple or their family regardless of how the relationship evolved. The bond was fluid; many couples would take breaks and easily be reunited many times during its course. This was the norm, not the exception. An overarching appeal to Percivious and the subscription to the ultimate in altruism and the benefit of the whole rather than the desires of the individual helped this along. When the pressure to select the perfect mate and the suffering in the event of a relationship breakdown was removed, the XYZ were allowed to choose their partners honestly, in favor of emotional connection above all else. And with this construct in place, most of them found mates for life.

As they neared their new home, an electricity had begun to run through the passengers aboard the *HELIX*. There was a constant edge to conversations and debates. It was now a race to finalize the preparations required to begin their new life on Orbyss II. They had all been waiting for this moment for decades, even before leaving Orbyss, yet they had also collectively survived such monumental obstacles together only to be faced with yet another: colonizing and terraforming a foreign world. And what a different home Orbyss II would be.

If Orbyss had been a beautiful garden, Orbyss II was a dark forest filled with hidden dangers and unforeseen perils. To the young XYZs, who had only read about their native planet, thoughts of landing on a new home had the opposite impact on those who had once enjoyed the vast oasis of Orbyss. Lamenting what once was prevented their parents from experiencing the excitement of what was to be. The excitement that their children were capable of. It was an old adage: you can't miss what you've never had. Although the young XYZs had learned everything there was to know about Orbyss, it was not the same as living there. This gave them an advantage, and their anticipation for the new planet had stimulated not only their creativity but also their desire to produce the incredible technology they had subsequently invented.

They pushed each other during the long hours spent honing their science, and more than just science was the outcome.

Tirus found every excuse possible to work closely with Vanae; it seemed that the closer they came to Orbyss II, the more he sought out her company. It was as if he had her captured, somewhat, aboard the ship, but perhaps when they left, she might drift away from him somehow. He was positive that their bond would continue to grow, and he could not imagine life without her. And it would have been as simple as it was in his mind had it not been for Rahl.

Rahl brought out a side of Vanae that Tirus didn't care for, one he felt was best left dormant. Rahl realized he had tapped into something undiscovered and was addicted to bringing it to the surface, especially for the benefit of bystanders and the shock it guaranteed. It was a drama, really, just for show at first, but lately, Tirus worried that it might be more. And the longer it went on, the higher the stakes became. While the *HELIX* returned to intrastellar travel and the fusion engines were put to sleep as the *HELIX* closed in on the distance to Orbyss II, the intensity of the flirtation between Vanae and Rahl made up for the speed the ship had relinquished. Rahl's invitation to live in the moment was an aphrodisiac for Vanae, one which her heart seemed addicted to and her head cautioned her to avoid.

The thing was, Tirus and Rahl had been competing since either one of them could remember, and if they placed the situation under a microscope, it may have revealed that it had very little to do with their true feelings for Vanae at all. It was the perfect storm. Their ongoing challenges, the countdown to Orbyss II, and now Vanae, who seemed to encapsulate it all. It was as if whoever she chose was the ultimate victor and all else would be forgotten. This was the mood as they finalized plans for the space walk scheduled for the very next day. The one Vash had reluctantly agreed to now that the *HELIX* was stabilized back at intrastellar speed.

Herriden had advocated for it for years. The design of the suits and the supporting equipment would make the experience like no other. They had all been working towards it for what seemed like forever. After evicting them from their hideout, Vash helped them get set up in their own lab, one she could oversee day and night. While they continued to use the casings for testing, as they were the perfect size and structure, it was only allowed with either herself, Grynn, or Shal present. While, at first, the young XYZs had resented the involvement of their parents, they soon came to realize just how much experience the older generation was able to offer. Fledgling theories quickly translated into bench tests, which, in turn, rapidly progressed to full-blown beta testing, and as a result, some of the most advanced technologies their species would ever take credit for were created. It was invention at hyper-speed, and the generational gap dissolved, as did the usual barriers between parent and child. Suddenly they were equals, everyone's idea considered, everyone's contribution acknowledged.

Today only the junior members of the team were present. Herriden was leading the preparations for the space walk, which required the incorporation of Vanae's suit modifications and also a hybrid suit/vehicular design she and Tirus had worked on together. Eelaa had also run the equipment through multiple rounds of preliminaries; they were all confident, and after her own rotation of testing, so was Vash. However, she had requested a number of changes to the safety features, and the four of them would not only be required to make them but also to test them before they were allowed to leave the ship.

They could have been finished at least an hour earlier. It was Tirus who held them up with his seemingly never-ending hypothetical scenarios. He had so many questions that Herriden had started to wonder if this was Tirus's way of staying in Vanae's company, and Herriden shot her a look that said as much, to which she replied with a smirk. The only one who did not seem to mind Tirus's onslaught of questions was Eelaa. One would think that she would have heard enough from her brother for one day, but the truth was that she was in no hurry to leave Herriden's company, not that she would have admitted it.

As if in answer to Herriden's predicament, Rahl and company entered the pod. Ever popular, ever calculating, he carried with him what looked and smelled like lunch. Vanae was the first to comment, lips in a petulant pout and brow furrowed in response to what appeared to be a feast he was unwilling to share.

"I'm hungry . . ." she volunteered with annoyance at his lack of hospitality.

"I'm hungrier . . ." he replied in a seductive tone, one that was impossible to ignore and easy to translate.

Before the crowd could respond, Vash followed Rahl's small posse into the pod. If she noticed the shaking heads and rolling eyes, she refused to acknowledge it. It was obvious to them all that, in her opinion, they all wasted immeasurable time on nonsense. Precious time she refused to squander.

"So, let's see them. Did you make the changes?" Vash's careful inspection revealed that not only had they incorporated her suggestions but that they had also added a few of their own.

"OK, well, let's head down and test them." Vash wanted to get this finalized. At first, she had dug in her heels. The last thing she wanted was for her babies to float around outside the *HELIX*, especially after the tragic end to what had been the first *HELIX* space walk. However, they were all about to leave this ship for good in less than a year, so she had better get used to them roaming around outside the protection of the starship.

"We'll meet you guys down there. Just going to grab a bite . . ." Vanae called back to the group as she started to follow the plate Rahl carried in the opposite direction.

They all looked to Vash to put an end to it, but the extent of the situation between Vanae and Rahl had escaped her, for the moment. Vash had more important things than Vanae's escapades to worry about.

CHAPTER 39

TIRUS

3.04 (Early Morning) / The *HELIX* / Nineteen
and a Half Years of Interstellar Travel

Tirus's cold skin was streaked with the sweat that steadily pooled beneath him. As the night terror took hold, he couldn't escape it, not this time, not ever. Tirus had thought all this was behind him, but then, he hadn't ventured outside the ship for nineteen-plus years. He had been foolish, believing that time had blunted the impact of that tragic day. As he looked at himself in the mirror now, he met the eyes of the small, scared child who had survived only thanks to Herra's sacrifice.

Tirus knew the others would not judge him if he told them he couldn't join them. They would offer only their support, their empathy. It would be completely understood that it was just too painful for him, that he was terrified he would freeze out there, that he would be overcome and not be able to perform. But something deep within him refused to give in to the fear. It turned him inside out, and he wanted to claw at his own skin, but anger rose within him, one directed at the angst, a fighting spirit born of rage that refused to give in to the terror.

It was terrifying and it was all-consuming, as it always was, lingering in the sinister night like an unseen predator. But it wasn't going to define him, not this time, not ever again. Two things drove him to fight through his personal nightmare: Vash and Vanae. There would be no shot at the captain's seat if he skipped the space walk, and there would be no shot at Vanae if he stayed behind while Rahl left the ship in her company.

Sleep had yet again eluded him. So Tirus decided to complete the prep for the others and double-check the equipment. The last thing they needed was an equipment failure. He headed down to the air lock where they had organized the apparatus required for the walk. Seeing the suits lined up made him nauseated. They lay supported by the floor of the air lock due to the weight of the accessories, like fallen soldiers awaiting burial. A knife twisted deep in his abdomen as he relived the worst moment of his life, just at the sight of them. His resolve started to wane, and his hand shook as he reached for the connection piece that would attach the first suit to the propulsion device he had built alongside Herriden and Vanae. It was a compact personal vehicle, an accessory to their suits, complete with navigation. It would allow them to literally travel outside the *HELIX* wherever they needed to, as if they were walking as naturally as they would inside the ship. The vehicle would create a seamless experience. Their first steps off the starship would feel no different than the ones they had taken aboard only seconds before, if everything went as planned.

Lost in self-inflicted torture, Tirus was startled by the hand that suddenly rested on his shoulder.

"How are you holding up?" Herriden's voice was filled with sympathy, and when Tirus turned to meet his gaze, he saw only compassion in his friend's eyes. It was at that moment that his resolve returned. The promise he had made to Herra flooded back to him, and if he had wavered before, now he was determined; he had to be out there to save Herriden if it came to it. The decision was clear: the real reason he had to go through with this was not for himself; it was for Herriden and the promise he had made to his beautiful mother.

It was no surprise to Tirus that Herriden had come looking for him, also not able to sleep. Perhaps losing Herra was more abstract for him, but Herriden had felt his best friend's anguish as he had watched it take its toll on Tirus over the years as he stood by helpless to rid him of the pain. When Herriden couldn't find Tirus in his pod, he headed to the air lock guessing correctly that he might find him there. That was when Vash arrived, having woken to Herriden leaving their pod. She was the lightest sleeper, ever sensing impending danger or a missing body from the nest.

It crossed Vash's mind on more than one occasion, as well, that Tirus may be struggling. He was much too brave and proud to ask for help, but any of them could imagine the terror he must be feeling. Vash had considered finding a reason for him to stay behind in order to spare him reliving the nightmare. However, each time she had approached him and hinted at the prospect, he would stop her dead in her tracks, insisting that he was not only up to the task but was also looking forward to it. Reluctant to decide for him, she had let it go, and after he deflected her second and third attempts, she decided to give up and focus on the stars instead during their ritual morning visit to the observation deck.

As Vash joined them in the air lock, her suspicions were confirmed; both Herriden and Tirus were busy preparing the equipment, double- and triple-checking the connections, energy storage, and calibration.

"I see we are getting an early start," Vash volunteered. Not that she would admit to it, but she was a little nervous herself. It had been more than twenty-five years since she had left the ship, so long that she had a hard time remembering the feel of anything other than the gentle rise and fall of the ship beneath her feet.

Vash fell in line, assisting in the audit of the equipment. Everything had been carefully prepared for months, even years, prior, but she had witnessed too much of the unforeseen take place to leave anything to chance. They had almost finished the inspection when the full crew arrived ready to suit up and take the first steps off the *HELIX* after more than nineteen years of travel. It was both momentous and exhilarating, feelings that could only exist with the presence of adventure, danger, and the unknown.

"I think we are ready to go here; I am just going to check in with Grynn and Shal to make sure they are prepared to assist us from the control pod, if need be."

As Vash left the air lock, Rahl came to stand beside Tirus. Their relationship had always been shadowed by competition, but Rahl wanted Tirus to know that he had his back today. Had Tirus not been battling his own vacillating emotions, he may have been able to recognize Rahl's gesture as it was intended. However, he continued to fight off the storm that today had accumulated within him, and he mistook his words as a challenge.

"Are you up for it?"

"Of course, Rahl. The question is, are you?" This brought a smile to Rahl's face. He was relieved to see that Tirus was holding his own, despite what must have been a difficult prospect after what had happened all those years before.

Herriden, taking in the exchange, decided to take the lead. "OK, so once we leave the air lock, we will all proceed in single file. The walk will last exactly four hours. The first hour will be spent testing the equipment, the remaining three inspecting the *HELIX* for any surface damage or erosion that undoubtedly has occurred during our nearly two decades of travel. Please remember to check your own pack for all safety equipment you hopefully will not require. Once we leave the air lock, we will begin by testing the propulsion thrusters. All of us will remain together throughout the duration of the walk."

"Yes, yes, we have all been over this at least a million times. We are ready to get out there! Can we please move it along?" Vanae had always been quick to lose patience with her older brother. To her, Herriden was a baby grandpa, ever monotonous, ever mundane.

"OK, I think we are ready to go! Is everyone good?" Vash was back from her trip to the control pod, and as she scanned their faces, it would seem that her final box could now be checked off. They were all as ready as they would ever be.

It was surreal how something potentially dangerous could embody the rhythm of a snail. On board the ship, anything exciting had an element of speed or uncertainty that required precision, physical strength, or both. Now as they left the *HELIX*, the silent star-filled landscape that stretched out endlessly before them seemed incapable of exposing them to peril. It welcomed them as a newborn child would be welcomed into their mother's arms as they entered the world. And as each of them left the air lock in turn, they were overwhelmed at the sight. The suits and propulsion vehicles worked perfectly together, just as they had been designed. And it was not long before their single-file line began to disintegrate as the wonder and joy of walking in space took hold. They could not help but play in the sea of stars they had just stepped into.

As expected, it was Vash who finally brought them back to reality, only after she had had some fun herself. It truly was a magical experience, and Grynn, through transmission, enjoyed it right alongside her.

"OK, enough, let's start putting the equipment through the paces! Let's see just what your 'inventions' can do!" Vash looked over to Vanae, Tirus, and Herriden as the challenge left her lips.

Taking in their expressions warmed her heart, all of them sporting face-splitting smiles and laughing like when they were children. To be the one out there enjoying it with them suddenly brought tears to her eyes. It had all been worth it to see them this way. Even Tirus had begun to relax. It crossed her mind that this was probably the most therapeutic thing for him.

It seemed that they would conquer what before had been a tragic end. This time, with all the brightest minds aboard the ship, space would be theirs. But as it happens, if you skip a step, your results cannot be guaranteed. And this morning, even Vash had forgone her early-morning routine with Tirus. One that could have changed their plans that day, one they would come to regret.

At first the dust that swirled around them was negligible. They noticed it lightly collecting on the creases of their suits before they could detect it in the surrounding void. Perhaps if they had been more experienced at walking outside the ship, it would have served as more of a warning. But what was supposed to have been a perfectly clear day in space was now showing early signs of a shower.

They had ventured out approximately six kilometers from the air lock in order to complete their inspection of the ship when the minute particles became visibly noticeable. It wasn't enough to alarm them; ancient relics of supernovae or shattered planets brushing by the HELIX had been a regular occurrence throughout their many years of travel. They all recalled the incident back in the twelfth year of their trip when a "relic" half the size of the ship almost ended their existence. However, Vash had decided that they should cut the walk short and make their way back to the air lock now, just to be safe. She knew this would be met with disapproval—they were like toddlers with a new toy—but they could easily finish this tomorrow or any other day, for that matter, now that they had proof that their suits and accessories were a success.

"OK, let's head back. The dust is getting thicker, and I don't think we should tempt fate," Vash transmitted to the rest of them.

"The suits are designed to function in much worse than this. I think it makes sense to test the suits this way, to ensure their functionality." Vanae was not going back to the prison ship without a fight.

"This was plenty for day one. We have six kilometers to cover to get back to the air lock, which is plenty of time to 'test' your suit in this dust," Vash replied.

But just as the words left her mouth, the sound of meteoroids pelting the far side of the *HELIX* drowned them out.

Grynn was now transmitting frantically to Vash that a meteoroid shower had come out of nowhere. They needed to get back to the air lock as fast as possible. It was easy for him to swiftly navigate the *HELIX* away from the incoming onslaught, but not with the six of them on a space walk hovering just off its exterior like frightened flies.

They had plenty of backup energy to make it to the air lock at top speed; this was not Vash's concern. Her heart stopped at the thought of losing any of them to the storm. The suits were not built to withstand the impact of large meteors. And from the sound of the space rocks ricocheting off the port side of the *HELIX*, she wasn't sure the ship would hold up either.

"What do you want to do, Vash? It's your call." Grynn felt sick. He started reliving the original *HELIX* space walk in his mind. He could not lose Vash the same way he'd lost Herra, and his voice cracked as he finished the last of his words to her.

He felt helpless and knew he could not go through this again. Grynn didn't wait for her reply. "I am coming out there!"

"No, you are not going to do that." Vash's transmission to him felt foreign, like someone else was relaying her thoughts. "Send Shal to the air lock with the Enseven. It will protect us from the shower and get us back to the *HELIX* more quickly than we can get there ourselves."

Grynn turned to address Shal, but having eavesdropped on Vash's transmission, he had already left the control pod.

As Shal navigated the impressive vehicle through the corridors of the *HELIX*, he barely noticed the stunned faces of the passengers who had no idea the craft even existed. He wasted no time as he closed the air lock doors to the ship behind him and then opened the ship's exterior door to the vastness of space that now held both his children hostage.

There was no time to test the cruiser. Shal was forced to become a rescue convoy expert under fire, and he hoped against hope that the Enseven would not also be required to serve as an ambulance. He tore through the distance that comprised the length of the *HELIX* in a craft only his son could have designed. As he neared their location, it was difficult to make out the emergency lights that had been activated on their suits through the thick dust of the shower.

As the dust particles morphed into a hailstorm around them, the joy of the walk was soon abandoned. His own worst nightmare coming to life, Tirus had begun to panic as the death of Herra started playing like a movie in his head. They were all terrified and had started to plan where the best possible place to take shelter would be outside the ship when the lights of the cruiser came shining towards them.

Vash had never been so grateful to see Shal in her entire life. As he positioned the craft directly above them, they quickly reassembled the single file they had so easily abandoned not twenty minutes prior. It was imperative they board as quickly as possible and get back to the *HELIX* in order to avoid any casualties.

It was in that moment that Grynn transmitted Vash's greatest fear. That the *HELIX* was about to initiate the preservation sequence it had been designed to automatically deploy upon threat of catastrophic damage to the pods. Unless he overrode its initiation in the next eight seconds, it would commence.

The starship was designed to take a hit; Lenacyth was the strongest material Orbyss had ever known, but as an additional safety precaution, in order to minimize potential damage to the ship as well as its passengers, the *HELIX* could relinquish control to each individual pod. Each one becoming a self-directed space shuttle, complete with its own navigation and power source in case of emergency and during colonization.

With seconds to make a decision, Vash became nothing more than the captain of the *HELIX*. She would sacrifice herself and both her children if it meant saving the ship to ensure the survival of the species. She had no other choice.

"Do not override the sequence."

"Vash, but—"

"You heard me."

She looked up at Shal, who had also received the transmission reply, and he could only shake his head back to her as they both helped Eelaa into the Enseven. Next was Vanae, who had trouble keeping her balance against the shower of rocks and debris that had picked up in both size and speed.

"The sequence is commencing in five . . . four . . . three . . ." Grynn delivered the last seconds out loud, aiming to change her mind as each digit reduced by one, his voice growing louder with intensity as the countdown closed in on zero.

Shal screamed down to her, "Get in here, Vash! The *HELIX* needs its captain, we all need you." But she refused to board until their children were all safe inside the shuttle.

The sequence commenced, and the giant ellipses that were their living pods took flight. Fused together, they formed the spiral shape of the ship, from which the *HELIX* had received its name. As they gently detached, it was like watching a murmuration of starlings in outer space. They were melodic, participants in an intricately coordinated dance, elegantly avoiding the space rocks and each other.

As the pods moved in formation and away from the core of the ship in order to avoid the meteoroids, only the Enseven seemed out of sync. It held its position as the space rocks pummeled at its strong but not impenetrable defensive shell.

Desperate, Vash could not make out anything through the dust and hail as she searched for signs of Herriden, Tirus, and Rahl. She transmitted to Herriden, calling his name. But the reply that came back to her was from Rahl. He had been struck by debris, and while he was unharmed, he had lost navigation and was now drifting, being pulled along by the storm.

Tirus stood beside Vash, and as she motioned to him to board the craft through the swirling haze that engulfed them, he slowly backed away from her.

She screamed at him to get on, determined not to lose a life that could be spared. But he shook his head in reply. He had vowed to protect Herriden, and if it meant giving his life, as Herra had given hers, so be it.

Rahl's transmission brought with it a form of echolocation that had survived their evolution and original migration to land. While the shower made it difficult, Tirus had a general idea of where Rahl had drifted to, and he was certain Herriden had located him, as well.

About fifteen meters ahead, he could vaguely make out Herriden's outline, continually pelted by debris. Both he and Rahl seemed to be drifting into the vortex, and Tirus knew he had not a moment to spare. As he reached Herriden, he could see that his suit had taken a beating, and although it did not seem compromised, he wasn't sure it could withstand another blow.

"Get back to the craft. Your suit is damaged. One more hit, and I will be saving you too," Tirus pleaded.

"No, I have this, I just have to make it to him," Herriden retorted.

Tirus grabbed Herriden, turning him around to look into his eyes. "You need to get back." There was no need for further words or transmission. Herriden knew Tirus would keep the promise he had made to his mother regardless of the cost. Logic won in the end. Herriden also knew his suit may not even hold up long enough to get to the cruiser, and after he reluctantly embraced Tirus, he headed back through the storm.

Tirus could now make out Rahl's emergency indicator some thirty meters beyond. He needed to pull Rahl to safety. He had learned many years before on his first space walk that he would have to secure them both to a fixed structure on the exterior of the *HELIX*. But where? He couldn't see anything through the incessant meteoroid hail, now the size of a fist.

As Tirus approached Rahl, he could easily recognize the terror on his friend's face. Rahl had all but accepted the end, but true to his nature, he refused to dissolve the twenty-three-year-long challenge they had carefully cultivated.

"Oh, it's you. Of course, they would send you over here to fetch me."

Relieved to see that Rahl was yet unharmed, he bantered back, "I wasn't about to let this opportunity slip past. I have been waiting for this day for as long as I can remember."

Tirus linked up with Rahl's suit. He hoped he had enough power left to get them both to safety but still could not imagine where they could possibly go, as their visibility had been all but lost to the storm.

Then they received the transmission from Vash. "Tirus. Rahl. Vanae has secured the cruiser tracking to your suits. You are four meters away from the observation dome. It's straight ahead. If you can navigate through the debris to the underside of the dome, it will shelter you. We are on our way."

Tirus didn't wait for her to finish; he immediately set out towards the observation dome with Rahl in tow, trying to avoid the largest meteoroids, which was onerous, as he could barely make them out through the dust and haze.

Shal tried his best to head in their direction, all the while dodging the meteoroids. He was terrified for his son. How could this be happening again? Shal decided in that moment that no member of his family would *ever* leave the *HELIX* again.

Tirus could tell he was nearing the edge of the observation dome, not because he could see it but because he could feel a reprieve from the storm behind the shield it provided. The dome was a structural contradiction. The *HELIX* hood ornament offered a window to the stars while it deflected their storms.

It was magnanimous; the one pod that could have spared them this mess in the first place would be the one to give them a second chance.

The base of the dome was a massive saucer. It had already begun to shield them; however, its protection came at a price. The curve also captured the meteoroids that crossed its open lip. The speed of the largest ones slung them through the dome's basin, altering their projection with an unpredictable outcome. So, while the storm may have lessened, now Tirus and Rahl were left to dodge the largest meteoroids from within the bowl.

It was nearly impossible for Tirus to navigate both himself and Rahl, who outweighed him by ten kilograms, around the space rocks while remaining within the safety of the saucer. It seemed to want to repel anything that entered it. Tirus's battery was almost empty. Once they lost their power source, they would undoubtedly be flung back into the storm, and judging by the size of the meteoroids now entering the dome, they wouldn't stand a chance.

"You have to let me go, Tirus. We can't keep this up."

"If I do that, you will have nothing to hold on to, Rahl. No, it's both of us or neither of us, either way."

As he held tightly to his suit, Tirus could feel Rahl's body relax a bit in relief at the prospect of not being left behind. Rahl had made the offer not knowing what Tirus's response would be. He could now fully imagine what it must have been like for Tirus, at five years of age, to be fighting for his life against the harsh will of space.

Out of nowhere, a blinding light shone down upon them. Tirus wasn't sure if it was the storm, the *HELIX*, or his father. As the craft he had built himself, now battered by the storm, gently floated towards him, tears filled his eyes. They might make it after all. He just might survive space a second time.

As the Enseven entered the basin, it seemed to create a pathway directly behind it for two of the largest meteoroids the storm possessed. Tirus knew that he would either die right then and there, with Rahl beside him, or they would both make it onto the craft. It was now or never, and just as the craft entry opened for them, a massive meteoroid was launched on a trajectory that seemed intended for the two of them.

It was a reflex for him. Herriden took command of the cruiser's controls from Shal. He arguably had far more practice at driving the craft than Shal. Herriden had won race after race through the casings ahead of both Tirus and Rahl. He hoped that now it would serve him well. He needed it to. Herriden wasn't the most daring driver, but his reflexes were unparalleled.

To choose which was more terrifying, the colossal meteor rolling towards them or the tremors it created beneath their feet, would have required a complete detachment from the situation. As the meteoroid closed in on them, Rahl and Tirus instinctively raised their arms to shield their faces in a hopeless attempt to avoid a crushing end. Eyes closed, they both assumed the meteoroid had struck them when the force of the air pressure from the opening of the craft closed in around them. It enveloped them like an invisible net. Once they were aboard, the cruiser immediately exited the shallow basin at top speed, scarcely avoiding collision with the mammoth rock.

It was an impossible rescue at an impossible speed, and no one other than Herriden would have dared to attempt, let alone accomplish, it. The timing and accuracy were both milliseconds and millimeters from failure.

Space was not to win that day. They could hardly breathe, huddled together on the floor of the craft. The entire group stayed locked in an embrace as Herriden navigated them back to the protection of the *HELIX*.

CHAPTER 40

VANAE

8.08 (Evening) / The *HELIX* / Later That Night

She watched Tirus slowly drift across the pool from where she stood. Vanae hovered just one step inside the pod that housed the lagoon and waterfall.

Tirus had insisted he needed to be alone following their return to the *HELIX*, wanting no witness to his surrender. As he floated on his back, water disguised the tears that poured from his eyes but not the tremors that shook his body, and Vanae felt vindicated in her decision to ignore his request.

She had looked for him first in his pod and, not finding him there, had initiated a search. She wasn't sure what had led her to this place; perhaps she just felt him there. All she knew was that after Tirus had rescued Rahl, she felt drawn to him.

He appeared exhausted and spent to her scrutinizing gaze. All his pain released into the water. Perhaps it comforted him while camouflaging the deliverance from his fears from so many years ago, not to mention those from today.

He didn't notice her approach the water. He had abandoned the suit that had saved his life on the artificial beach they had borrowed from Orbyss. She discarded hers, as well. It covered his, lying haphazard on the sand, and together, the garments briefly glowed in recognition of each other. A sign of things to come if Vanae had her way.

He went still, floating, resting just above the surface, giving in completely to the water. Vanae decided he didn't deserve any further surprises that day, so as she came up behind him, she softly whispered his name so as to not startle him. Her long dark hair floated around her, extending an invitation of its own. She was a mermaid, surfacing from the depths, and as he turned to face her, it crossed his mind that he may be hallucinating due to the trauma.

He didn't imagine it happening this way. He didn't want to feel this vulnerable. Not in front of her. And that was what she found irresistible. He would be hers.

In her mind, it was the only end to what had been a harrowing day she would never forget. Something changed for her when Tirus entered the craft behind Rahl, exhumed from the underside of the observation pod. She hadn't pictured Tirus a hero until that moment. And the fact that he had rescued Rahl made his transformation even more potent.

Vanae had more experience than Tirus, being that it was his first time. Therefore, he had no choice but to follow her lead. Perhaps he had been waiting for her, if he was honest with himself. In any case, he had been mistaken that the exhaustion he felt as a result of fighting not only for his own life but also Rahl's was insurmountable. Desire conjured what he assumed he was incapable of.

Her kiss stopped his questions as well as his breath. It didn't matter because, at that moment, he would have given her whatever she asked for. They seemed designed for each other. Her wet skin pressed against his own as if they were already one. Tirus abandoned himself to her, just as he had abandoned himself to the water only moments before.

She covered an impatient breast with his hand and sighed at the touch. It was designed to both erase his suffering and satisfy her desire. As he entered her, conscious thought drifted away in the pool that surrounded them. Only they existed together in time and space.

From the pod entry, it was obvious that this was their first time. The water echoed their frantic consummation, thrashing through them, a hurricane for the senses. Neither one was lucid, lost in a world of their own invention. At least that was Rahl's thought as he watched them from the sand.

He entered the pool, the same way Vanae had, undetected. They were completely oblivious to his presence as he came up behind Vanae and traced the length of her spine arched in pleasure, a response to feeling Tirus tremble beneath her.

Tirus felt her stiffen in acknowledgment of Rahl's seductive hello, and it woke him from his trance. He opened his eyes to look at her, but he also took in Rahl standing just above her shoulder. There was a moment of tension as the next move hung in the balance. Were they in or were they out?

Tirus had just spent hours literally sandwiched against Rahl from what he could recall. And now facing him with Vanae between them both, he had to question if he hadn't actually survived at all, if instead, this was where you found yourself at the end of things.

Rahl whispered something to Vanae that brought a smile to her face, and Tirus felt weak. His head spun as he tried to decipher what was real and what was his imagination.

For Vanae, it was exhilarating that Rahl would join them. He knew exactly how to please her, and at that moment, Rahl could think of no better way to express his gratitude, a gesture extended to thank Tirus for saving his life. In the moment, it made sense. The act was celebratory—they had outmaneuvered space, and they had won. Tirus's consent came in the form of his welcome to Rahl, as he pulled them both closer towards him.

Their three bodies fused together, protruding suggestively at multiple angles above the surface of the water. They formed a living sculpture. Each was a perfect specimen, and their unencumbered abandon made the performance exceptionally erotic. Recovery came swiftly for the trio. Passion taking over, taking Vanae over, yet again. In the years to come, the scent and taste of salt water mixed with their own desire would bring them back to this moment countless times.

Hours passed, and eventually they made their way to the sand. They drifted in and out of sleep, consciousness, and a place somewhere in between. For the XYZ innocence could not be lost; to seek intimacy was innocence unto itself. Although disputes between the trio were not uncommon, compromise won that night. Deliberately avoiding light, they stayed in the shadows, beneath the stars, not wanting day to come.

Eventually they did succumb to the evening, in the wee hours. As they lay upon the shore, spent and breathless, a smile escaped Vanae's lips. If either Tirus or Rahl noticed, they made no mention, perhaps content in the assumption they had pleased her. Ironically, what amused her had nothing to do with either of them. Her thoughts had turned to Herriden, and just how wrong he had been when he told her that nothing good could come of this.

CHAPTER 41

VASH

5.68 (Morning) / The *HELIX* / The Next Day

She felt like she was sleepwalking as she made her way down the well-worn path leading to the control pod. She tried not to relive the event, which was made difficult as she passed by a group of little ones who had already fashioned themselves toy living pods so that they could recreate their own adventure from the day before. As they chased each other down the length of the corridor, each child seemed to take on their own unique role in the game. It was either play therapy or just play, depending on how each one had experienced it—either from inside their family pod or the body of the *HELIX*. The looks on their parents' faces told a different story; obviously, they had no desire to relive the event. But their expressions quickly changed to smiles of gratitude as they recognized Vash. If they were traumatized, one could only imagine how Vash must have felt, having experienced the entire ordeal from outside the ship.

As she entered the control pod, Vash was relieved to find that both her children, Herriden and Vanae, had beat her to it. Exhausted with relief, she had collapsed into bed soon after they had made it back to the ship. She had fallen into Grynn's waiting embrace, and once Dexl had tended to their collective cuts, bruises, and scrapes, Vash found she had nothing left. Satisfied they were all safe now, and that none of them would be venturing back outside the ship anytime soon, she crashed. As soon as she entered their pod, she fell fast asleep, her first insomnia-free night in as long as she could remember.

Seeing her two children, along with the others, now at the helm of the *HELIX* alongside Grynn and Shal was incredible; she could not have been prouder. She had chosen her successors wisely. Vash finally had her team, a team no one would question, with Herriden eventually taking the lead. After he had saved them all, no one would challenge his leadership. She would never need to defend him.

"So, what are you all doing up here?" she teased.

"I thought it was best to keep an eye on the troublemakers," Shal quickly offered in their defense, interjecting before any of them had a chance to reply.

"Well, from what I witnessed yesterday, you are all light-years from piloting this ship, and if I were you, I would already be in the lab making the necessary adjustments to those suits based on the beating they took yesterday." They all looked at her dumfounded, at a loss for words after her unanticipated command.

"I'm not joking." Vash was not about to let their egos swell any more than they already had.

Both Grynn and Shal smiled and shook their heads, relieved to see that Vash had also fully recovered.

As the future successors reluctantly left the control pod, Vash could hear the rumblings of which modifications they would start on first, and she couldn't help but smile at Shal and Grynn. She was glad it was just the three of them now, because she needed their help.

The second thing that crossed her mind that morning, right after the whereabouts of her family, was their new home, Orbyss II. Their close call had driven home the fact that they should be prepared for the same, or potentially worse, once they reached their new planet.

The *HELIX* had performed too and, in many cases, exceeded expectations. But it had also provided them with a false sense of security. They had been very lucky for many years, but that luck could turn in a second, and yesterday had been a harsh reminder of that fact. Their ability to problem solve on the fly, and Vash's own uncanny ability to see ten chess moves ahead, had served them well thus far. However, they were about to head into completely uncharted territory. They were scheduled to arrive at Orbyss II six months from now, a planet they knew would be much less hospitable than Orbyss. But beyond that, they ultimately knew very little about it. Looking at Orbyss II through the high-powered telescopes aboard the ship had educated them on the terrain, gravity, and weather, but they knew nothing of the humidity, precipitation, atmospheric temperature, potential vegetation, or climate variability.

Not one to waste time, Vash just came out with it. Shal and Grynn had learned long ago not to question her demands or her timing.

"We need to send satellites out ahead of us to Orbyss II now."

"OK, agreed, but not all of them." Shal had no desire for further surprises either. But they had limited cargo space, and only twenty satellites were brought aboard the ship prior to leaving Orbyss. They could potentially build more if need be, but if he were to subscribe to Vash's line of thinking, their time was better spent constructing what they would require for survival on their new home.

"We should send three now," Shal continued after some consideration. He had been shaken by the storm and wanted to ensure, or at least improve, the likelihood that a satellite would make it to low Orbyss II orbit. The satellites travelled twice as fast as the *HELIX* during intrastellar travel, so if all went well, they should start receiving updates in three months' time.

"I agree; let's send three to Orbyss II, but also another three to orbit its sun. The more we know, the better." As the words left her mouth, she felt confident they would not question her request.

Vash wasn't about to waste their last months aboard the *HELIX* staring at Orbyss II through a telescope wondering what catastrophes their new home might conceal when, instead, time could be much better spent inventing what was required to ensure that colonization went smoothly. After yesterday, Grynn and Shal had to agree with her line of thinking. None of them wanted to narrowly survive another space walk. And now that they had been outside the ship, who was to say that the new home they had so carefully selected would be any kinder than what met them just steps outside their temporary front door.

Shal didn't waste a moment. He headed straight for the cargo hold that housed all twenty satellites. State of the art, roughly the size and weight of a car, they were his most prized inventions, coming in second only to the submersive designed to bury the DNA time capsule into Orbyss's core.

As he brought his sextuplets to life and began to put them through their paces, he wondered what they would discover as they circled their new home to be—that was, if they were able to make it there in one piece, sailing through the harsh storms of space.

CHAPTER 42

GRYNN

2.08 (Afternoon) / The *HELIX* / Three
Months Prior to Landing on Orbyss II

The closer they got to Orbyss II, the more Grynn started to panic. Not only had he failed to recognize that he was not as strong as he thought he was, but now he understood clearly that the strength he did possess was entirely dependent upon Vash and his children. Ultimately, he was the adult, the father figure, much loved and respected not only by his own family but all those aboard the *HELIX*. They had not been mere spectators; they had mourned alongside him at the death of his parents and wife, and they had celebrated along with him once his fortune had turned. If only he could see it that way—a turn in fortune. Not that he was ungrateful, of course; it just seemed to him that when you had lived and then relived the nightmare, you had no option but to question if it just might haunt you again, regardless of whether you deserved it or not.

The past months were a flurry, this time from within the ship. Grynn had taken over the inspection of the pods. Once the meteor storm had passed and the *HELIX* recalled its pod army of fifty thousand back into formation, the arduous task of assessing the damage and performing any associated repairs took precedence. They were all astonished at how well the *HELIX* had held up, considering. Only exterior surface damage had been detected, nothing that impacted the functionality of even one pod. While it was a terrifying experience for the occupants trapped inside during the shower, Grynn had done well with his design by securing a magnetic field that engaged once dispersion was initiated. All furniture and fixtures, including their suits, were immediately fixed in place. This meant those wearing the suits were subject to an automatic full-body seat belt, while each pod did its best to avoid impact with the unfriendly meteors.

Vash had slipped into the same mechanical coma she had exemplified prior to the *HELIX* taking flight; only, this time, Anae was not around to temper her. Grynn did his best to set her mind at ease as much as he could, but her lists of potential scenarios they may face were already endless, and she had been pushing everyone to the point where they weren't sure it was a good idea to leave the ship at all. Vash had managed to terrify almost everyone, with the exception of Vanae. Vanae seemed to have absolutely no fear at any time, ever. Hers was a unique and infectious optimism. Vash, on the other hand, planned for the most horrific outcomes imaginable, dragging them all reluctantly behind her. It was an advanced breed of pessimism, and if it weren't for both Grynn's and Shal's attempts to lighten the mood, Vash may have been successful in luring them all over to her dark side.

Away from the teens' parents, excitement and anticipation ruled the day. While Vash's future successors carefully incorporated all of her endless suggestions in terms of the modifications to the suits and vehicles, their focus had independently turned to the simulations. Post space walk, they were fixated on rebuilding the meteor shower within a simulated environment, and when they presented their model to Vash, she lit up. They had managed to recreate not only the physical characteristics of the storm but had also programmed the simulator to run probabilities and solutions for infinite scenarios. It was an advanced algorithm produced through a direct interface with the *HELIX* computer cores that had captured all storm data. It had initially been Rahl's idea, but it was Vash's dream come true. And now that the satellites were due to reach their destination, she could hardly wait to incorporate scenarios for Orbyss II based on the data they had collected.

Today, Grynn sought out his soulmate at the helm of the control pod. Vash was the easiest passenger to find on the ship, permanently glued to her seat for the most part.

"Grynn! I was just about to come find you! They made it!" This was Vash's welcome, the warmest Grynn could recall for quite some time.

She was obviously referring to the satellites she'd had Shal send out three months ago. There was little else she had talked about for so long.

"That is wonderful!" Grynn mustered as much enthusiasm as he was able, considering he knew the satellites would now take her even further away from him.

He and Vash brought up the feed from each satellite on the giant monitor of the control pod so that they could observe them simultaneously.

"Look at that, love! It's beautiful!" Grynn said. A close-up of the terrain on Orbyss II brought tears to her eyes. Vash and Grynn experienced their new home together, for the first time, not from the distant lens of the *HELIX* telescope but up close, as if they were already there. It was like they could reach out and touch it.

"Grynn, we have to show the kids!" Vash exclaimed after the two of them had taken in the feed from all three satellites across all angles of the planet for more than an hour. She set out in search of Herriden and Vanae.

Grynn had decided to stay behind. The perpetual feed of their new home gave him a small amount of comfort. The planet was raw and untamed. It looked severe but at the same time beautiful, especially the strip down its center they would call home. From the satellite feed, they could identify the glistening proof the water on its surface was liquid, plentiful, and potentially pure, just as they had suspected. And as the planet stood still in a foreign, almost dignified, manner, Grynn felt relief instead of fear for the first time since their return from the space walk.

He could not seem to drag his eyes away from the monitor taking in the video from one satellite after another. The labeled feeds, "S1," "S2," and "S3," all offered a glimpse of their new home at unique locations on different sides of the planet. However, he could not help but be drawn back to the life-supporting terminator zone of the perpetu-ally stationary planet. Stationary due to its extreme proximity to the red dwarf sun. And Grynn was left wondering what it would be like once they landed there. An almost instantaneous reminder, it was then that he recalled Vash's request for the additional three satellites meant to orbit its sun, as well. He shook his head; of course, they would be online soon enough, but it stood to reason that it may have taken them a bit longer to take position. In any case, Vash would soon be on the hunt for them. She did not require a reminder from him, and hopefully she could enjoy the moment as she shared the feeds from Orbyss II with the others.

Vash was not the only one capable of predicting a fateful future. And with that thought, he left the pod, no longer wanting to take in the sights. He could no longer enjoy the three feeds equally displayed on the monitor, knowing full well that S4, S5, and S6 were still inex-plicably missing.

CHAPTER 43

VASH

5.08 (Morning) / The *HELIX* / The Day
Before Landing on Orbyss II

It had been three months of clandestine conduct. No one could be allowed to guess at her theory, and she required all her faculties to ensure the secret held. She had even gone so far as to request a sleep aid from Dexl, as slumber continued to evade her. It was vital that Vash possess a clear head because she could not afford her fear to enter the minds of her crew. True to her nature, she refused to let it rule her, not until there was empirical evidence to support it. And at this point, nothing conclusive could be confirmed. Even if her theory held weight, and the very worst came to be, ultimately, she believed that they had to try, that they had no other option.

A celebration had taken place as the *HELIX* entered low Orbyss II orbit. To have the passengers look out their pod windows at their new home for weeks on end seemed almost cruel; however, it was not to be helped. They needed to investigate well ahead of entry. Today would be the first time they set foot on the planet, and Vash knew it would be vital for her crew to be at their best, especially as she had decided she would not be accompanying them. She feared Grynn could not take it if she left the ship with them. If she were honest with herself, she had lost the desire for adventure, and she felt she could do more from the helm of the *HELIX*, especially at this proximity. This was to be her protégés' mission; they were the ones destined for it, and Vash would rather guide them through it than slow them down. Her eyes and her mind were much faster than her hands and her feet these days.

The past three months had been the most stressful in her existence. They had flown by in a millisecond, or, at least, it had felt that way. The feed from the three satellites in orbit provided a constant to-do list. She had been right to send out the satellites ahead of their arrival. Today Vash couldn't imagine having gone in blind without them. They had learned an infinite amount of information and incorporated every-thing they required into the designs of the suits and vehicles in order to make themselves at home.

Life on Orbyss II would be nothing like it was on Orbyss, nothing like it was on the *HELIX*, which resembled their past life as closely as possible. Vash worried about the comfort level of the passengers and how they would take to this harsh new home where freedom would come at the cost of comfort. They would not be able to experience this brutal albeit beautiful new planet as they had on Orbyss. Their suits on Orbyss had offered comfort and safety, but they were by no means nec-essary. In fact, they had all happily abandoned them whenever appro-priate, sometimes even when it was not. This simple enjoyment would not be possible on Orbyss II, at least until they terraformed the termi-nator zone to the point of improved atmospheric conditions.

The severe temperature on either side of the planet was lethal. While the habitable strip in the center was conducive to *some* life, they could not weather the radiation-filled atmosphere from their new sun without their technology. Vash knowingly sent both her children and their closest friends into this extreme climate to go explore on their own. Something she could have never imagined before this day.

She would have to seek them out far in advance of their departure. If possible, they would avoid her, knowing that she would probably run them through a last-minute departure pop quiz. The simulator was the only reason Vash agreed to any of this. The level of sophistication they had achieved was astounding, even to her, and the ability to push them through its endless testing gave her all the confidence she required regarding the suits and vehicles. Orbyss II could do its worst; she'd put them through more than she believed the planet was capable of, with the only blind spot being the absence of the feed she had expected from the satellites sent out to orbit Orbyss II's sun. Unfortunately, they had been lost. From what they could decipher from the last data collected, it looked as if the satellites had been burned by the sun itself, and this mystery was what kept Vash up at night.

Tirus had been correct when he had noticed the decreased luminosity of Orbyss II's parent star. This, coupled with the loss of the satellites, meant its days were numbered, but why? Their new sun did not possess the properties of Orbyss's sun and was likely much closer to the end of its life. Orbyss II might not be the forever home they had hoped for, but the potential for millions of years was a strong estimate in its favor, and proof that water rested on the surface they would inhabit made the prospect of terraforming Orbyss II not only possible but highly probable especially when one considered how much their technology had advanced while aboard the *HELIX*.

Upon entering the air lock, Vash realized she had made it just in time. She caught Herriden as he was taking his first steps onto the Explorer, the last to board. The multi-passenger vehicle had been designed specifically for the rocky terrain on the red side of the planet, but unlike all other vehicles, it could also maneuver the icy field on the blue side, as well. It was triple reinforced with Lenacyth and able to withstand a barrage of insults from both above and below, not unlike the Enseven, only with eight impenetrable wheels capable of providing flotation if necessary.

Thanks to the orbiting satellites, they had already identified that life existed in the waters of the planet. Primitive organisms identified in the midline consisted of photosynthetic life far beneath the surface, which appeared to be well adapted to the intense conditions found on the ubiquitous planet due to extreme sunlight on one side and perpetual darkness on the other. It was no surprise that these plants only inhabited the terminator zone that the XYZs were also hoping to share. From what they could glean, as recently as only a month ago, small amphibian-like creatures had been identified swimming between the dense leaves of the plants, living in what could only be imagined to be an underground system of caves that would provide the necessary protection from the extreme conditions found on the surface.

As such, they would attempt to land the Explorer at coordinates that would not disturb the life that already existed on the planet. They would also place existing life on the planet as the priority when it came time to land, ensuring that the pods did not disturb the areas supporting life of any form.

Herriden's eyes widened in surprise as Vash made her way towards them. It was obvious they had just realized they would not escape without her inquisition masquerading as a farewell. It was no surprise to Vash; this crew had been bubbling over with excitement for the past three weeks. If it seemed cruel to the passengers to park the *HELIX* just kilometers from Orbyss II for three weeks' time, it was absolute torture for this lot, and it had been all she could do to keep them on the ship. She was both relieved and terrified to send them down there, but she had complete faith not only in their ability but also in the functionality of the equipment they had developed.

They were a tight-knit group, and she knew they had each other's backs, so instead of putting them through an unnecessary last-minute final exam, she took Herriden in her arms and held him tightly. Simultaneously, she glanced up into the Explorer and exchanged smiles with each of them, transmitting to the group that she would be watching them, so they better not do anything to mess this up for her, to which they laughed in reply.

From behind the window within the interior entry to the air lock, she watched the Explorer leave the *HELIX*, tears in her eyes and heart hammering in her chest. Grynn, Shal, and Moda all came to join her, taking front-row seats to the start of a new life as their children led the way.

A surge of cheers and applause filled the Explorer as well as the *HELIX* as Herriden navigated the cruiser away from the starship and towards their new planet. They could hardly wait to set foot on something other than the starship for the first time in their lives.

The speed of the Explorer was impressive, never before matched. It was designed for hasty departures if necessary, the ideal vehicle for a narrow escape. It made the navigation of the Enseven they had piloted during the meteor shower seem rudimentary. All vehicles destined for Orbyss II had been enhanced in terms of navigation, speed, stability, and strength. Lenacyth had reached new heights, its evolution guided by Moda's and Eelaa's careful hands. Sond had passed everything he had learned during a lifetime dedicated to botany along to his daughter, and Moda, in turn, had passed along the inheritance to Eelaa. The contributions of mother and daughter were key not only to the structure of the vehicles but also to the material of the suits.

As Herriden closed in on the last few kilometers prior to entering Orbyss II's atmosphere, they braced themselves for what would undoubtedly be a precarious entry. A planet in perpetual war with itself, light against dark, heat against cold, fire against ice—and this war created weather to match. As the Explorer made its entry, a planet-wide hurricane welcomed them and shook the Explorer to its core. It was almost impossible to navigate through the storm, and Vash could sense their angst all the way from the *HELIX* control pod.

Her voice immediately calmed the crew. "Keep going, it's going to lessen up as you near the strip."

They had set exact coordinates for landing, an area well away from where life had been identified but close enough to explore within a comfortable range should a quick escape become necessary.

The Explorer took position to land and touched down upon the ice. They could all hear it as it started to crack, but it did not give way to the water running far beneath it. They had technically landed on a river that's surface always remained frozen, disguising the waterway that flowed far beneath it.

As they left the craft, the cold temperature automatically called their suits to respond, offering optimal protection from the elements.

"I don't think we should leave the Explorer here. What if the ice doesn't hold?" Tirus was reluctant to leave his "baby" in a suboptimal location.

Herriden laughed back at his best friend. "Those are nothing more than surface cracks from the impact of landing. The ice is at least a mile thick here. We can test it if you want to?"

"Let's not waste our time measuring ice when we could be staking our claim on the best place to pitch a tent." Vanae was in disbelief over how attached Tirus had become to the vehicles; they were nowhere near as important as the suits, in her opinion.

Much of Vash's study of the new planet had focused on where best to colonize it. She wagered a strong guess and had delivered the coordinates to the group weeks ago. This was their bet, but how close did she actually get? They wouldn't know for sure until they stood on the spot for themselves.

The quintet made their way towards the exact spot Vash had provided, marching along an icy path. A snow-lined red carpet complete with snowflakes as confetti and howling wind as the band. They walked on, an anxious excitement filling their suits, which protected them from the temperatures well below freezing that surrounded them all.

It was intensely cold on this side of the planet, the one that had never peered into the face of its star, covered in frozen oceans and forgotten land masses. But as they made their way towards the habitable zone, the weather began to change. The clash of the cold and hot pressure created the winds of a hurricane, and the group was forced to make use of their personal vehicles just to stay in position as it pummeled them.

Vash had eyes and ears on them through the Explorer, as well as through each of their suits, and she guided them through the storm, just as she always had. As they made their way farther into the terminator zone, they were enveloped in light that suddenly penetrated the storm. On the other side of the hurricane was a reprieve, and their suits automatically adjusted to the oasis. It was just as they had seen it on the satellite transmission from the comfort of the control pod, a Zen-like garden where water caressed the surface and plants could be identified far beneath the surface. Their new home would be an area about 480 kilometers in diameter. A concentric ring with an ideal climate—from what they could tell, the only one in existence on the planet.

Eelaa removed a container from her pack. She could not wait to get the water sample back to the *HELIX* lab in order to test it. To witness water running freely, as far as the eye could see, in ribbons from beneath the ice fields quenching the blazing swells of fiery mountains that faced the sun on the other side. As they looked out onto what would become their new home, they could easily imagine recreating what they had only ever read about or seen pictures of: life on Orbyss.

They ran like children, splashing through the shallows, in awe of what surrounded them.

"OK, enough, it's time to get back to the ship!" Vash had seen all she needed to. Once they took the exact measure of the area and its immediate borders, she could then pinpoint the best place for landing once they returned to the ship. From Vash's perspective, there was nothing more to be done, and the longer they stayed down there, the more that could go wrong.

As they boarded the Explorer and it lifted off to return to the *HELIX*, the excitement and hope that filled the cruiser were contagious. Their first steps on their first planet were beyond what they could have imagined. It was their destiny, and the five of them felt a blissful hope for the future, one unlike anything they had ever known. They were finally home.

CHAPTER 44

HERRIDEN

6.56 (Evening) / The *HELIX* / Later That Night

It was a moment unlike any other. One for which Herriden had no comparison. One he could not effectively describe. The endless questions from the passengers, the cheer when they had first entered the ship from the air lock upon their return. He had felt an energy he would never forget. Touchdown on Orbyss II was surreal, almost as if it hadn't happened at all. In reality, the first steps on their new planet were blissfully uneventful, but what they symbolized was great. There would be life after Orbyss, and life after the *HELIX*, the only home Herriden had ever known.

Finally, Vash was ready to give the green light on entry to Orbyss II for the 107,379 passengers aboard the ship. She was as close to 100 percent as she was capable of getting, and if Herriden thought that after having made the decision she would head to her pod to get some rest, he would have been mistaken.

Fully knowing this would be the case, he gave up on celebrating with the rest, and instead, he shadowed her as she circled the *HELIX* obsessively checking on anything and everything that crossed her mind. Safe assumptions were to be questioned. Multiple connections that had never failed prior were suddenly not to be trusted. It was a ceremonial dance as she drifted from one end of the ship to another, trying to outsmart fate, which had cruelly made her the one, the only one, who seemed to be able to prevent its potential malevolence. In her mind, she alone was able to circumvent its unforgiving challenges. The one soul able to appease it.

It was well past midnight when Herriden suggested they head to the control pod. The party had long ended, and everyone was making last-minute preparations to land, if they weren't already fast asleep. They had all left for their living pods hours ago in order to secure them for entry.

Vash looked exhausted, and Herriden decided he was going to attempt to distract her and, if successful, try one last time to convince her to get some rest, even if it was only for a couple of hours.

"Mom, you know what, we never reviewed the footage of the landing. There is something I want to show you." A look of strain crossed her face; she was incredulous that he would wait till now to inform her that she had missed something. Herriden laughed at her expression, reading her mind, and shook his head. "Hey, come on, I wouldn't do that to you."

In all the excitement, they had forgotten the bet. How close had Vash come to calculating the sweet spot, the concentric oasis that would become their new home? Herriden brought up the footage and ran the corresponding data. He was confidently guessing and desperately hoping she had been correct, fearing that if she were wrong, it would send her into a further spiral of self-doubt that she would take out on the ship with a new round of inspections.

As it turned out, she had been *incorrect* . . . by .00000056. They both laughed. Even his mother had to agree that this margin of error held no significance. Suddenly her smile faded and her face fell slightly. The lost satellites haunted her, not that she would share this with him, but the fact that they were still missing plagued her constantly and wouldn't leave her head. She had spent countless hours, sometimes literally staring at the control pod monitor willing them to show themselves, but they never appeared. Shal had tried to put her mind at ease, and finally she relented that they may have been damaged or, as Herriden suggested, a plethora of other issues may have befallen them, including the possibility that they may still be on course to reach their destination. But the apprehension would not leave her. How could all three satellites that were sent to Orbyss II be accounted for and the other three sent to orbit the planet's sun go missing? This was what kept her up at night, more than all of her other worries.

Determined not to waste this last night aboard her ship, especially the rare opportunity to share it with her son, now a grown man, Herriden and Vash relived the footage of the crew's landing through to the end. When he eventually closed the file, he noticed another was open on the control pod's screen.

Vash noticed his discovery and smiled. "You caught me reliving the past." It was a family photo album of sorts. Vash's favorite memories of their lives aboard the *HELIX*, a ship that captured everything for them. The *HELIX* recorded the very best and the very worst of their existence without prejudice—candidly, beautifully. "I guess I needed to say goodbye," she offered by way of explanation.

They perused hundreds of hours of footage together. They laughed and cried, remembering life aboard a ship that would not let them forget. A vessel that had protected them not only from space but had also provided the comforts of Orbyss so that even those born aboard could not just imagine but also experience their first home.

Many times, Vash thought about waking Grynn and Vanae to join them but then decided against it. There was something therapeutic in sharing this moment with Herriden; it seemed important and necessary somehow. A last lesson aboard the *HELIX*, from one captain to another. Only, this time, she wasn't passing along instructions on *how*, she was passing along instructions on *why*. Why it had been so important to get it right, all of it. Because they might not get a second chance.

Now Herriden saw the ship in a new light; he saw it through her eyes, fully, for the first time. It struck a new appreciation within him for who she was, why she did the things she did. He could now see for himself what she protected. Not just the physical survival of the species but the survival of their essence, their innocence, their culture, their way of life. The things that made them who they were. It was her

responsibility to ensure that they carried on intact—mind, body, and soul.

Herriden was not to be the victor that night; Vash had won. Not only on one but on two fronts. She had almost perfectly identified their new address, and she had also avoided sleep entirely. The two of them continued to relive their best moments aboard the *HELIX* until they experienced its artificial dawn together, for the last time.

CHAPTER 45

VASH

5.00 (Morning) / Orbyss II / Day One on Orbyss II

It was as if a colossal metronome kept an unfaltering pace for the pods as they elegantly drifted away from the *HELIX* and seamlessly entered the atmosphere of Orbyss II, the hearts of the passengers aboard each pod keeping time. A flawless symphony, every instrument joining at just the right measure, at just the right moment, in order to play just the right note.

If there was ever an expression of Vash's genius, it was embodied by the living pods' entry to Orbyss II. As they made their way surely through the storm brought on by a hostile planet at war with itself, they did so with the accuracy and assurance only Vash could have conducted.

It took them less than nine minutes to reach the landing strip where they would come to rest. An almost flat runway carefully selected by their captain. The snow-lined path was not visible until seconds prior to landing due to the winds and blowing snow that obscured it from sight. The youngest of the passengers had not experienced the substance before, and they could scarcely contain their excitement as their small hands pressed against the windows of the pods in a futile effort to touch it.

Beyond what the passengers' imaginations could produce was the entry to their new planet. The black carbon fiber of the Lenacyth comprised the shell of each pod, in complete contrast to the icy white glacier beneath it. As they neared the surface, the lower lip of each pod made contact with the snow, and heat from the friction melted the surface, leaving water to rest at the top. They hit the ground, one after the next, separated by only thirty seconds. The surface water created by the first pods to land took flight as each new pod entered. The substance, unfortunately unfit for their consumption, nevertheless created a fantastic display like fireworks between the pods as they touched down. It was an ethereal fountain, composed by Vash, their debut and finale, together as one. Fifty thousand seeds planted to the music of the overture that had played for years in her mind, now taking hold in the garden of Orbyss II, five deep, a hundred meters between them each.

The control pod would be the last to enter, and as she watched the innumerable living pods land from the heart of the ship at the helm of the *HELIX*, tears escaped her eyes and rolled down her cheeks. They fell in a mixture of relief, testimony, and gratitude at having had the honor.

As Vash prepared herself to leave, Grynn, Vanae, and Herriden by her side, she decided to make one last trip to the second control pod within the emergency ship. It was an exact replica of hers, the space that had housed her greatest joys and worst fears. The only difference that could be identified was the captain's chair. While hers was well worn, especially at the arms, this one was like new. They would leave the emergency ship in low Orbyss II orbit in case of, as its name suggested, an emergency. It offered her comfort to know that there was a quick and easy getaway for them should the worst present itself. Before she left the pod, she decided to leave one item behind. A small token she had always kept with her, a model of the *HELIX* Vanae and Herriden had built together many years before. Somehow it didn't seem right to separate this toy ship from the real one, almost like taking an infant from its mother's arms, so she found a safe spot for it to rest, hoping they would never *need* to return to it.

Shal would remain on board to finalize the emergency ship protocol and initiate its anchor sequence. Besides taking the new role of emergency ship, the *HELIX* also became a battery for them, suspended up in space, should they require additional energy. The naked, pared-down version of the ship was deceptive without the pods. But make no mistake, it was an unsurpassed power source, and now it would assist them with the energy required for colonization.

As Vash reentered the control pod to the excited welcome of her family, she could not help but smile in return. It was their turn now, and they waited for her to take the lead. As she expertly navigated the control pod to the end of the living pod rows, she took in the collective transmission of cheers from the passengers already safe on the ground.

The pods had landed so smoothly, so effortlessly, it would have been unimaginable if they all hadn't witnessed it for themselves. The pods could barely contain their enthusiastic contents, and it was all that parents could do to keep their little ones in place while they observed Herriden, then Grynn, followed by Vash and Vanae, leave the control pod after its landing.

Following a cursory look around, Vash transmitted to each passenger that it was safe to join them, and as the pods released their eager passengers into a new world, they were surprised as each felt their suit immediately adjust to their surroundings. A winter wonderland to the inhabitants of a starship, many of whom had never encountered anything other than stars suspended in the black of night through the windows of the *HELIX*.

While the children and many parents played, the crew started their mission to put in place the holding tower that would be used to collect and treat the water they would require to successfully colonize the planet. Later that day, they would survey the coordinates of the location destined to become their new city. One they would build in cooperation with the life and landscape it touched. The crew was already bursting with ideas for its design. Vash was sure it would be a Lenacyth palace as she surreptitiously eavesdropped on their conversation. She had pondered many of their ideas herself and had to admit she was at least as excited as her children were to begin designing their new home.

The days leading up to entry had been stressful, but now as they walked across the snowy terrain, Vash felt secure; she felt at home. It was not Orbyss, but it felt familiar somehow. For the first time since they had left Orbyss, she felt at ease, that somehow her burden would be shared with this wild new planet. If anyone could tame it, it would be her, and a renewed energy coursed through her veins as they made their way towards the jewel of the planet.

As they stood at the location where they would build their new life, there was not a dry eye. They had made it. And as they looked up, a never-setting sun welcomed them. The crew embraced each other, grateful to have experienced it again, this time alongside their captain.

Shal, still aboard the *HELIX*, made his final round to ensure all was well on the emergency ship. He entered the *new* control pod to take in the sights, and he joined in their tears from the privacy of the ship's helm. Vash's hasty departure seemed to leave an unquiet behind, and Shal felt the need to double-check the function of the pods.

At first, he thought he was mistaken, but a second and third check confirmed it. It was odd, as he reviewed the data, that it would be off. The formation, timing, and position of the pods were just as they had agreed; it was the location of landing that was off, by a full sixteen degrees. While it did not provide cause for alarm, and Shal decided against alerting Vash unnecessarily, it disturbed him. Her calculations were never off. Even a degree would have surprised him. Perhaps it had been intentional, and she had observed something she wanted to avoid on the terrain. That was not unlike her; she often made last-minute decisions and would fail to inform either himself or Grynn. She also liked to keep secrets to prevent unnecessary fear, and quite likely, this was something she had decided upon in the wee hours and neglected to share. Shal knew her well, and there was no way Vash would have slept for a second last night. He had not either.

A light went on in the engine room, Shal's lair, and he left the control pod without delay, further thoughts of the miscalculation forcibly pushed from his mind. He would be spending some time on the emergency ship until everything was functioning perfectly, or at least to his satisfaction.

Perhaps if he weren't called away to the engine room by the red indicator light, he would have noticed another indicator signal insistently flashing a flurry of incoming data. It likely would have taken him some time to notice it, as it was not prioritized as urgent. Although maybe it should have been. The multitude of data points coming in was from the satellites nearly four light-years away pointed at Orbyss; however, instead of one set of data per year, as expected, there was at least one every ten minutes, and the frequency was increasing.

CHAPTER 46

MODA

To choose the most eager amongst them would have been difficult. However, upon close examination, the winner would have undoubtedly been Moda. No one was more excited about exploring Orbyss II than her; a close second was her daughter. Orbyss II was a botanist's dream come true, and to begin building a database of plant life on the planet was something she had dreamt about ever since she had learned of their decision to colonize it. For the past three months, the constant stream of information from the orbiting satellites, S1, S2, and S3, provided proof of photosynthetic life, and it had kept Moda up for nights on end as they approached Orbyss II. It had kept Eelaa awake as well, on the opposite end of their family pod with similar fantasies about what they would discover once they set foot upon their new home.

Now that they had landed safely, Moda was not inclined to waste a moment, let alone a day. She and Eelaa prepared to set out early to survey the belt that inched along the hot side of the planet just next to the edge of the terminator zone. They took the necessary precautions and provisions and planned to be back prior to evening. They were so filled with excitement, they refused to detain themselves a moment past daybreak; the only shadow that dared touch their enthusiasm was the thought that Sond would have loved to have been there with them.

They would be the first to make use of the Vid3s, versatile motorcycles engineered with a Lenacyth shell and frame intended for commutes to and from the hot side of the planet. The cycles would easily fulfill the requirements for the pair's transportation. Speed was low on the list of priorities, but should they lose track of time, it was nice to know it was available to them if they needed to get back in a hurry. As they left their snowy touchdown point and ventured through the habitable zone, they were struck by the beauty of the planet, such biodiversity within only a 480-kilometer span.

While Moda and Eelaa were overcome with anticipation, Vash was full of doubt in the early hours. Something wasn't right; she could just feel it. It had been another sleepless night for her. The pods had been planted a full sixteen degrees off course, and for the life of her, she could not imagine why. If any calculation was more important than this one, she couldn't recall it. She had run through the numbers more times than she could remember, and she had made Grynn and Shal run them alongside her in order to double- and triple-check the accuracy. So how could the pods have possibly landed so far off? She was just about to transmit to Shal that the navigation on the pods may have been damaged when she noticed the incoming satellite feeds from Orbyss, which indicated that she had more than a thousand annual data points to review.

At first, Vash was dumfounded. She shook her head, knowing that it was likely an error, perhaps some malfunction. But as she methodically opened each feed on the control pod screen, the satellites' data points revealed there had been no mistake.

While her heart screamed at her to call out for Grynn and the crew, her head advised against it. She needed time to think this through, not just the impact of the information she had received but why she was receiving it now. How was it that she could be flooded with data points every ten minutes from Orbyss when there was only supposed to be an annual update, as there had been while the HELIX was travelling between Orbyss and Orbyss II? Too much was happening too fast for all of this to be a coincidence. "Think, Vash," she said aloud to herself. Satellite feeds from Orbyss—data points in the thousands, satellites to Orbyss II's sun—lost; the pods landing sixteen degrees off course; and the luminosity of Orbyss II's sun diminished. Then it hit her like an atomic bomb going off inside her brain. Her blood ran cold as she transmitted to Shal. She needed him to deploy three more satellites, this time behind Orbyss II's sun. Far above and behind it. And she hoped against hope that all they would reveal was the infinite starscape of space.

Shal was conveniently in the engine room when he received Vash's transmission. His cooperation came at a price, and once she had shared her worst fears, he sprinted to the cargo hold to release the satellites. They needed to be dispatched at full speed. He wanted to believe this was just Vash's paranoia getting the best of her, as usual, but the sinking feeling in his stomach as the cargo air lock closed behind the satellites immediately following their departure told him otherwise. He scolded himself for not paying more attention. If she were right, they should have connected the dots well before this. But even now, facing the worst, the desire to believe in the new planet, a planet they had taken two decades to reach, seemed to supersede his analytical mind. They had put everything into Orbyss II; it embodied their hopes and dreams for the future, not to mention all sentiment and thoughts of starting a new life in a new home. The power of the planet was supreme, and it overrode logic, even for the most skeptical, even as the voice inside Shal's head told him something was very wrong. Following suit was no use. He scolded himself for imagining the worst without proof, only with Vash's hunch and her catastrophic thinking as his guide. In any case, they would have a definitive answer soon enough. The satellites would begin their transmission in less than four hours.

As Moda and Eelaa made their way to the hot side of the planet, they stopped to mark areas in the terminator zone that they would come back to survey on the back half of their trip. As much as they yearned to take a closer look now, it did not serve well to carry the specimens with them, as they would only weigh them down and may even deteriorate as they made their way into the heat.

"Look at that formation! It looks like there is an opening. Like it might be a cave." Eelaa pointed to a large brilliant-red rock protrusion that jutted out from the ground defiantly, its face, the mouth of the cave, turned away from the hot sun.

"How far away is it?" was Moda's reply. She wanted to head straight for it but relied on her daughter's expertise to ensure that it was safe—personal interest giving way to ensuring the safety of her children, as always.

"It's within the safe zone for the suits and vehicles, but it's a hundred forty-seven kilometers away, so if we want to check it out, we should go straight there, in order to have time left to collect these samples afterwards."

It was all Moda needed to hear, and a bright smile stole her face. "I'll race you!" she challenged her daughter as she engaged the motorcycle and accelerated quickly away from where Eelaa was left sitting with no choice but to stop with her navigation efforts and quickly try to catch up with her mother.

As their clock crept towards the four-hour mark, both Vash and Shal sat paralyzed when they should have been celebrating the arrival at their new home with all the others. Grynn was out surveying the terminator sweet spot with the rest of the crew. Even he was not immune to the building momentum of excitement created by the thought of designing a crown jewel for Orbyss II.

For Vash and Shal, it was an excruciating waiting game neither one wanted any part of. Vash on the ground and Shal up on the ship. It seemed that the only truly safe place for them in the universe was aboard the *HELIX*.

Then the satellite feed filtered in first from S7 and then synchronized messages from both S8 and S9. The twin control pods displayed them in real time as both Vash and Shal sat in identical seats 280 kilometers away from each other.

There was only silence, no transmission. No recognition of each other witnessing exactly the same feeds. They were at a loss for words because their hearts couldn't accept the truth as quickly as their minds were able to process it. It was almost as if, if they didn't acknowledge it, it wouldn't be true. However, the truth was directly in front of them, relayed through the eyes of the three satellites, as plain as day. The singular reason for everything they had been questioning was now displayed larger than life on the twin control pod monitors. The planet was shifting due to the depletion of the gravitational pull from its sun. The border between the habitable zone and the searing heat of the sun was marching ever closer to them as Orbyss II spun towards its dominant star. It was quickly being devoured by a supermassive black hole that lurked directly behind it.

In their excitement, Moda and Eelaa had dropped their vehicles at the mouth of the cave. Hot, dry winds still whipped at the mouth of the cavern they had coerced open long ago. The cave entry was no more than four by eight meters across, and they did not want to disturb anything they might find, so they proceeded on foot. Half a kilometer into the dark opening, they came to a pond below the high canopy where the cave opened up. The ceiling was twice as high at this point, and the lights emitting from their suits illuminated stalactites far above their heads. They glistened as the light reflected the crystalized minerals each were composed of. It was as beautiful as taking in the stars aboard the *HELIX*.

"There must be a waterway that runs through the terminator zone. I think we found a spring, Eelaa. Not bad for our first time out!" Moda was beyond excited at their discovery and could not have been happier that they had decided to head straight for the cave.

As she knelt down beside the pool, her eyes widened at the rich vegetation, some of which floated on the surface of the water. The almost iridescent light-green algae had never seen the light of day. In an effort not to damage its delicate structure, she removed her cumbersome safety gloves.

"Mom, do you think that's safe?" Eelaa was safety first, whereas Moda led with her heart when it came to plants, and she nodded and smiled at her daughter in an effort to ease her worries. The gloves protected against anything harmful, including toxins in the water, and Moda was determined to collect an intact specimen of the delicate algae, like watery lace that floated on the surface of the pool.

As the water enveloped Moda's hand and her fingers reached the underside of the plant, she suddenly lurched forward into an unnatural position.

"Mom, what's wrong?" Eelaa assumed something had startled her.

"It's nothing, love." Her mother pulled her hand towards her and stumbled back against the stalagmites that lined the perimeter of the pond. She held her hand to her chest and winced in pain.

"It *is* something! Look at your suit!" Moda's suit had already identified the lethal toxin and began to cut off circulation at her forearm. "You should have never removed your glove!" Eelaa was sick with worry. What seconds before had been one of the most precious moments they had ever shared was now quickly turning into a nightmare.

Moda tried to focus on Eelaa's words in an effort to soothe her, but the pain that shot through her arm at the bite she had received prevented her full attention. She was dazed by the defensive measure delivered by the planet's most hostile life-form, a primitive albeit venomous form of sea snake that made its home beneath the cover and safety of its food source. And this one had been lunching on the very algae Moda had chosen to retrieve as her specimen.

It hadn't even occurred to her that something large and lethal might inhabit the planet. All life they had observed in the terminator zone was next to microscopic. Nothing that should give them reason for caution or fear.

Moda's suit alarm emitted a bright-red light across her face that was now dripping in sweat. Eelaa knew they had to get her to the medical pod where Dexl could examine her as quickly as possible. It was her only chance. "Mom, we have to get out of here," Eelaa screamed at her mother's red face, blinking in unison with the alarm.

Moda had never felt such pain; she was weak and dizzy, but she had no choice. She had to convince Eelaa they would both make it back.

With as much strength as she could muster, she got to her feet. Desperate to keep her balance, she adjusted the weight of her pack and, in order to disguise her stumble, started off towards the entry at a quickened pace.

"Yes, Eelaa, you are right, we need to leave now," she shouted behind her.

As they reached the mouth of the cave where their personal vehicles waited, Moda could feel adrenaline coursing through her veins as she tried to hide the emergency monitor of her suit from her daughter's frantic eyes. Since they had entered the cave, forty minutes had passed, and despite the fact that they had left both vehicles well within the shade of the cave door, Moda's now lay wind whipped and burning in the sun. It was hot to the touch, and she pulled her unharmed hand away from it instinctively as it burned through the protective layer of the suit's outer glove. A second later, the worst was realized when she summoned the vehicle to life and there was no response.

It was a detail that went unnoticed by Eelaa because it was at that moment that Vash commanded them all back to their pods immediately. They had exactly fifteen minutes to take their place in their respective family pod or their safety could not be guaranteed. If Vash and the others weren't aware that she and Eelaa were missing, they soon would be; therefore, Moda had no time to spare. She choked back the tears that threatened to fall as she looked into her daughter's face.

"You heard that, right?"

Eelaa nodded.

Moda fixed what she hoped was a convincing smile on her face. "Well, let's get going," she transmitted. "We don't have a second to spare."

Moda created a shield with the vehicle and her good arm. As the wind spiraled at the mouth of the cave, it created a vortex so that mother and daughter could not make one another out. As its momentum increased, they could not see within three centimeters of their faces.

Instead, they would be forced to rely on the suits' navigation, and this was what made Moda's subterfuge possible.

"Mom! The suit is not holding up. The heat is burning me!" Eelaa transmitted as she started her return.

"I know, Eelaa, mine's burning me too." Moda was terrified for her daughter. The thought of losing Eelaa made her forget her own pain entirely. She continued choking back her tears. "We just have to hurry; we are almost there. We will make it, love."

Moda watched Eelaa's progress on her own suit's navigation display that was synced with her daughter's, and continued to transmit to Eelaa's until she had made it safely back inside the terminator zone. In between their conversation, she transmitted to both Shal and Tirus in confidence. She told them she loved them, explained the situation, and asked that Tirus be there for Eelaa as soon as she arrived, and she shared her daughter's coordinates with him. These were their final moments together. The last time in the universe she would share with her family, and she asked that they both pass on her love and consuming regret to her daughter.

Now alone, save for Shal's heart-wrenching sobs, Moda watched Eelaa's progress on her navigation screen and kept up with her faux transmissions, pretending to be right beside her. While her heart remained with her daughter, her body walked back into the cave, back towards the lethal pond that had stolen her life. Ultimately, she had no malice for the creature in the water; if anyone was at fault, it was her, overeager to make the acquaintance of all life on the new planet. But now, in her final moments, as she stared pensively into the pool, the skin of her suit burning into her flesh, she wondered if the venom that would soon take her life had also caused her to hallucinate, as the pond's water had started to boil.

CHAPTER 47

VASH

5.65 (Morning) / Orbyss II / The Same Day

A bright light reflected off every surface Vash's eyes rested upon. It seemed meant to blind her while simultaneously drawing her attention. She knew better than to panic, but the lack of sleep and the blinding rays were making it nearly impossible for her to suffocate the fear that rose within her. Adrenaline kicked in and then a pounding; she could feel her heart beating in her chest, echoing in her ears, and the world blurred before her as her hand shook at the controls.

"How much time do you think we have?" Herriden had never seen her this way. She seemed to have aged fifty years in the last five minutes.

"Herriden, if you continue to ask questions you know full well I have no answer for, then it's over for us, we won't stand a chance." Vash regained her composure only thanks to his presence. Her children alone allowed her to dig so deeply within herself, deep enough to fight off her own fears, so that theirs would not have to be realized.

She continued, "Now listen to me because I literally do not have time to repeat myself. Find your father and Vanae. You need to leave immediately for the *HELIX*. I will join you after the last pod departs."

"And leave you down here alone? No way!"

"Herriden, you are not leaving me down here. If you don't start listening to what I am saying from this very moment on, we are all going to burn down here. Get your father and sister up to the ship so that you can organize everyone once the pods reassemble. I'm not telling you this as an attempt to dissuade you; I *need* you on the other side. I need you to take charge of the *HELIX*, and I need you to do it right now. You wanted to be the captain of the HELIX, so what the hell are you waiting for? *Go!*"

He enveloped her in a crushing embrace that brought tears to her eyes, tears he would never see. He raced from the control pod in order to carry out her orders exactly as she had commanded. He knew that the only way to save her now was to do exactly what she said. They all needed her, and it was up to him to make sure she completed the mission, one that would hopefully save all their lives.

Vash had done it. She wilted into her seat. She had managed to achieve his compliance while covering the display for the control pod's exterior protective shell that was already reading amber and climbing quickly towards red. Vash felt sick. The Lenacyth had never been engineered to withstand the intensity of the heat from the red side of Orbyss II. She watched from the control pod window and held her breath, hating each second that passed that did not take her family's pod back to the *HELIX*.

If it were up to her, she would be right behind them. If she had only herself to worry about, her family would be the first to leave Orbyss II and never look back. But instead, she switched the pod's monitor to the surveillance of Tirus. He was making good time and had almost reached Eelaa. She had to survive. Shal was overcome with grief at having lost Moda and was barely holding himself together. It was now up to Vash to ensure that the rest of Shal's family made it back to him alive.

"How is she? Please tell me she made it."

Tirus's voice choked at the sound of Vash's. "Her suit indicates that she is breathing, but she is unconscious, she won't respond to me, Vash."

"You need to get her to the medical pod as fast as you can, Tirus! Dexl knows that you are coming and is waiting for you. He will assist as soon as you can get her there. You are not to wait for him to start administering; you are to leave immediately for the *HELIX*. Do you understand me?"

Tirus transmitted a "Thank you" back to her. Which forced fresh tears from her eyes. To sit helpless in her control pod seat, resting on the surface of Orbyss II, a now non-tidally locked planet turning ever closer to the fire, was more than she could stand. She felt helpless without the *HELIX* beneath her feet. Everything she had ever done, all the planning, preparation, and care she had taken, would be for nothing if they couldn't get back to the ship. Anxiety threatened to take over her; she could barely stop the thoughts of blame and regret long enough to realize that self-loathing was a luxury at this point. One cannot imagine the height of self-hate that comes at a moment when you realize thousands of lives have been impacted by your decisions and your failures. And she wished for her own death instead of having to attempt to bear the pain of potentially watching them all die on Orbyss II alongside her.

Out of the corner of her eye, she detected movement. The medical pod lifted slightly, then rose six meters. Her tears fell again as she transmitted to Herriden.

"You need to follow the medical pod back to the ship now. You need to be there to help Eelaa."

He didn't bother to transmit back, knowing it would provide more assurance for her to see their family pod lift off and follow the medical pod up to the *HELIX*.

"Shal, I need you to initiate the reconfiguration. The medical pod and my family pod are en route. Can you do that?"

She felt sick as she waited for his reply. "Of course, Vash. I am already on it."

She wanted to say she was so sorry, so very sorry. That this was all her fault, and that she could never make this up to him, but she wanted the chance to try. But she stopped herself. She knew that would be too much for him to take, so all she had left to say was: "Confirmed, they will be arriving in three minutes."

She didn't imagine it would happen, that she was even capable of it, based on what she had experienced only moments before, but now that she was confident they would make it, she completely regained composure. It was the difference between night and day. Now she could think clearly again. To know that at least her family had made it out alive was all she needed in order to do what was necessary to save the rest. She looked down again at the pod's exterior monitor as it approached red and decided to turn it off. Watching the countdown would not serve her, not now. She needed to complete the calculations. And she could not afford to be wrong because she couldn't rely on Shal to check them, not in his state.

She waited for Herriden to confirm that they had made it. He needed to take over from Shal in order to complete the reconfiguration of the rest of the pods.

"I am ready." Herriden's transmission gave her new life. As his words echoed in her head and hope rose within her chest, she transmitted the command she had been stifling with angst for the last twenty minutes.

"All passengers depart immediately for the HELIX. I repeat, all passengers depart immediately."

Before her transmission was complete, the first of the pods lifted. Their passengers did not realize it yet, but now they were under the command of a new captain. Tears chased each other down her cheeks, and Vash desperately tried to wipe them away so that she could continue to inspect the pods for even the slightest signs of failure. Her eyes darted from pod to pod as she held her breath, willing them to leave Orbyss II's atmosphere as gracefully as they had arrived. One by one, they disappeared until she watched the very last of them climb out of sight towards the safety of the *HELIX.*

That moment was to be her last chance. She could have made it had she left within four seconds, assuming a position behind the last pod. But she refused to leave without confirmation from Herriden that they were all ready. That they had made it. She was the ultimate captain, the one who would go down, instead of the ship. She surveyed the sky, desperate that none of them would fall back down towards her. She waited and waited, then turned in horror as Grynn entered the control pod.

"You didn't think I would actually leave you down here alone, did you?" Grynn entered the control pod relieved to have made it to her through the scorching blaze of a planet on fire.

Vash bolted from her seat, straight into his arms. His suit burned through hers, but she didn't care; she barely noticed. The remaining tears she had left her eyes, and as the pod emergency alarm sounded that its protective shell had been compromised, she silenced it. There would be no leaving Orbyss II for them; this would be their grave, their crematorium.

To feel his arms around her gave her the comfort and strength she needed to accept their fate, one he had already embraced many years ago. Herriden transmitted that all pods were in place, and as they awaited her arrival, she transmitted back to him, "Thank you, thank you for sending him to me."

CHAPTER 48

HERRIDEN

7.12 (Morning) / The *HELIX* / Later That Day

Herriden's initiation as captain of the *HELIX* would be baptism by fire. He took his seat at the helm of the twin control pods aboard the ship in synchronicity, as Vash claimed hers on Orbyss II below him, with Grynn now at her side.

"Will you guys please get up here?" Herriden transmitted to them.

"No, we have a few things to run over first. There is plenty of time," Vash lied. Herriden knew something was up, and already he felt the impatient weight of the *HELIX* take position upon a new set of shoulders, his shoulders, and he thought better than to question her, especially with Shal, Vanae, and Tirus present.

"OK, so where are we heading to, once you guys board?" Herriden was not about to let her get away without a fight. "I assume you don't want to stick around for a front-row seat to Orbyss II's destruction and risk getting sucked into the black hole right along with it."

Vash laughed despite herself. So, he was capable of humor, albeit sarcasm, at a time like this. That was a good sign.

"No, right you are. But as it turns out, we are going to use the means of our destruction to our advantage. You are going to slingshot the *HELIX* around the black hole. We are headed to Orbyss III, Herriden." Vash wanted them all to hear it. The sooner they got over the shock and accepted the plan, the sooner they would be out of harm's way.

Her words shook Shal out of his grief. "Vash, this is insane, the *HELIX* was never meant to withstand . . . Our modular control systems cannot support this even if the infrastructure . . ."

At that moment, Dexl entered the room, without waiting for acknowledgment and without saying a word. His expression said it all, and Tirus stole the words from his lips. "Eelaa!"

Dexl nodded, and Shal and Tirus sprinted behind Dexl to the medical pod where Eelaa was fighting for her life.

A fresh set of tears washed Vash's face. But she was out of time; they all were. They had to remain on task, and her next words replaced the worried expressions on her children's faces with ones of shock. "You will not fail at this. You can't!"

She continued, "Herriden, I need you to retrieve something from the space directly under the control module." Shaking his head in disbelief of what was happening, he somehow managed to comply. He didn't know what he had expected to find, but he never would have guessed it would be the model of the *HELIX* he and his sister had built nearly fifteen years prior.

"Why are we looking at this?" Both Herriden and Vanae stared at the toy as if they didn't recognize the ship on which they had spent the last twenty-plus years of their lives save for one night and the equivalent hours of one full day on Orbyss II.

"I need you both to remember this. Listen very carefully to what I am about to tell you. This ship is the first example I can recall of the two of you working together to create something worth saving. I have kept it with me for all these years. It is precious, and it is a symbol of what you will do together today and for the rest of your lives. As long as you remember that together there is nothing you can't accomplish, the *HELIX* will protect you; it will stay intact, just like this ship you built."

Vash paused for a moment; this next part would be tough. She was grateful it was just their family. They needed this moment alone, together.

"We won't be joining you. The control pod exterior has been compromised, and its engine has ruptured. You will be leaving without me and your father, but we will be with you every step of the way."

"*No!* I am coming down to get you both!" Vanae was on her feet and heading towards the control pod entry. Fury crossed her face as angry tears streamed down her cheeks. She felt betrayed.

It was Herriden who stopped her. He had known long before Vash said the words. Vash had forgotten momentarily that her pod was linked to his and that all indicators, even the one signaling that the shell of her pod had been compromised, were identical. Now that she had confirmed there was no error, that her control pod's exterior had failed, he had nothing left to hold on to but his sister.

"You will never make it back, Vanae. You can't leave," was all Herriden could manage. She melted to the floor, and he wanted nothing more than to follow her, but instead, he turned to Vash on his screen. His eyes met his mother's as both she and Grynn placed their hands up to the monitor. Herriden and Vanae, now standing behind him, both repeated the gesture, and they said their last goodbyes to their parents from low orbit of the planet intended to offer salvation that instead had delivered slaughter.

Vash very deliberately took her seat, ushering Herriden to do the same. They all followed her mechanical actions, terrified to stray from her lead. Now that farewell was accomplished, Vash, as expected, would become binary. There was no time left for further tears, regardless of how desperately they were deserved.

"The only way you can avoid being consumed by the supermassive black hole that exists behind Orbyss II's sun is by reaching interstellar speed. It is going to be very difficult to navigate, especially against the pull of the hole's gravitational force. It will also be difficult to navigate the trajectory of the curve the *HELIX* will be forced to take. But it is possible."

She continued, "Vanae, I need you to double-check my calculations while I run through the details with Herriden."

Had they had more time, she would have put everything through simulation, multiple times. Perhaps it was a blessing, because if her plan was destined for failure, at this point, she didn't want to know.

Herriden's suit worked double time against the sweat that continually pooled on his skin. The more his mother explained, the more his fear mounted. She could sense his terror.

"Herriden, you aren't going to do this on your own; I will be right with you the entire time." Her son seemed to relax slightly, and tears pooled in his eyes.

"No time for tears, son. Tell all the passengers to leave their pods. You may be left with only the emergency ship if the pods are lost, so you need to move all the passengers now."

He did as he was told, indicating via transmission that all passengers were to seek a safe spot within the emergency ship. Even in her delicate condition, Eelaa would have to be moved, as well. There was no other option.

As he finished the transmission, he could almost feel the questions and concern of the passengers. They had expected to hear from Vash, their captain, and so she set out to put their minds at ease, transmitting a follow-up to Herriden's command as if she were the one at the helm. She informed them of their trip, that they would be attempting to travel to Orbyss III and the only way to get there successfully on the power they had left was to slingshot at the edge of a black hole using its immense gravity to propel the *HELIX* to near light speed.

Following her transmission, the evacuation of the pods accelerated as they uniformly made their procession to safety. For those who could recall it, it was much like when they had first boarded the ship. The only detail Vash left out was that she would not be joining them. It was no matter. They had all accepted that Herriden would be the next captain long ago.

Vash began to relax, despite the fact that the monitor on the exterior was well into the red, and she and Grynn could hear the searing hiss of the Lenacyth shell as the sun burned through the control pod's protective layer. Orbyss II was now rotating at an ever-increasing speed due to the ongoing decrease in the gravitational pull from the sun. Soon the control pod would be completely compromised, and they would not survive the temperature for more than fifteen or twenty minutes.

"Herriden, can you confirm that they have all evacuated?"

"I'll go," Vanae said. "But before I do, you should know that your calculations are perfect, Mom. I can't find an error." Vanae hid her face as the last of her words dropped off and she was overcome with emotion. She couldn't believe this was happening.

"I'm proud of you," Vash shouted out to her before Vanae left the pod. "I'm so very proud of you both, I always have been, and I always will be."

Herriden and Vash went over the plans and discussed how he would need to take over manual control of the ship. "It is going to feel like the ship is breaking apart, but I need you to believe that won't happen. The *HELIX* can take much more than you think. It is strong, just like you and your sister. Promise me that you will believe this. You cannot fail. You cannot give up."

He nodded in reply just as Vanae reentered the pod to confirm that they were ready.

Herriden initiated the sequence to deploy the nuclear fusion engines, which could only be accomplished from the control pod aboard the ship as a safety measure, and the countdown began. True to her nature, Vash needed to ensure everything was in order, and Herriden watched from his seat as she prepared the last of the required instrumentation settings for the *HELIX*'s next trip from her own controls on the ground. The sure strokes of her hand commanding the starship, the indicator lights responding to her effortless touch; it was what she had been born to do. He watched the sequence display on his own board as if it were a self-playing instrument, when he knew that nothing could be further from the truth.

He had to stay sharp and follow her every move. Just in case. Just in case he lost her too soon.

"OK, Herriden, you're ready now." The thrust of the engines pushed the ship slightly forward. The unmistakable roar of their ignition echoed through the *HELIX* as he pointed the ship high above Orbyss II's sun at an angle that would take it safely around the black hole.

"Remember, I will be with you." She smiled at him, her face on the feed of his monitor. "Everything, all the new data we have collected from the satellites directed at Orbyss, is there for you. You will need to study it all, and there is one more thing you and only you must know right now, as we do not want to alarm the others with even more than they have already suffered. The satellite data from Orbyss is changing rapidly. The annual data points have been received at an alarming rate, which is ever increasing. Our proximity to this massive gravitational field has slowed down time compared to that on Orbyss. The field is so immense that it pulls time into the black hole, and therefore, many years may have passed on Orbyss compared to the twenty years that have passed here for us. Orbyss may have changed dramatically. It may even be habitable again. However, if there is life, you need to promise me that you will never harm it. Orbyss may no longer be ours, Herriden. You need to respect that."

There was so much to convey, but she tried to say as little as possible. He had an overwhelming task ahead of him. Orbyss could wait. If there was one word to describe Herriden, it was Percivious. This was clear to her now. Her son, Herra's son, embodied the definition, even to the extent of his own demise. Herriden was not only capable but made it a priority to put others first, in every situation, even should it be undeserved.

There was no further time to lament, no time to second-guess or question themselves. Vash watched the *HELIX* leave low Orbyss II orbit on her pod's monitor and make quick work of its path. As Herriden took over manual control in order to manage the curve, the shaking began. Vash watched from their shared display the exterior of the ship, as the pods shook in tandem with the acceleration. Herriden was terrified as he held tight to the controls, too terrified to scream. That was not the case in the emergency ship as passengers held on to one another, their tears and cries fully consuming the air around them.

"You are good, you are right on track. I told you there would be turbulence. Just hold on tight." It scared her to see the veins protrude from her son's red neck, and to watch his face jolt. His body, clearly visible on her monitor, echoed the ship's leaps, made visible on the feed. She could only imagine their ride, the horror of it, but they had no other choice.

As he made the curve round to the zenith of Orbyss II's dominant star, she could see it now, clearly displayed on her monitor from the *HELIX*'s exterior feed. The relatively small black circle, devouring Orbyss II's sun. To watch it being consumed filled her with fear, dread, and compunction. What had she done? What if they didn't make it? She almost screamed at Herriden to turn back.

He sensed her dismay. "I can do this, Mom. Trust me, I've got this."

If he didn't trust his mother's almost flawless calculations, he trusted Vanae's. Just as Vash had commanded, they would do this together, and it was with Vanae's help that he stayed on course. She seemed fearless, composed. There seemed to be no question in her mind that they would make it, and she steadied him.

For Vash, it was terrifying to watch them pick up speed. The feed on her monitor started to flicker. She wouldn't be able to see them much longer. Before she could verbalize her final goodbye, the monitor went dead. Vash and Grynn were left with nothing but the heat, hiss, and smell of their burning pod.

She did the only thing she could think of at that moment. She transmitted to her son, "I am still with you, just open your eyes."

It was evolution, strong enough to conquer space. And after Herriden let her in, Vash continued to navigate the ship with him, safely past the black hole, travelling at three-fourths the speed of light, looking on through her son's eyes.

CHAPTER 49

EELAA

She opened her eyes. As they adjusted to the screen at the foot of her bed that monitored her every breath, she realized she had no recollection of what had happened, where she was, or how she had ended up there. Her head pleaded with her to go back to sleep. The throbbing pain at her temples reigned over lucid thought, and the only thing numbing the agony from the burns that covered her body was the steady drip of neuromodulators, which were due for a top-up.

A distant memory nagged at her; it was small droplets, at first, that rapidly accumulated, then washed through her mind like a tidal wave. Everything. Moda. The fire that burned through her as they fled together from the hot side of Orbyss II. She had to find her. Where was her mom? Why wasn't she beside her?

Dexl was notified by the medical pod interface as soon as Eelaa had regained consciousness. He rushed to her aid despite also having to tend to the onslaught of injuries suffered by many of the passengers during their adrenaline-fueled jaunt around the black hole. The *HELIX*, once again their savior, had not gone unpunished. It was now a pared-down version of itself, having lost nearly half the pods to the force of the hole.

The emergency ship had saved them and was functioning as well as could be expected, but with only one of the four nuclear fusion engines spared. Shal and Tirus worked double time in order to maintain the centrifugal force needed to simulate gravity as it had been prior. The *HELIX*, despite running on only one of four engines, was maintaining its extreme speed from the slingshot maneuver.

No one had slept, save Eelaa, since leaving Orbyss II. It was all hands on deck, especially for Dexl, who literally could not keep up. But he needed some good news, and as Eelaa's monitor displayed her activity in the medical pod, he immediately left the grand foyer directly outside the air lock that had become their makeshift sick bay. He had been desperately waiting for any sign of her recovery. She needed to hold on. Her burnt body was barely staying with her. Dexl had done everything he could under the circumstances. He cursed when they were forced to move her and would never forgive himself for not fighting harder to keep her in the medical pod, which, by some miracle, had managed to stay with the ship. He would never forgive himself, now knowing that it could have protected her throughout their slingshot around the black hole.

Dexl navigated the beds and bodies as quickly as he could manage, ignoring requests for his attention with a raised hand. It was never ending: the injuries, the lacerations, the cries. They had suffered 8,212 casualties due to high-speed impact. Neither the suits nor the ship had been designed to retain the magnetic safety function required. The turbulence was crippling, for both the ship as well as its passengers. The *HELIX* was a bird caught at the edge of a hurricane, flying for its life. Herriden, sitting at the helm, refused to blink, refused to let a second pass without his full concentration. All hope began and ended with him, but he did not stand alone. Vash had remained with him till the end, as long as she could.

He had not realized that she was gone until well after they had left the hole behind. It was Dexl who entered the control pod to find both him and Vanae, two shaken leaves fallen to the floor, behind the control board in an embrace anointed by falling tears. He offered his assistance and his hand. All three knew that comfort was a luxury they could not afford, one that would have to wait. And in that moment, the crown was passed on to Herriden, Vash's successor. A coronation well before its time. One without cause for celebration, one neither coveted nor envied.

Herriden raced a half pace behind Dexl on his own path to the medical pod. Dexl had transmitted to him as soon as he had been notified that Eelaa had regained consciousness. Ultimately it had been Herriden's call to move her. He could not bring himself to leave her in the medical pod knowing full well it might be torn from the ship and left drifting in space. There would have been no opportunity to turn back to retrieve her. And so it was, both of them pining away for her to return to them, based on the decisions they had either fought for or against, decisions they had made on her behalf.

As Dexl and Herriden entered the room, they both took in her searching gaze. Her blue eyes, seemingly the only feature left untouched by the fire of Orbyss II.

"Eelaa, it's Herriden. Oh, Eelaa, do you remember what happened? I know you are in a lot of pain, but—"

She stopped him with a hoarse whisper. She seemed determined to speak.

"My mom?"

He shook his head as tears filled his eyes. Tears that surprised him only because he thought he was incapable of crying more, so excruciating had the past five days been for them all.

Herriden tried not to put any weight on her body, imagining her discomfort. He knelt beside her, and they both cried as Dexl administered more of the medication that kept her pain at bay. They were both motherless now. Left with only the *HELIX* as surrogate.

CHAPTER 50

VANAE

5.72 (Morning) / The *HELIX* / Three
Months After Leaving Orbyss II

Vanae wanted out. Back on the *HELIX*, or what was left of it, she felt locked in the trunk of a car. Without her mother to buffer the weight of the ship and its constant demands, life had become more stifling than Vanae had thought possible. Every minute of every day seemed filled with one of a hundred tasks that required immediate attention. Vanae and Herriden could barely keep up, and on top of grieving both their parents, they were left to manage what Vash had kept hidden.

Both of them had a renewed appreciation for what their mother had shouldered, the quiet burden that gradually consumed her. Vanae was constantly asking the same question: How in the world had she done it all? What Vash had accomplished, the responsibility she and Herriden now shared, was nearly impossible to believe. Vash had directed the circus while her two children had been designing suits and racing crafts. Vanae wasn't sure she would have extended the same courtesy now that she stood in her mother's shoes. Vash had sheltered them all, and it had gone largely unrealized and unappreciated.

Arguably, Shal had always been there to assist her, just as he helped Herriden and Vanae now, despite his grief. But it had become abundantly clear that the split had always been eighty/twenty, Vash/Shal. Now all of them had been forced to come together in order to manage the ship in emergency mode as they tried to conserve what little energy they had left. In an effort to be pragmatic, at least until they figured out a way to make it to Orbyss III, the ship ran at low power, and they literally coasted on the momentum garnered from the gravity of the black hole. They would continue to travel at nearly half of the speed of light, but would it be consistent and fast enough to enable them to reach Orbyss III in a reasonable time frame? There was absolutely no way Vanae would tolerate both being born and eventually dying on this ship of disaster that had already taken so much from them. And this alone, this never-ending drift through space, was what tormented her. She could stomach being trapped on the *HELIX* heading towards a destination within a certain time frame, but being trapped on the *HELIX* with no idea if or when she would be getting off was more than she could take.

Herriden had banished her from the control pod on more than one occasion. It was impossible for her to just sit beside him and wait for the next emergency the damaged ship would conjure. He possessed the patience she lacked, and until they had a plan in place, Vanae needed to keep her brilliant mind occupied. Shal was the only one in possession of both the experience and expertise required to determine what the ship could take, and until he fully assessed the functionality of the *HELIX*, they would have no clear answers.

Grudgingly, Vanae agreed with her brother, and now that they were out of danger, and the ship and its passengers were stable, she and Herriden both decided she would turn her attention to the satellite feed they had been receiving from Orbyss. The satellites pointed at Orbyss, which they had put in place prior to their departure, delivered data from their position in the asteroid field in annual Earth time. Even as they had landed on Orbyss II, thousands of bits of data had been received. However, before today, they had been consumed with putting out fires on the *HELIX* following their escape. It was only now that Vanae would begin the arduous task of sifting through the feeds. It was like a puzzle with a million pieces, and she had no idea how long it would take to make sense of it all.

Since landing on Orbyss II, they had begun receiving a thousand transmissions per day; in other words, they were receiving a thousand Earth years' worth of incoming messages in one day. Now, realizing the fact too late, it was obviously due to the gravitational force of the supermassive black hole that had since swallowed Orbyss II.

As the *HELIX* had skimmed by the black hole, its ever-increasing gravity multiplied that time dilation by more than a hundredfold. Literally, hundreds of millions of years had passed on Orbyss, and consequently, the number of satellite messages had also increased exponentially. The only thing in Vanae's favor, the one thing she had on her side, was time. Until they decided how far they could travel, she had endless amounts of it, and what better way to make use of it than to find an answer to the question: What did the landslide of data they had received from the satellites contain?

She had become a cynic and fully expected the apparent increase in number to potentially be an error caused by their slingshot around the black hole, perhaps a multiplication of the same feeds, but she had nothing better to do than take a look. She had more respect for her mother now than she had ever had when Vash was alive. If her mother had wanted them to take a close look at it, then Vanae had to assume there was good reason. If anything, it was better than tending to the "baby," aka the *HELIX*.

Vanae was not suited to this, any of it. She craved action and adventure, at least a solid distraction. Sifting through image after image was arduous for her, and her mind began to drift just like the ship that carried her. Hours, days, weeks passed, and there was nothing of significance to observe. She was ready to quit, perhaps ready to give up entirely, when from the recesses of a disbelieving mind, something on the feed caught her attention. Hours of images at every angle revealed a dead planet, until out of nowhere, what had been a surface of strictly grey or brown, in all its kaleidoscope of shades, suddenly changed. On the north tip of the planet, there was now a contrasting area, one that had not been there before. It was black, or the darkest shade of blue. An undeniable indication of the presence of water.

Vanae's heart raced. She took a closer look at the next satellite feed from the same angle, and there it was, clear as day. Water. And water meant the potential for life. She sprinted from the living pod she still shared with her brother, which had fortuitously been spared during their hasty departure from Orbyss II. Vanae was overcome with excitement. She hardly trusted her own eyes as she raced to the control pod to show Herriden. Perhaps *she* had been the one to uncover the answer. Perhaps *she* would be the one to save them all from being lost in space. Perhaps *she* had discovered that their next home could be their first.

CHAPTER 51

HERRIDEN

The *HELIX* had become the hero's burden, and Herriden was ultimately its beast. He labored for the ship's benefit, night and day, so that
the remaining 99,167 passengers aboard could fulfill their purpose and
continue the species, even if that meant living aboard a starship travelling indefinitely through space.

Now there was a glimmer of hope aboard the *HELIX*. It seemed
Vanae, with her exhausting scrutiny of the satellite feed, had been
correct. And upon her vindication, she was incapable of keeping the
information to herself, so unlike her mother. The promise of water, a
renewal, a return to their original home, caused a current of excitement
to spread through the ship. A potential return to Orbyss breathed life
into passengers who had lost almost everything to Orbyss II, and their
thin escape from it. It seemed their luck had changed; no longer would
they be fated to inhabit a planet destined for destruction. They would
make their way back home—this time, hopefully for good.

Vanae had experienced nothing but exhilaration since her discovery was acknowledged by the crew. Shal, their biggest skeptic, had even begun to discuss a return to Orbyss, with the faintest spark of hope in his eyes. The possibility was especially potent to those of them who had grown up on the planet, the ones old enough to remember it. Even though they tried to contain themselves, their shared discussions transferred ripples of anticipation through to their offspring, who could only compare it to their parents' reactions in the days leading up to landing on Orbyss II. If they felt the need to share every memory, every rite of passage and anecdote that had shaped their formative years, then from what their children could discern, they were headed to paradise by returning to Orbyss.

Herriden wanted nothing more than to deliver their fantasy, but he had been through too much to make any promises, even to himself. He smiled and nodded in response to their enthusiasms, but that was as far as he went. It was especially challenging to manage Vanae, who would have teleported back immediately had the option presented itself. In her head, she was already on Orbyss, and she and Tirus spent hours discussing not only how best to return but also what to do first once they arrived.

For Herriden, it was exhausting, his attempts to keep the crew's feet on the ground. It didn't help that ground only pertained to the floor of a starship. He had grown old before his years; the *HELIX* was like having a perpetual newborn with chronic colic. It demanded his attention both day and night, and now that Vanae had discovered water on Orbyss, she had little time for what was supposed to be a joint venture. It would appear that Vanae had no inclination for mothering, even if it was required by the ship on which her life depended. In her head, she was fully justified in devoting her attention exclusively to the satellites. That was her contribution, one just as, if not more important, than checking off the daily tasks required to keep the *HELIX* afloat.

If it weren't for Eelaa, Herriden feared he could not have kept his head. There were many times he wanted to rid himself of Vanae, relinquish her access to the control pod indefinitely and take over Vash's old role in its entirety. But in those moments, he found Eelaa. She was an elixir, the solution to whatever plagued him—in most cases, Vanae. She was the one to remind him just how much they needed each other.

That he and his sister were opposite sides of the same coin. Vash had found magic in the pair, and she had known just how to extract the very best from each of them. She had fashioned the ultimate captain for her starship out of her two children. But everyone knew that Herriden was always meant to be at the helm, and this was what Eelaa so eloquently would remind him of, time and again. That only he could save them all at the end of the day. It was her strength, despite everything she had lost, that kept him still in the face of the storms only the *HELIX* seemed capable of placing in his path. It seemed to blow hard at him, as if it wanted to show him just how ruthless it could be, that it hadn't accepted him as its new master, even if its passengers had long ago.

Eelaa had escaped Orbyss II with her life, but barely. Her scars had transformed beauty to horror. Everything had mutated due to her burns, including her voice. The only thing that remained intact was her unending empathy—the essence of what made her who she was, the most beautiful amongst them. For Herriden, for all of them, it was inconsequential; they saw Eelaa as she had been, would always be. The only reminder of the dramatic change was the immature response to her disfiguration by the very young XYZs. She would smile at them in return and win them over despite her grotesque appearance. She was something that could never be destroyed or forsaken.

It was generally assumed that she and Herriden were a couple. It was as if they had always been destined, and now more than ever, they were an embodiment of love conquering all. This sentiment was attached to the couple by an abundance of well-wishers. Everyone aboard the ship expected they would soon share their own pod and family. Even with Eelaa's limited mobility, due to the severe burns that had charred through to her bones, Herriden refused to see her any differently than how he remembered her; to him, she was exactly the same. It would be difficult for her to care for a child, if she were capable of having one, but the fact mattered little to him, if it even entered his thoughts. Herriden already had his hands full with his firstborn, the *HELIX*. And a species who viewed every child aboard the ship with the same love and consideration as their own would be quick to come to Eelaa's aid if she were to have one, as quickly as Herriden's birth mother had made her sacrifice for his best friend.

CHAPTER 52

TIRUS

Tirus kept a vigil in the observation pod, despite knowing Vash would never join him again. It was his tribute to Vash and the mornings they had spent together staring out at the stars. It was the one place aboard the *HELIX* that remained virtually unchanged. The only difference being the celestial configurations ever in flux as they charted a new course to Orbyss.

Tirus laughed when Vanae entered the pod. Obviously, she had been searching for him for some time, judging by the impatient look on her face. She was insatiable, all the way round. Keeping up with Vanae was not for the faint of heart. But as for Tirus's heart, she kept it beating, fast.

He knew his time in the dome was done now, and that they would be heading back to the feed. Vanae had all but stolen him from his father, who was now on his own, more or less, to get them back home. Vanae had decided that Tirus's time was much better spent with her, instead of with Shal in the engine pods. Besides, Rahl could assist Shal, as he was much better suited to it, in her opinion. This left Rahl disappointed upon hearing her decision. Shal was no substitute for Vanae. Despite Rahl's passion for the ship's engines and the secrets they held, nothing could compare to his hunger for her.

It was a covert operation. Tirus and Vanae were closet anthropologists, digging through the satellites' feed for remnants, artifacts, anything they could use to piece together the story of Orbyss since they had escaped. They shared their esoteric findings only if and when they saw fit. Tirus knew that Herriden would be appalled by what Vanae left out. The volumes and volumes of data she skipped over in order to "get to the good stuff" were staggering. However, he placated himself, vowing in silence that if they did come across anything that would change their course, and Vanae refused to share the information in a timely fashion, he would do so himself. He was bound to her. She was a goddess to him, and he would go along with anything she asked of him—as long as it was best for them all.

"I should have started my search for you here, obviously. We need to get back to the data. I want to show you something!" Vanae's eyes lit up. It was evident she had discovered something new. He had to admit that it gave him immense pleasure to know that he would be the only one to share this latest secret with her, that she would seek him out first.

Once they arrived at the pod Vanae had claimed for her ongoing project, together they reviewed what they had managed to observe thus far. The initial water she had identified had progressively spread across the planet as the millions of data points from the satellites progressed in kind. From where they had left off, she estimated that water covered approximately 75 percent of the planet. It would seem that their original home had recovered from the assault of the asteroid and, not unlike their species, had also managed to survive the disaster. As they took in file after file, the images became more and more promising. Orbyss had indeed recovered nicely and was exhibiting many of the same characteristics it had embodied prior to their departure. Its daily rotation, its orbit around the sun, and its atmosphere were all similar to when they had left.

As Tirus and Vanae sat down at the imaging consul, which had become a permanent perch for the pair, Vanae could hardly contain herself.

"Look at this!" Far ahead, actually millions of years ahead of where they had last been studying the data, she pulled up a file.

"There, can you believe that! It's not brown, it's not blue . . . that is *green*!"

Tirus moved the file directly in front of him and enlarged the image. "I'm not sure, Vanae. That could be a false color image. It could be an incorporation of infrared light . . . or it could just be sediment."

"Yes, of course. I thought of that too. But how do you explain this?" Vanae pulled up another file, at least another ten million years later, in the exact location. And the image was undeniable. Not only was there vegetation on Orbyss now but there were forests. The feed would bring immense hope not only to the crew but to every passenger aboard the *HELIX*.

"Vanae! This is incredible! We have to let the others know! But, listen, you should have waited and we should have gone through them one by one, as we agreed to. What if you missed something? We need to document the findings in sequential order. We can't afford to miss anything. You know that!"

"So, what if I did miss something? Who cares? Look what I found!"

Tirus knew better than to continue chastising her. She was like steel. His words had no hope of making a dent. "We have to get this to Herriden. It's incredible, Vanae! The potential to pick up where we left off. This is beyond our wildest hopes and dreams!"

"You go tell him, Tirus! He would rather hear it from you anyway."

"No! You should come with me. This is your discovery."

"Yes, and one that he will no doubt criticize me for, just as you did a moment ago. Herriden will not look kindly on jumping ahead in the feed. He is much too tedious for that."

Tirus could sense that the rift that had started to form between Vanae and Herriden was securely in place now, and it troubled him. He made a mental note to see what he could do to help repair it as he kissed Vanae on the lips. Before he left her, he whispered a promise that he would return to her soon. She smiled back at him, a smile that stayed on her lips until after he had left but then pursed into a thin line of concentration.

She had sent him to Herriden by design. Now, more than ever, she felt vindicated in her decision, despite him castigating her exuberance.

In defiance, she pulled the feed from the most recent satellite transmission they had received and immediately displayed the file on the screen in front of her. She would waste no time for fear of Tirus's return or any number of potential interruptions.

As soon as she initiated the command and the corresponding image filled the center of her screen, her eyes widened in disbelief, horror, and wonder, all together, all at the same time. They screamed from within their sockets. A forest on Orbyss was nothing. Nothing compared to the images that had begun to blur her vision. Her hands shook on the console. She blinked through tears of disbelief and terror at a civilization like nothing she had ever seen or imagined. Not only was there intelligent life on Orbyss but there was an apex species, one that had taken the planet for itself.

CHAPTER 53

HERRIDEN

Herriden stood at the window of the control pod taking in the meteoroid storm that crossed their path as they entered Pluto's proximity. It was a storm and a planet of little consequence, more of a dust swell and conglomeration really, but it reflected his dismay. The path of what would come next was now obscured. His thoughts needed filtering, and he had no one to share them with, save Eelaa. Vanae had made her wishes abundantly clear when she shared the images. From her perspective, Orbyss was theirs. They were the original inhabitants, its protectors, and Herriden could not deny that they had taken better care of the relatively small portion of the planet they had inhabited, albeit hundreds of millions of years before. Resources were abundant, and given the intrinsic nature of their species, exploiting northern and southern climes would necessitate an undue burden on the planet due to the harshness of the environment at those extreme latitudes.

Yet, Vash's words repeated, running through his thoughts even when he rested his eyes.

Orbyss may no longer be ours, Herriden. You need to respect that.

Just when he thought he had conquered the *HELIX* and brought it to heel . . . now this. There would be no rest for the captain of a starship, wicked or not.

Nightmares plagued him, now that he had seen the most recent satellite feeds for himself, the images of human civilization captured over the past decade. He could barely process the data in his head. The numbers. Billions of people spread across the entire surface of the planet, a species so different from their own. They seemed to exist alongside, instead of with, each other, like infants at play, seemingly unaware of each other's existence.

Humans were a species that had advanced in certain areas well beyond what seemed to be within their reach, but yet they had failed to harness the full energy of their planet. It was as if they had stopped short before discovering the energy the planet produced naturally. They were detached from nature, and the science they had adopted seemed to ignore what was so obviously right in front of them: Their buildings a product of defensive protection from the climate, from each other, instead of intelligent living structures that gathered energy from everything they came in contact with. A reliance on fossil fuels, when all their energy could have easily been accomplished through photosynthetic construction and intelligent energy. Worst, beyond all these missteps, was their advancement in warfare. The atrocities he had witnessed, at the hands of this species, the destruction of the planet and each other, left him with feelings of disgust and dismay. He feared for them, all of them. How could they have possibly prospered and managed to multiply to the extent that they would cover most of the planet, and yet the resources and attention they allocated to the means of its destruction resembled a suicide? It was a global death wish from what he had observed, and as he continued to follow the storm outside his window, he mourned for a planet he had never known.

Part of him agreed with Vanae, and that part won out. How could he question her logic? How could any of what they had seen be for the best? The images displayed on the feed were no good for anyone or anything concerned, most of all the life of the planet. But what did that mean? Vanae had made her wishes clear; she would go down there and claim what was theirs. But Herriden understood that she had no idea just how dangerous that might be.

The XYZs were peaceful; they had not developed in the event of war or an industrial revolution; they never fought for territories, never had reason to defend themselves from greed, envy, or power. The success of the individual was reliant upon the success of the whole. Individual goals that ran against shared goals were absent in XYZ culture, because the achievement of shared goals was the only measure of a positive or negative outcome. To fail was to fail at contributing to the collective. The individual's success was measured entirely on their contribution to achieving a collective success, never on how well they satisfied their own individual desires or those of an elite or powerful few. It was ironic; perhaps if they had evolved on a path similar to humans, the XYZs would still be on Orbyss. They would have just destroyed the asteroid on its path towards the planet before it ever reached them. But destruction never entered their minds, and they were committed to an experience that respected all life and the circumstances it brought with it. Herriden could only agree that this philosophy had served them when he reflected upon what they had accomplished and the combined characteristics of all XYZ that surrounded him on the ship. And if this was their philosophy, if this was Percivious, the ultimate in altruism, self-sacrifice in order to benefit others with no regard to reward or reciprocity, then he needed to come around to Vash's line of thinking. They needed to respect the planet's new apex species, respect humans, even if they disagreed with most of what this new species represented.

So, what were they left with? What were his options? Herriden would have given anything to have his mother back. Just for an hour. Just for a moment. What would Vash have done? These humans were so different from them. His instincts told him, from the hours of data he had studied, which reflected hundreds of years on Earth, that they should avoid contact entirely. He had to believe that Vash would have felt the same. He had to wonder, had his mother also skipped ahead, just like her daughter, and witnessed some of the same feed available to her during her time on Orbyss II . . . would Vash have concluded that Orbyss was no longer theirs? Despite what had been, and that their path was to locate a new home, on another new planet. As much as he hated to do it, he pondered changing their course for Orbyss III. However, he knew all too well that they did not have the energy required to make the trip. And as of yet, they had no idea how to replenish their resources and repair the *HELIX* so that it could give more than anyone could expect in a time frame that would produce an arrival on Orbyss III within their lifetimes.

What could he do? It was an impossible situation. All passengers' hopes and dreams had grown to such an extent that to announce that they would not be returning to Orbyss would be like extinguishing the flame of their future. After all they had been through, he just couldn't do it without a solid plan in place. But what? What would the plan be?

"Herriden, come up here to the observation dome. You have to see this!"

Tirus's transmission broke through his melancholy and snapped him back to the storm outside the window that had somehow dissipated, seemingly unable to keep pace with the storm that possessed his mind.

Herriden entered the observation pod to find Tirus and Vanae at the telescopes, pointing and gesturing wildly, arguing over what they were observing.

"Look at this!" Vanae grabbed Herriden's arm and pushed his head towards the lens. "What do you think that is?"

"Some kind of satellite?"

"That's no satellite, Herriden! Look at the size of it!" She laughed at him in reply.

"Well, what do you think it is?" Herriden didn't even want to ask the question. His sister exasperated him.

"No idea, but I'm about to find out."

"No, you are not!" The worst of Orbyss's feeds played through Herriden's mind. What if it was from Orbyss? What if *they* had put something in play that could destroy them all?

He continued, "You need to figure out what that is from inside the *HELIX*. No way you are going out there. It looks to have Orbyss origins, based on what we have seen. So, go figure out what it is, Vanae. If you would have cataloged the feed sequentially like you agreed to, you would already recognize it. Now it's going to be like looking for a needle in a haystack, hundreds of millions of years high."

"Let's make a bet. I'll have it for you within the hour."

"You're on." Herriden shook his head as Vanae marched towards the pod she had sequestered for her feed investigation over the past years. He had to give her that; being stuck in a room sifting through satellite feeds would have been torture for someone like her, and that pod undoubtedly felt like a personal hell, a cell within her *HELIX* prison.

CHAPTER 54

VANAE

1.91 (Early Afternoon) / The *HELIX* / Eight Days Later

Herriden had won their little bet. The massive feed unfortunately got the better of Vanae. But if it hadn't been for her fit of anger, she might have never found it. It was exactly as Herriden prophesized, a needle she might never find, when, in frustration, she started calling up random feeds, and suddenly there it was. August 20, 1977, at CCAFS Space Launch Complex 41, manufactured by the NASA Jet Propulsion Laboratory. The *Voyager 2* space probe, launched sixteen days before its twin.

One hour had painfully stretched to eight days as they started coasting because Vanae refused to move a meter until she had figured out what it was. She was bringing that probe on board the *HELIX* if it killed her. And now that she knew it wouldn't, her older brother would no longer have an excuse to stop her.

She raced to the control pod, her body dank with sweat and a smell that not even her suit could contain. She hadn't slept since she and Tirus had identified the spacecraft in the observatory. And now she had everything she needed to convince the others that they needed to collect it.

"Great! The crew's all here!"

"Look at you! Have you slept at all? You smell!" was Herriden's unwelcoming to his long-lost sister, who had all but disappeared.

"That's irrelevant, because here it is. Late, yes, but worth the wait. This is what you've been waiting for."

Vanae brought up the feed of *Voyager 2* and gave them a crash course on when, why, and how the probe that floated directly outside the control pod window came to be there.

"So, now, big brother, it's time to collect it."

A light sparked in Herriden's eyes. He had been staring out at the probe for days, secretly contemplating whether they should just take the risk of capturing it. The *HELIX* had run diagnostics from the exterior of the ship, and he knew there was no substance present that would potentially set off a reaction that would harm them. But he wanted Vanae to learn her lesson, and so he waited. If he knew his sister, she would find it, no matter what. And so it began, the retrieval of *Voyager 2*.

They decided to engage with the latest addition to their space cruiser fleet, the multi-passenger M10, in order to tow it inside the air lock. *Voyager 2* wasn't big, but it was heavy at 722 kilograms. The probe contained an imaging science system, an ultraviolet spectrometer, and potentially much more—at least, that was the hope. Quite likely, it would provide them with a vast amount of information about Orbyss, much more than their own satellites could hope to capture.

The crew quickly put together the plans for its retrieval. Herriden wanted minimal exposure for the crew. He and Tirus would attach a line to the probe from the safety of the cruiser and, once a secure attachment was in place, tow the probe back into the *HELIX* air lock. Once inside, a scan would be performed to further ensure the safety of the foreign object, and then their examination would ensue.

It took some convincing. Vanae was not one to be left behind, but after he agreed that she would lead the examination—only if she promised to take a shower—she reluctantly gave in. As Tirus and Herriden headed out towards the probe, they laughed together. The last time they had been in a cruiser, it had saved their lives from the meteor shower. It was a shared nervous laughter, and they had to shake their heads, wondering if, once again, they were tempting fate.

The attachment was simple; the cruiser collected intelligence from the *HELIX*, transferring instructions seamlessly from the starship. Towing the probe was easy work for the impressive M10, and the entire "mission" lasted approximately fifteen minutes.

A crowd had started to gather with the hopes of greeting them outside the air lock upon their return. The crew dispersed the crowd to the best of their ability, knowing the extent of the information they needed to keep to themselves. It was crushing to take in the excitement of the passengers, eager to return to their beloved home. Herriden refused to share what they knew about Orbyss and its dominant life-form until he had a solid plan for how to renew their trust after he crushed their dreams.

Once the safety scan was completed, Vanae was unleashed to do her work. However, she did agree to leave the probe intact. They would return it to its home in interstellar space once they had learned all they could from it.

Once inside the *HELIX*, the excitement to investigate the contents of *Voyager 2* was scarcely contained, and everyone could not help but be drawn to the twelve-inch gold-plated copper record, covered in aluminum and electroplated in an ultra-pure sample of the isotope uranium 238. Who could blame them? Cold steel stung their hands as they dissembled it until the gloves of their suits adjusted to the assault.

Vanae held the object up to the bright light of the examination table she had assembled in the air lock.

"I am going to have the *HELIX* run diagnostics on the object from the control pod. It will be able to extract and translate any meaningful information."

"I'm not sure we want that thing engaging with the *HELIX*." Vash's never-ending worries now seemed to attach themselves to Shal.

"It's safe, Shal. The *HELIX* can identify and destroy anything that would harm the ship or the passengers before it ever gets the chance." Herriden was dying to know what the shiny record contained as much as his little sister. The fact that it was from Orbyss made it that much more irresistible.

It was a walking race past the crowd, back to the control pod for the crew. They were all anxious to learn what the record contained. Secrets the color of gold from the planet that was once their own.

It took the *HELIX* less than four minutes to complete its diagnostics and begin translating the contents the gold record contained.

They listened in awe to Bach, Mozart, and Beethoven. Music not unlike their own. They took in the chants of the Navajo Nation and laughed at Chuck Berry's performance of "Johnny B. Goode."

It was at the end of the record that the *HELIX*'s sophisticated interface detected the B side of the record. Something most humans were unaware of.

In disbelief, they listened to human's knowledge of their own existence on the planet millions of years before. That the DNA time capsule they had buried had been compromised as a result of the disturbance of a massive water reservoir due to tectonic activity that ended Pangea. Not only had they identified the existence of the capsule but XYZ DNA had been identified within the population. Although, in 1977, it had not yet been identified that only an extremely small percentage of the population contained XYZ genetic markers, as it would be decades until universal DNA information was gathered. Not only were humans, the apex species, aware of XYZs but they were related to them. Humans were not their successors; they were their descendants.

The crew looked at each other in disbelief as they listened to the translation a third and fourth time. They optimistically believed, in light of what they had learned, that the "general" population was aware of their existence, not just a select few. And that the majority of humans bore their design, their DNA. It was this mistaken assumption that guided all their decisions with respect to Orbyss and the humans it sheltered.

Unfortunately, the "select few" not only suppressed the profound discovery of a prior advanced hominid species that lived on Orbyss hundreds of millions of years before their own evolution. But worse yet, even Carl Sagan, one of the most respected and influential astrophysicists of the day, who felt the world had a right to know, would be allowed a fleeting statement left only to interpretation before he took the secret to his grave:

"The spacecraft will be encountered and the record played only if there are advanced space-faring civilizations in interstellar space, but the launching of this 'bottle' into the cosmic 'ocean' says something very hopeful about life on this planet."

CHAPTER 55

HERRIDEN

1.36 (Afternoon) / The *HELIX* / Thirty-Seven Days Later

It took thirty-seven Earth days for them to complete their analysis and make a plan to return to Orbyss's proximity. Once they reassembled *Voyager 2* and carefully towed it back to the position it would have assumed given its average speed and trajectory, it came back online and began returning normal science data back to Orbyss immediately.

Herriden found it almost impossible to believe that they shared DNA with humans, although, from the knowledge gained through the *Voyager 2* and through the satellite data, they knew the human evolutionary lineage was based on a primate predecessor, unlike their own cetacean ancestors. Nevertheless, Orbyss was human now, and they all had to respect that, just as his mother had told him years before in the final moments they had shared. It was heartbreaking for him, and as he prepared to tell the passengers of their new plan, he tried his best to find words that would comfort and console while impressing upon them there really was no other choice, no better solution.

Having taken in the compilation from *Voyager 2*, Herriden was more convinced than ever that their new home would be Orbyss III. He did not voice his concern to the crew; however, based on all the data they had collected, he guessed that the days for humankind may already be numbered, and even though he had considered a rescue, he had no choice but to remain focused on the *HELIX*, his passengers, and securing the future of his own species. Orbyss was no place for them now.

The most efficient fuel source aboard the *HELIX* was intelligent energy, by far. In reality, XYZ required much less sleep than humans, and a significant amount of energy could be collected during their sleep hours; they had evolved so that collection had no or a very small impact on their function. The quality and duration of sleep were of little consequence to the descendants of cetaceans. Their only disadvantage in the collection of intelligent energy was their numbers. Had they the population of Orbyss, they could have made it to Orbyss III unassisted without issue. As it stood, they would need to make a pit stop in Orbyss's orbit in order to collect, through induction, the intelligent energy required to make it to their new home: Orbyss III, a moon-based planet five light-years from Orbyss. It was not ideal, but at least the planet orbited a star that was young. The last thing they needed was a repeat of Orbyss II.

With a population estimated at close to nine billion upon their arrival, Orbyss was the perfect fuel stop. They projected energy retrieval would take between twelve to fifteen Earth months depending upon the speed of transfer. They had no way to test it. However, armed with the information that they shared a genetic code with humans, they assumed a conservative transfer rate at half of their own.

The crew had already begun the configuration of a colossal induction device. There would be twenty of them in total. They would attach to the exterior of the *HELIX* in order to collect energy as efficiently as possible. Massive carbon-fiber platforms, formed of the strongest Lenacyth, would shield the pods while they collected the energy required for the *HELIX*'s next, and hopefully last, interstellar voyage. The passengers would forgo the view from their pods during collection, but that would be the least of their worries. They would be sacrificing something much worse, a return to their original home, Orbyss, in exchange for colonizing yet another planet. Besides, they had spent years stargazing; it would be an insignificant concession for a new home.

While Tirus and Vanae led the design of the inductive chargers, Shal and Rahl continued repairs of the battered *HELIX* from the sling-shot around the black hole, which included reconstruction of the three lost nuclear fusion engines they would require for the trip "home." Once again, they would reach a speed of 0.2 the speed of light. It would be thirty years before they reached their destination, but they needed the time. They had their work cut out for them. They would also need to begin plans to rebuild the *HELIX* pods required for colonization of Orbyss III once they began collecting enough energy from Orbyss, alongside collecting the energy required for the voyage.

Herriden left all this to his crew; he had other plans. If XYZ shared DNA with humans, then there was no reason he could not potentially transmit to them. He had already begun countless hours studying Orbyss's languages, customs, and history. Vanae was all too eager to abandon the feed to him, and alongside the plethora of data collected from *Voyager 2*, Herriden had years of work ahead of him. A force beyond him screamed at the importance of it, a force impossible to explain. He was compelled to understand these human cousins, just in case he could help them if the opportunity presented itself.

And with plans in place and already underway, it was time for Herriden to break the news to the passengers. His words fell like his tears as he told them with great certainty that they would not be returning home. He transmitted as he spoke in order to fully engage all on the *HELIX* that Orbyss belonged to a new species and it was no longer theirs. He whispered that they would travel and inhabit a new home, and as he felt a grim silence fall over them all, he made a promise, loud enough to reach the very back of the crowd that had assembled. That they would survive, they would go on, and they would succeed at colonizing Orbyss III.

CHAPTER 56

THE HELIX CREW

5.23 (Morning) / The *HELIX* / Eight Earth
Months Behind the Dark Side of the Moon

A constant hum filled the *HELIX* engine rooms as the induction of intelligent energy continued without pause. In cooperation, Orbyss provided a never-ending supply of energy, as night existed for half of the planet at any and all times, thanks to its never-ending spin. It was foreign to Herriden and the crew, as all they had ever known was a fleeting, stationary planet that took almost everything from them. The only thing that escaped them was that this sleep on Orbyss had become a restless sleep, akin to perpetual insomnia, that, unbeknownst to the XYZs, failed to satisfy human requirements for healthy function, as the *HELIX*, night after night, slowly absorbed the energy the XYZs required for their trip.

The ship had already collected almost half of the energy it needed for its voyage to Orbyss III through intelligent-energy capture, thanks to the efficient design of the induction discs Vanae and Tirus had built and the staggering population of contributors on Orbyss.

Herriden had called the crew together, ready to share what he had discovered. He'd been diligent in his study of humans, which bordered on obsessive when combined with his attempts to reach them. For the past eight months, he had transmitted to Orbyss with a systematic methodology that alternated every hour, every day, every week. It was an exhausting exercise, but one he had been determined to complete alone.

His results had been extremely disappointing, until today. He had relied upon images and subtle suggestions. He transmitted messages that were like silent movies in an attempt to overcome language barriers. If he were speaking directly to humans, it would have been easier. Herriden was now fluent in the planet's top ten languages. But this was different. Attempting to transmit to beings that were likely unaware that they possessed the ability to do so was frustrating. From what he could infer from the data he had observed to date that divulged only evidence of audible or gesture communication between humans, he had no reason to believe that he would ever be successful, just a nagging compulsion to continue against all odds or reason.

He had perfected his transmission "dream," which he had hoped would have a better chance of success based on what they knew of their own species. It was inspired by the first transmissions received by XYZ infants, transmissions from their parents that triggered their unique ability in a dreamlike state of consciousness. Making the assumption that transmission would also be new for humans, like infants, Herriden created the dream he had been transmitting consistently for the past seven of the eight months since they had stationed the *HELIX* behind the moon.

It was an image, a representation of all XYZ, meant as a greeting, a symbol of how they would appear if encountered, wearing a suit, including the digital information that displayed across each of their chests. After the introduction, the dream was set up to communicate their need for assistance. Herriden had struggled with how to communicate the energy transfer best, and then, with Eelaa's help, he had finally decided upon a visual that resembled construction, of something being built that required the participant's assistance. The dream was dependent upon the recipient's preference, in a hope that it would be more memorable and engaging. Herriden's suggestion encouraged the recipient to select a task they could relate to, one that would initiate the dream sequence and how it would manifest in their mind. Once it took hold, if Herriden's assumption proved correct, they would then understand the reason for the XYZs' need for the inductive energy capture and, eventually, if all went well, lead them to direct communication through transmission. Only, he had had no indication of its success, until now.

He looked at the crew, deciding how best to share the news. When he caught Vanae's eye, she immediately knew that something was up, just by the look on his face.

"I know that look. What's going on?" Vanae wasn't one to waste even a moment; she was happy to take the lead.

Herriden smiled back at her. Since the inductive energy capture had commenced and was producing at a rate that exceeded their projections, the relationship between brother and sister had vastly improved. With the success of the inductive platforms behind her, Vanae had set out on a mission to improve their speed. If Orbyss III was the only chance of getting off this ship, then the faster they made it there, the better. In the absence of any supermassive black holes along the way, they were going to have to rely on their own initiative, and none amongst them was more determined to get off the *HELIX* than Vanae.

"Well, I can go into a long explanation of what I have been working on in seclusion, but it's probably best if you take it in for yourselves." Herriden did little to hide his excitement.

He reached for the control pad and brought up a file the *HELIX* had recorded just that morning. That was the beauty of the intelligent starship; it captured everything. Nothing entered or left the *HELIX* without its permission or recognition.

And there it was for all the crew to hear. The first transmission they would receive from Orbyss, 390,000 kilometers away.

"Stop!"

It stunned the crew and silenced the room. They saw an image next.

A young boy, a human, on Orbyss. A cap of electrodes covering his head, his name, Albert Xavier, displayed on the monitor to his left. Eyes open, staring straight ahead. All captured through Herriden's own eyes, as Albert let him in unknowingly, his defenses weakened from his dream.

Shortly after, in recognition of the young boy's age and the English language that he had transmitted in, Herriden responded back with Brahms's lullaby, one he had discovered during his study of human culture. He wanted this boy, Albert, to understand that he would not harm him, that he was there to help and protect him. It was a combination, a connection with the boy's culture and a mixture of his own, a gesture, this lullaby in English, transmitted in an attempt to comfort Albert and ease the boy's disturbance.

CHAPTER 57

PASCALE LAURENT

The success of the joint venture between NASA and SpaceX had reached new heights. Moonwalking via a combined government/commercial venture was child's play. Much grander plans had been on the table from the very beginning, and now that an unidentified object had been confirmed by the second Chinese Chang'e probe on the dark side of the moon, they were working both day and night to launch a new hybrid starship/fighter jet. One capable of not only exploration but also the initiation of an attack and, if necessary, defense, if deemed pragmatic or profitable by SpaceX and NASA.

Pascale, head of the ESA, had been invited to the launch; it was her intel, her connection to what went on in Malcolm's lab, that had initially secured her invitation. None of them were yet the wiser that Malcolm, head of research at Genetech, had completely shut her out. In reality, it was now of little importance, more of a diplomatic courtesy and an effort to contain what was going on behind the SpaceX doors. The combined hubris found at SpaceX was of epic proportion, and besides, they would be making "contact" of their own soon enough.

Despite the fact that they had not requested her daily update for a week, Pascale continued to reach out to Malcolm. Half out of regret for how things had ended and half out of a desire to potentially remain valuable to the project depending on what she discovered. In Pascale's experience, one's days were severely numbered when one was just along for the ride.

SpaceX was already surveying the *HELIX* twenty-four seven from the lunar STARLINK satellites positioned within optimal distance to the starship. If only the general population knew that the "altruistic endeavor to provide global internet coverage" was not as it seemed; rather, the STARLINK satellites, all forty-two thousand of them, were, in actuality, spy satellites homed in on the *HELIX*. They were now fully aware of the ship's size. Where the Chinese probe had only captured a visual of the head of the *HELIX* observation dome, STARLINK satellites revealed the full length and composition of the starship. The first data set from the satellites had lit a fire that only discovering a twelve-kilometer "alien" ship could. They captured its exact position, and now there was compelling evidence of a significant population of aliens on board. The only thing left to do was to get up there as quickly as possible and see it for themselves.

It was an operation under such secrecy that none of those involved were allowed to leave the SpaceX base under any circumstance.

They held all the cards, all the intel, or so they thought. What they did not know, what no one knew, was that direct contact with the "aliens" had already been made.

CHAPTER 58

HERRIDEN

1.44 (Afternoon) / The *HELIX* / Ten Earth
Months Behind the Dark Side of the Moon

What if they were killing them? There was no ignoring this. Not any longer. The data from the satellites displayed the full impact of a global pandemic. And Herriden could not help but think that *they* had potentially created it. It wasn't affecting all humans identically; there were differences in the impact, but the longer it went on, the more severe the symptoms grew. Reports of car crashes were up 317 percent, and a significant surge in diabetes, heart failure, and strokes had been reported, as well as a plethora of workplace accidents. The indicators were alarming, and they tormented him without reprieve. These humans, their cousins, were not like them; they were not nearly as strong as the XYZs from what Herriden could ascertain. And while it seemed impossible, he still wondered if the inductive capture was to blame for their suffering.

Herriden hated to sit by, a helpless witness to their suffering. He had been watching their decline for months, refusing to turn the finger of blame towards himself. It had been easy and convenient to over-look induction as the cause. His reason for pause was understandable, taking in the considerable and constant damage humans managed to inflict on the planet and on each other. The pandemic was much more likely a product of their own destruction. He had begun the investigation of everything that could be the potential cause as soon as signs of their deterioration had materialized. Everything organic, pollutants, viruses, anything environmentally related, and when nothing consistent emerged, the thought that it might be the induction would not leave him, even though it made absolutely no sense. It should have absolutely no impact on these human cousins of theirs. They had been so careful, setting induction at a level that would not have adversely impacted even the most vulnerable XYZ amongst them. But regardless, he had to be sure.

He needed to significantly reduce the collection in order to measure the impact. He needed to do so immediately. What was initially supposed to be a quick, unnoticed, and unobtrusive energy capture with no anticipated consequences was quickly unraveling before his eyes. Vash's words haunted him. They would have to find another way to make it to Orbyss III. They had not yet collected the energy required for the trip, but it mattered little; they would not sacrifice the inhabitants of the planet that once belonged to them. Not under any circumstance. Not even to save themselves.

CHAPTER 59

VANAE

4.92 (Morning) / The *HELIX* / Twelve Earth
Months Behind the Dark Side of the Moon

"*No way!* I won't let you! You can't do this!" Tears stung Vanae's eyes as they started a slow path down each cheek towards her strong jaw, set in defiance to Herriden's unbelievable suggestion. She had placated his bizarre obsession with life on Orbyss, even turned the inductive energy capture down to a fifth of its original amplitude at his command, losing almost all hope of collecting what was required to reach Orbyss III. But now this, his madness, it was more than she could take.

"Vanae, I have to. I have to try. What if we did this to them? What if I did this to them? Regardless, we have to try to save them."

"Herriden, how can you leave now? How can you leave with the latest information we have received demonstrating that the humans have almost completed a ship capable of attacking the *HELIX*? What in the world do you hope to accomplish? What if they attack you before you even make it down there? Their history is rife with unending violence, destruction, and greed."

"Come on, Vanae, you know the likelihood of that."

"What if they attack the *HELIX*? We have no way to test against what horrific nuclear weapons they may have on board. What if the inductive shells can't protect the ship? What if the Lenacyth is unable to withstand the assault?"

"They are trying to figure out how to communicate with us, Vanae. They are trying to figure out how to communicate with you, now, because I'm going to Orbyss, and I'm leaving right now."

"You are *not* leaving me here! I am furious with you! How can you do this to me? How can you do this to all of us? *We* need to leave! We all need to leave for Orbyss III! Why can't you see that you are going to get us killed? What about the passengers aboard this ship? Do you care nothing for them?"

"I care for nothing but them. How can they trust a leader without an allegiance to our biological makeup? You are asking me to turn my back on everything we have ever stood for. You are the captain now. Just like you always wanted, so start acting like one."

"Stop, Herriden!" Vanae started chasing him towards the cargo hold as he made his way to the *HELIX* stable in order to select a ride for his journey to Orbyss. Simultaneously, she began transmitting to the rest of the crew the insanity of Herriden's plan.

Her transmission launched Tirus into a sprint for the hold from his current position alongside Rahl and Shal in the engine room. All three were desperately trying to devise an alternate solution in order to reach Orbyss III prior to the end of their lives, using the depleted amount of energy they continued to capture from Orbyss.

As Tirus rounded the corner, it was a near miss as Herriden took the curve towards the hold entry at a breakneck pace. A confrontation with his best friend was something Herriden had hoped to avoid. Having Vanae in tow was bad enough.

"What are you hoping to accomplish, Herriden? You are not going down there!" Tirus couldn't believe this was happening.

Herriden was angry at Vanae for alerting them. "If you mean Orbyss, then, yes, I am going down there. Please do your best to sort out our collective futures here with Vanae and find a way to get us to Orbyss III."

"Look, I understand, it's a terrible end to this. I can't imagine what you are up against here, but this isn't the answer."

"OK, Tirus, so what is the answer, *my friend*? While you were busy building inductive platforms strong enough to kill those intended for collection, I was discovering all I could in order to learn about them, help them, if possible. And now, as it stands, I am the *only* one positioned to potentially save them. Are you going to go down there, Tirus? What do you even know about them?" The anger Herriden felt he could not project at his sister suddenly found itself directed at Tirus.

"Stop, Herriden, listen, this has nothing to do with Tirus." Vanae had never seen her brother this way, nor Tirus, for that matter. It seemed that Orbyss and its nine billion inhabitants had culminated in a planet-wide aggression the planet since their departure millions of years prior, and that aggression was now manifesting itself in the XYZ due to their proximity.

"No, maybe we should have this out, Vanae. Maybe this is exactly the time and the place for this," Tirus replied, towering above Herriden. And he made his height felt as he blocked Herriden from entering the hold.

Herriden would later regret it. Not the sting and the swell, but his manipulation of a friend, a brother, really, in order to escape to Orbyss free of guilt and turmoil. "Yes, Vanae, perhaps this is the time and place for Tirus to apologize for stealing my birth mother from me."

The blow met Herriden's bottom lip, left to right, across his jaw. Vanae and Eelaa, who had also joined them just in time to witness the display, screamed in unison. Herriden had suffered much worse at the hands of untested vehicles, suits, and the apparatus that accompanied such inventions. But never at the hands of another XYZ. It was not their way. Not their way to respond, but also not their way to incite. The very fabric that had held their society together. Everything that made it possible for them to leave Orbyss and now return had been dependent upon shared goals and self-sacrifice. To physically, intentionally, harm another ran counter to this foundation and, until this moment, had been unheard of. Discovering they were capable of violence towards each other immediately shattered the very essence of what made them who they were. It was the end of their inculpability and simultaneously the beginning of a movement that would lead to either its restoration or its demise.

Herriden's suit did not react in time to prevent contact. Now that it had witnessed interspecies aggression for the first time, it would adjust its protection accordingly. The data was immediately incorporated and uploaded so that the *HELIX* interface could respond in kind. Deliberate aggression between XYZ was now possible, where, prior to this moment, it had never occurred.

Tirus was sick at his own reaction. His eyes locked with Herriden's in the hope of finding understanding and forgiveness as Herriden wiped the blood from his face. It was as if the more they learned about Orbyss and the closer they came to its surface, the more they became infected by humans and the aggressive nature that had evolved with them, especially now that XYZs were reliant upon humans for the energy required to find a new home.

"She made me . . . she made me promise to protect you." Tirus stood still directly in front of Herriden. He was unable to move, struck by the colossal impact of his actions, and he was unable to believe that Herriden would leave them all to go down there in an attempt to save a species worse than he could have ever imagined.

At a loss for words, Herriden pushed away from Tirus and headed towards the M11, an update on the M10 designed for reconnaissance of Orbyss II and now redesigned for exploration of Orbyss long before they knew of its new occupants. Any doubts that he was making the right decision were now laid to rest thanks to his best friend's cataclysmic breach.

Vanae sprinted to the control pod in order to copilot what would be a twelve-hour voyage for Herriden. She had no time to process what had just happened. So much like her mother, her focus went immediately to protecting the crew, the passengers, and the ship, in that order. She had to make sure that Herriden's shield was active. There was no need for a goodbye between her and her brother. Thanks to Vash, they were as connected as twins, and they always would be, come what may.

Only Eelaa's voice could stop Herriden in his path at that moment.

"You would leave without a goodbye," she whispered as she joined him at the entry of the cruiser. She tasted the blood still fresh on his lips as his mouth covered her own. A kiss that tasted of the bitter, stale iron of their fate since reaching their destination on the dark side of the moon.

As the cruiser door closed and Vanae's voice came online, Herriden took in the faces of the crew. His crew, who would ensure the survival of their species, and of the *HELIX*, no matter what. Relief poured over him as he made his way to the air lock, where, upon Vanae's countdown, he would leave the *HELIX* for Orbyss.

For months, he had somehow known that this was his destiny. For months, he had watched insomnia plague the lives of people who continued to try their best to continue, despite the disorder. It was relief he felt, yes, because now he could try to help them. But he also felt relief because, if he was honest with himself, he longed to walk amongst them, longed to feel the weight of their existence for himself, longed to experience what was once his ancestors' home, longed to walk alongside Orbyss's new apex species.

CHAPTER 60

HERRIDEN

8:56 p.m. / A Midwestern Cornfield Bordering Lake Michigan

A successful atmospheric entry left Herriden full of excitement and hope. His ship had performed as required and was transmitting his coordinates by the nanosecond back to control. He had secretly been concerned about the effectiveness of the heat shield but now realized he had worried unnecessarily. The modifications had solved the issue, and he was seconds away from his predetermined landing point. Seconds away from his first landing on Orbyss.

He remembered the time-tested formula for the selection of the optimal landing site: low habitation, low terrain, low resistance to impact, low surveillance, and high potential to hide the ship post entry.

Accelerating through space towards his destination made him realize he was hesitant, but now, as he felt the force of the deceleration from the water and watched the light disappear completely from above, he lost all fear.

The force of the impact pushed the ship through the bottom of the lake into the subsurface sediment. It was like being caught up in an avalanche. He no longer had control; the sediment of the lake floor substituting snow. He opened the automated hatch, and as water and debris poured into the cockpit, he laughed to himself, gasping deeply. He couldn't get any more hidden from sight than this.

He left the craft, crawled up through the lake floor, and swam to the surface. It flashed across his mind that it was like he was being reborn—reborn to this planet his ancestors had left behind hundreds of millions of years before. The water was cold, and he shivered as he trudged through the mud towards the shore. The air was dense with humidity and the smell of decaying vegetation. An incredible revelation engulfed him as he realized he was breathing and surviving on an alien planet.

Reconnaissance had demonstrated that a rural location, with minimal population per square meter, just following harvest was the best place and timing to avoid collision or sighting during landing. The dense brush surrounding the lake provided all the privacy he needed, and the timing at dusk increased the likelihood that its inhabitants would be scarce. Had his entry been observed, it would undoubtedly be misinterpreted as a meteor or "shooting star" and be wished upon rather than investigated.

In any case, the opportunity had already passed. His ship was no longer visible, buried beneath the lake floor. Regardless, Herriden performed his detailed investigation of the area for any signs that his entry and landing had been witnessed. Satisfied his arrival had gone unnoticed, he allowed himself a personal account of the surroundings.

He breathed in the air to fill his lungs and felt invigorated; the oxygen content of Orbyss's atmosphere was almost double that of his home. It was interesting, he thought, as his "home" world had become a misnomer. It was this planet, Orbyss, that was actually his home world—or at least that of his ancestors. Herriden's planet had been completely obliterated; all of them were now interplanetary refugees.

As he looked up to Orbyss's moon, he felt tears run down his cheeks, a reminder that he wasn't dreaming any of this. He had never experienced a sunset, let alone the beauty of the night sky full of stars while his feet were planted firmly on the ground, exquisite courtiers in attendance to a full harvest moon. At that moment, he experienced an epiphany, the tragic irony of his entire species, just a few thousand kilometers away behind the moon, yet so close to home. Herriden recalled the countless debates as their ship gradually made the epic voyage to its current location. The impossible acceptance to which they were forced to succumb—inflicting trauma on these hominid cousins—was innately counter to their nature. Not only were they exploiting the apex species on Orbyss, who had evolved during their 280-million-year absence, but the Homo sapiens were clearly suffering as a result of their unavoidable actions. It was their fault, the insomnia pandemic. They had created a global crisis in an attempt to collect the energy required to find a new home. And even if their intentions had been honorable, the harm they had caused could not continue and had to be corrected.

As clouds drifted across the lonesome moon, Herriden wondered what would happen next. What would be the impact of their actions, and what would be the consequences?

ABOUT THE AUTHORS

J J Cook and A J Cook, MD, attribute the creation of the Percivious Trilogy to the marriage of their unique skills and perspectives.

J J Cook's background in marketing across a spectrum of industries—technology, finance, and the arts—brings insight and depth to characters spanning an array of disciplines, ages, countries, and cultures.

A J Cook's current role as a pediatric urologist and director of fellowship education at the Alberta Children's Hospital has allowed him the opportunity to author and contribute to numerous published studies and hone his writing skills, while his experience as a surgeon—as well as the relationships he's developed with his young patients and their guardians—has contributed credibility and realism to the narrative.

They hope this novel—and trilogy—shines a light on something the world seems to have forgotten: altruism and its impact on society, something that needs a voice now more than ever but also a platform where it will be heard.

CPSIA information can be obtained
at www.ICGtesting.com
Printed in the USA
BVHW060227140222
628766BV00005B/12/J

9 781777 377465